MURDER MOST ICY

Hayley rushed ahead blindly, not knowing where she was going, just hoping and praying she would find her father soon, when suddenly she heard his voice calling faintly in the distance. "Hayley?"

"Dwight, where are you?"

"Over here!"

She followed the sound, her steps now urgent as she navigated the labyrinth of trees and snow. As she burst through a thicket of trees, reaching the north end of the pond near the boathouse where the note on the napkin had instructed Dwight to go, she finally spotted him. His features were etched with cold, his eyes filled with both recognition and a quiet plea. As their gazes locked, time seemed to suspend itself, and in the deafening silence, the cracks began.

Dwight didn't dare move.

Hayley could plainly see the terror written all over his face.

The ice beneath her father's feet trembled.

Then with an explosive crescendo, the ice shattered and Dwight's figure plummeted through the splintering surface, disappearing into the icy abyss below . . .

Books by Lee Hollis

Hayley Powell Mysteries
DEATH OF A KITCHEN DIVA
DEATH OF A COUNTRY FRIED REDNECK
DEATH OF A COUPON CLIPPER
DEATH OF A CHOCOHOLIC
DEATH OF A CHRISTMAS CATERER
DEATH OF A CUPCAKE QUEEN
DEATH OF A BACON HEIRESS
DEATH OF A PUMPKIN CARVER
DEATH OF A LOBSTER LOVER
DEATH OF A COOKBOOK AUTHOR
DEATH OF A WEDDING CAKE BAKER
DEATH OF A BLUEBERRY TART
DEATH OF A WICKED WITCH
DEATH OF AN ITALIAN CHEF
DEATH OF AN ICE CREAM SCOOPER
DEATH OF A CLAM DIGGER
DEATH OF A GINGERBREAD MAN

Collections
EGGNOG MURDER
(with Leslie Meier and Barbara Ross)
YULE LOG MURDER
(with Leslie Meier and Barbara Ross)
HAUNTED HOUSE MURDER
(with Leslie Meier and Barbara Ross)
CHRISTMAS CARD MURDER
(with Leslie Meier and Peggy Ehrhart)
HALLOWEEN PARTY MURDER
(with Leslie Meier and Barbara Ross)
IRISH COFFEE MURDER
(with Leslie Meier and Barbara Ross)
CHRISTMAS MITTENS MURDER
(with Lynn Cahoon and Maddie Day)
EASTER BASKET MURDER
(with Leslie Meier and Barbara Ross)

Poppy Harmon Mysteries
POPPY HARMON INVESTIGATES
POPPY HARMON AND THE HUNG JURY
POPPY HARMON AND THE PILLOW TALK KILLER
POPPY HARMON AND THE BACKSTABBING BACHELOR
POPPY HARMON AND THE SHOOTING STAR

Maya & Sandra Mysteries
MURDER AT THE PTA
MURDER AT THE BAKE SALE
MURDER ON THE CLASS TRIP
MURDER AT THE SPELLING BEE

Published by Kensington Publishing Corp.

DEATH of a GINGERBREAD MAN

LEE HOLLIS

Kensington Publishing Corp.
www.kensingtonbooks.com

Chapter 1

"Mona, for the love of God, could you *please* slow down?" Hayley begged as they shot down the rural US-1 road in Mona's white pickup truck toward Salmon Cove in Downeast Maine.

Mona, with one hand on the wheel, fiddled with the radio tuner knob on her console with the other. "I'm sick and tired of listening to this yacht rock station. It's going to put me to sleep. I need something peppier." She settled on a hard rock station playing a Led Zeppelin classic.

Hayley's head pounded from the relentless thumping beat as she shouted over the wailing voice of Robert Plant. "Mona, are you even listening to me?"

Mona was tapping her hands on the steering wheel to the music as Hayley's eyes settled on a porcupine waddling across the ragged paved road. "Mona, watch out!"

Mona suddenly gripped the wheel with both hands and veered sharply to the right, tires squealing, to avoid a roadkill situation. Oblivious to his near-death experience, the docile porcupine continued on his way to the other side.

"I saw him," Mona said defensively.

Hayley reached over and lowered the volume on the radio and shot Mona a disapproving look. "The roads are still icy from the last winter storm and I really would love to survive long enough to see the New Year."

Mona let up on the gas and the speedometer ticked back down from seventy-five to fifty-two. "Happy?"

"Look, you're the one who desperately wanted me to come with you on this last-minute road trip. I still have a ton of Christmas shopping I need to get done and you-know-who arrives on Monday."

Hayley was referring to her mother, Sheila, who was flying up from Florida for the holidays with her boyfriend, Carl. Hayley had been disappointed that her now two grown children, Gemma and Dustin, were not going to make it home for Christmas this year. Gemma was swamped producing a Christmas special for her Food Network show in New York while her boyfriend, Conner, was in London wrapping up a six-week run in a West End play and would not be back in the States until Christmas Eve, while Hayley's son, Dustin; his girlfriend, MacKenzie; and their son, Eli were planning to spend the holidays with MacKenzie's parents in Baton Rouge. So when Sheila had broached the topic with Hayley about traveling to Maine and visiting until just after the new year, Hayley could not very well use the excuse of having a full house. In addition, she had made the decision to close her restaurant,

Hayley's Kitchen, for the rest of December with plans to open it back up in early January after hosting a private New Year's party there. Her husband, Bruce, who was a big fan of Sheila's longtime beau and fellow sports fan, Carl, encouraged her to bite the bullet and extend an invitation, which Sheila eagerly accepted.

"I'm doing you a favor getting you out of town for some rest and relaxation before Hurricane Sheila blows into town!" Mona exclaimed.

Hayley noticed the speedometer creeping back up past sixty miles an hour. "You call this Mr. Toad's Wild Ride rest and relaxation? My heart's racing like it's competing in the Indy five hundred!"

"I wanna get to Salmon Cove before dinnertime," Mona insisted. "And in case you've forgotten, we are dealing with a serious medical emergency!"

"Your dad just left this morning. I'm sure he'll be fine without his blood pressure meds until we get there."

Mona's father, Bubba, had set out at the crack of dawn that day for an ice fishing weekend at the Butler family cabin in Salmon Cove, which was about a three-hour drive from Bar Harbor. When Mona's mother, Jane, realized her husband had left his bottle of high dosage lisinopril pills behind, she had tried calling him to turn around and come back. But like Mona, Bubba usually turned his phone off whenever he embarked on a road trip in order to shut out the outside world and focus on his time alone and quiet peace of mind. Jane slipped into a panic, with visions of poor Bubba clutching his chest out on the ice and dropping dead from a massive coronary. Mona tried calming her mother down, explaining he would most likely be fine for a couple of days, but Jane was not having it. She had demanded Mona immediately get in her truck and personally hand deliver her father's lifesaving medicine to him. Mona at first tried calling the local pharmacy in Salmon Cove to see if they could help, but given the town's tiny population, especially during the cold winter months, it turned out to be already closed for the whole weekend. Mona had finally relented and agreed to drive down to Salmon Cove, but managed to strong-arm Hayley into accompanying her.

The plan was to arrive around six with Bubba's meds, spend the night, then set out in the early hours back to Bar Harbor, allowing Bubba his much-cherished solitude until his return home Sunday night.

Mona had not been back to Salmon Cove in years. She had spent many summers at the family cabin and even had a childhood romance with a local boy, Corey Guildford, which had been rekindled when she, Hayley, and Liddy had traveled there for a girls' weekend away and had gotten mixed up in the suspicious death of a visiting travel writer. Corey tragically perished in a lobster boat accident and Mona had returned for the memorial service and adopted Corey's golden retriever, Sadie, who was still alive and well. Mona was so grief-stricken by the loss of Corey she could not bring herself to return to Salmon Cove.

Until today.

Hayley suspected Mona pressuring her to tag along on this quick there-and-back trip was for some much-needed emotional support. Although Mona rarely displayed feelings other than what could best be categorized as annoyed or really annoyed, Hayley instinctively knew that she had never fully gotten over Corey. Especially now that she had divorced her deadbeat couch potato husband, Dennis, after over twenty-five years of marriage and was free to explore a new relationship. It was so sad to think of the lost opportunity with Corey. Hayley had been a firsthand witness to the close bond that had formed between the two when they reunited six years ago.

Hayley glanced over at Mona, who was no longer tapping along to the Van Halen song that was now playing on the radio. She was staring straight ahead at the empty road, her eyes glistening, no doubt thinking about the late Corey Guildford the closer they got to Salmon Cove.

Shivering, Hayley asked, "Mind if I turn up the heat a little bit? I'm freezing!"

"Suit yourself," Mona grumbled, her lead foot pressing down on the accelerator some more.

Hayley glanced at the speedometer. It was back to hovering near seventy miles an hour. "Mona, I don't mean to be a pest, but if you're not careful, we're going to be pulled over for speeding."

Mona sighed. "Would you stop worrying so much, Hayley? We're not going to get pulled over! There's no one else on the road for miles! You're always worst-case scenario!"

Just then, through the rearview mirror, both of them could plainly see a flashing blue light closing in on them from behind.

"You've got to be kidding me!" Mona cried. "What's the speed limit?"

"Fifty-five. You're going seventy."

"The cops never pull you over for going a mere ten miles over the speed limit! What kind of speed trap is this?"

"You're going fifteen miles over the speed limit and that whole 'cops never pull you over for going only ten miles over the speed limit' is just a myth!"

"It's true! It's a thing!"

"It's not a thing, Mona. Sergio told me so."

"What does he know?"

Hayley bit her tongue. Her brother-in-law had been the police chief of Bar Harbor going on twenty years now. She was reasonably confident he knew a thing or two about the habits of law enforcement.

The light-blue squad car was right on their tail now.

"Mona, I really think you should pull over."

"I think I can outrun 'em!"

"Mona, don't!"

"I'm just joshing you, Hayley. Jeez, when did you lose your sense of humor?"

"About five miles back when you nearly squashed a poor unsuspecting porcupine!"

Mona flipped the blinker switch and pulled over to the side of the road, rolling to a stop in a patch of gravel. The police car followed and parked directly behind the flatbed of Mona's pickup truck. Hayley stared out the passenger-side mirror to see a tall, imposing female officer get out. She wore a blue fur-lined parka over her police uniform. Her dirty blond hair was pulled back in a bun and she wore sunglasses even though the weather was gray and gloomy.

Hayley immediately recognized her.

It was Sheriff Daphne Wilkes.

Hayley, Liddy, and Mona had clashed with the very stern and strict Salmon Cove sheriff on their last trip to the area. Wilkes had even arrested them for breaking and entering: A long story from a lifetime ago. She did not suffer fools lightly and had at one time given them a police escort to the edge of town to insure they left after several warnings to stop sticking their noses in official police business. Hayley was under the impression that Sheriff Wilkes would not exactly be thrilled to see them and held her breath as she approached the driver's-side window.

Mona rolled down the window and muttered in as friendly a tone as she could muster, "Afternoon, Sheriff."

"Do you know why I pulled you over?" Wilkes barked.

Mona nodded. "I may have been going a few miles over the speed limit."

Mona was smart enough not to trot out her "ten miles over the speed limit" theory. She also had recognized Wilkes and was presently trying to avoid eye contact.

"Eighteen miles over, to be exact. May I see your license and registration, please?"

Mona signaled Hayley to pop open the glove compartment and fish out her registration as Mona searched her bag for her driver's license. Wilkes's eyes narrowed as she seemed to recognize the two women, but remained mum until Mona handed her the Maine state license and she read the name.

Her eyes nearly popped out of her head. "Mona Barnes?"

Mona turned to face her, offering her a weak smile. "Nice to see you again, Daphne."

"Sheriff Wilkes," she corrected her gruffly before leaning down to peer over at Hayley sinking down in the passenger's seat. She moaned. "And you too?"

"Hi, Sheriff! It's been a while! You look great! Have you done something with your hair?" Hayley blathered on, desperate to keep things light.

"No. I always keep it pulled back in a bun. Just like I did six years ago. Only difference is a few more gray hairs, which I got the last time I saw you two."

Mona chuckled.

Wilkes gave her a bemused look.

Mona's smile quickly disappeared. She rummaged in the cup holder and raised the bottle of lisinopril. "We're not planning to stay long, Sheriff. My father's at the cabin this weekend and he forgot to pack his blood pressure meds, and so Hayley and I are just dropping them off, and then we're heading straight back to Bar Harbor, no hanging around, no dillydallying. Quick in and out. Very stealth."

Wilkes nodded. "I see. So you promise you're not going to keep popping up around town, making my life miserable. Is that what you're trying to say?"

Mona nodded vigorously. "Yes! Absolutely! You let us go with a warning, and I will give you my personal guarantee that you will not lay eyes on us again. Right, Hayley?"

"That's right!" Hayley piped up.

"I also promise to adhere to the 'no more than ten miles over the speed limit' rule so you won't have to worry about pulling us over for speeding again," Mona added.

Wilkes frowned. "You know that's not a real rule, right? That's not a thing!"

"Yes, sorry," Mona mumbled, chastised. She refused to look over in Hayley's direction because she didn't want to have to endure her "I told you so" smirk.

"Okay, then," Wilkes said. "Consider this your final warning."

As Wilkes strolled back to her squad car, Mona carefully and slowly shifted the gear to *drive* and pulled back onto the road for the last seven miles to the Butler family cabin in the isolated woods just outside Salmon Cove.

Chapter 2

As they barreled down the dirt road toward the Butler cabin that was set back in the woods a few hundred yards from the frozen lake, Hayley immediately noticed Bubba's battered Ford Maverick parked in an open area next to a thicket of trees alongside two vehicles Hayley didn't recognize.

"Looks like your father has company," Hayley said as Mona strained to get a look at the other two cars parked next to her dad's truck: a black Mercedes-Benz covered in mud and a shabby two-door jalopy with visible rust, scratches, dents, and faded paint belonging to someone who obviously did not invest a lot of time in its care and maintenance.

Mona screeched to a halt in front of the cabin and hopped out of the truck, trudging through the snow over to the parked cars to get a look at the license plates. "The Mercedes is from New York. The trash heap is from New Mexico."

"So they obviously don't belong to locals," Hayley

concluded. "Did Bubba mention having visitors this weekend?"

Mona shook her head. "Nope. He didn't say much of anything, except that he'd be home Sunday night."

They hustled back to the cabin. When Mona reached for the door handle, Hayley stopped her. "Maybe you should knock first."

"What the hell for?" Mona sniffed. "This place belongs to me just as much as it does to Dad!" She shoved the door open and marched inside with Hayley close behind her. There was no one in the cabin, but there was evidence that more than one person was currently staying here. Besides the unmade bed in the main bedroom, there were two cots set up, one in front of the fireplace, the other over near the recent bathroom addition. Mona's mother, Jane, insisted the long-standing outhouse behind the cabin be burned down in favor of a septic tank and running water from a nearby well. Both cots had two pillows and wadded-up sheets and thick gray blankets tossed across them, suggesting they had recently been slept in. Hayley wandered over to the kitchen area to see three plates on the table, scraped clean but with tiny remnants of bacon, egg, and breadcrumbs. In the sink on top of a pile of dirty dishes were three coffee cups and three shot glasses. A virtual liquor store's worth of booze was on the counter, as well as giant bags of potato chips, snack nuts, and Chex Mix.

"Okay, right now I'm feeling an awful lot like Goldilocks, who has come home to find three bears living in her friggin' house!" Mona exclaimed.

"Who else do you think is staying here?"

Mona shrugged. "Beats me. Every December it's the same. Dad comes here to get away from my mother for a few days and do some ice fishing in peace. He's never said one word about anyone else joining him."

"So what do you think? Is he having some kind of secret affair?"

"With more than one woman? Dad doesn't strike me as a guy who would date Kendall and Kylie Jenner at the same time! He's a little more conservative than that!"

Hayley noticed three overnight bags stuffed in the corner of the cabin. She walked over and bent down to inspect them.

"Dad's is the scuffed-up gray gym bag. I've never seen the other two before," Mona said.

Hayley unzipped the Travelpro Platinum Elite Carry-On Spinner and opened it up. It was filled with expensive men's sweaters and slacks and designer shirts. The other duffel bag was stuffed with cheap pullovers and fraying jeans and a couple of moth-eaten sweaters. "Okay, this is definitely some kind of boys' weekend, with one rich dude and the other barely getting by."

Mona scratched her chin, dumbfounded. "What is he up to? Who are these guys?"

As if on cue, the door to the cabin was suddenly flung open and Bubba stood in the threshold, red-faced. "Mona, what the hell are you doing here?"

Mona reached into her coat pocket and yanked out the bottle of pills she had been dispatched to deliver. "You forgot your friggin' blood pressure meds! I came all the way down here to save you from a possible coronary and that's how you talk to me?"

Bubba snorted and shook his head. "Well, you could've called and given me a heads-up that you were coming!"

"I *did* call you, doofus! Check your phone. Mom left three messages and I left two. But let me guess. You didn't want to be disturbed, so you turned off your phone!"

Bubba mumbled something inaudible.

Mona leaned forward, turning her left ear toward him. "What was that, Dad? I didn't hear you!"

Bubba cleared his throat. "I said you may be right about that! But come on, I wasn't going to keel over just because I don't pop my meds for a measly couple of days!"

Mona marched over and grabbed a breakfast plate, raising it in the air. "Eggs? Bacon?" She plucked a shot glass from the kitchen sink. "Whiskey? You're a heart attack waiting to happen, Dad! I probably just saved your life!"

"You sound just like your mother," Bubba muttered.

Mona's nostrils flared.

She never liked being compared to her mother.

Hayley never thought Mona took after Jane.

But she was the spitting image in both looks and personality as her father.

A man in a black Moncler puffer jacket and carrying some firewood appeared just over Bubba's right shoulder. Hayley recognized him instantly. "Mr. Crawford!"

The man peered over Bubba's shoulder. "Hayley, is that you?"

It was Liddy Crawford's father, Elmer. After divorcing Liddy's mother, Celeste, when Liddy was in college, he had moved to New York, which would explain the license plate on the Mercedes and the expensive luggage. Like his daughter, Elmer Crawford was a very successful real estate agent, handling high-end properties in Manhattan. He had also come out as gay later in life and was now living with his husband, Rocco, an interior decorator, on Park Avenue.

"Does Liddy know you're here?"

Elmer's face went white. "Uh, not exactly. Hayley, there is something you should probably know—"

Before he could finish his thought, the other mystery guest pushed his way through, also carrying an armful of firewood. "Coming through—I gotta put this wood down, my arm's cramping up!" The man stopped in his tracks at the sight of Hayley and dropped the wood, one piece nailing the edge of Bubba's right boot.

Bubba's whole face scrunched up as he yelled, "Watch it, Dwight, you nearly took out my big toe!"

Dwight.

Hayley could hardly believe it.

The man standing before them had shaggy gray hair and a scraggly beard. The lines on his aging face each had a story to tell. His body was hardly robust, but not slight either. The loose-fitting forest green sweater he was wearing made it hard to tell.

But it was the eyes.

The eyes gave him away.

They were the same as Hayley's.

Hazel.

With a hint of mischief.

And they lit up at the sight of her.

It was him.

Although Hayley had not seen him in decades, not since she was an eight-year-old girl, she recognized him on the spot.

This was her father.

Dwight Jordan.

He hesitated, not sure if he should step forward and give her a hug or wait for her to make the first move, so he just stood in front of Bubba as if his feet were nailed to the floor.

A stunned silence filled the cabin.

Everyone froze in place, not sure what to do or say next.

Finally, folding her arms, Mona turned to her father for an explanation.

"Uh, Mona, you know Elmer, Liddy's dad, and um—uh—you might not remember him because you were a little girl when he left Bar Harbor, but this is—"

"My father," Hayley interjected.

Mona's jaw nearly dropped to the floor. Then she collected herself and shifted into her typical best friend protective mode, worried about Hayley. "What's he doing here? How could you spring something like this on poor Hayley?"

"To be fair, we weren't expecting to see her . . . or you," Bubba said in a low voice.

Elmer finally stepped around Bubba and attempted to break the ice. "Mona, Hayley, it's lovely to see you both again. It's been a while. I keep tabs on you through Liddy when she comes down to see us in New York."

Mona wagged a finger in his face. "Well, she hasn't said squat about you or this little secret reunion you three got going on here!"

Bubba sighed. "Mona, calm down. Look, your mother and I were always close with Liddy's parents and Hayley's parents back in the day when we were young and just having kids. We did everything together, and when Elmer and Celeste divorced and Dwight and Sheila divorced—"

"They didn't divorce. He skipped town without telling anyone," Hayley said, feeling a strong need to correct the record.

"Right, well, you know Jane and Celeste and Sheila remained very close. They had been best friends since kindergarten. As it turns out, so did we. I've known Elmer and Dwight my whole life. So we've kept in touch over the years even though Elmer was in New York and Dwight was, well, traveling all over the place. Then, about five or six years back, we decided to get together here at the cabin in Salmon Cove to do some ice fishing and catch up on each other's lives. We had so much fun we decided to make it a yearly thing, every December before Christmas."

Hayley and Mona exchanged shocked looks.

Mona turned back, eyes boring into her father. "Why the hell didn't you tell anybody?"

"Frankly, we didn't say anything to anybody because we figured if your mothers found out all hell would break loose and we just wanted to avoid any un-necessary family drama," Bubba said sheepishly.

Boy, oh boy, Hayley thought to herself. Despite their efforts to keep these annual clandestine ice fishing trips a secret, word was about to get out. And there would be no avoiding the intense spray of tumultuous incoming family drama that was about to be uncorked.

Chapter 3

In preparation for their secretive boys' weekend at the Butler family cabin in Salmon Cove, Bubba had loaded up a cooler with live lobsters, fresh clams, and scallops from his daughter Mona's store. Hayley watched in awe as Dwight, a master chef according to family lore, whipped up a mouthwatering five-course extravaganza of a meal, serving a classic New England clam chowder, seared lemon garlic butter scallops, a fresh salad, a lobster risotto for the main course, and for dessert, a Maine blueberry pie with crumbled topping and a scoop of vanilla ice cream. Hayley had never remembered having such a full stomach when it was finally over at eleven-thirty that night. Bubba rolled out a pair of sleeping bags on the floor for him and Elmer so Hayley and Mona could take the two cots, while Dwight was given the one big bed as an award for his impressive culinary triumph.

As Mona, Bubba, and Elmer gathered around the

fireplace to keep warm and moan about their over-stuffed bellies while downing a digestif shot of brandy, Hayley got cracking in the kitchen cleaning up, filling the sink with water and dish soap to start scrubbing all the dirty pots and pans and dishware. It was the least she could do after her father had worked so hard to prepare such a spectacular dinner. Dwight begged off the shot and wandered in the kitchen to join Hayley. She could sense him hovering behind her, wanting to talk, but she kept her eyes glued to the task at hand, scrubbing the bottom of a pot caked with hardened risotto.

Dwight cleared his throat.

Hayley kept scrubbing and scrubbing.

He finally spoke. "I just want you to know, I never miss reading your column. Wherever I am in the world, I always keep up with my subscription to the *Island Times*."

"That's sweet," Hayley said in a low voice. "Thank you."

There was an awkward pause.

In the living area, Bubba was breaking out the Cuban cigars, handing one to Elmer and another to Mona.

"We should probably smoke these outside on the porch," Mona suggested.

"What are you talking about? It's twenty degrees out there!" Bubba protested.

Elmer had the good sense to realize what Mona was trying to do: Give Hayley and her father, whom she hadn't seen since she was a little kid, some space.

"Bubba, the last thing Hayley wants is smelling cigar smoke all night. Listen to Mona and let's take this outside."

Bubba grumbled a few four-letter words under his breath, but didn't argue anymore. He put on his boots and jacket and scooped up a lighter from the rickety old wooden coffee table and stormed out the door, followed by Mona. Elmer stood in the doorway a beat, and then turned his head toward the kitchen. "You coming, Dwight?"

Dwight shook his head and picked up a towel from the counter. "No, I think I'll stay here and help Hayley with the drying."

Elmer gave him a wink. He had not expected Dwight to join them outside. He quietly closed the door behind him.

Hayley handed the pot to Dwight, who began wiping it dry with the rag. She sighed at the sight of a tower of dishes stacked in the sink. "These aren't even from tonight's dinner. They're from dinner last night."

"And breakfast this morning," Dwight admitted sheepishly.

Dish duty was going to take a while.

And Hayley could not feel more awkward.

Her mind was still reeling from the presence of this man, this stranger, this father who she thought of often, but frankly had never expected to see again.

"Bubba tells me you own your own restaurant now," Dwight said, beaming.

"That's right. Apparently I get my culinary skills from you."

He chuckled. "That's for sure. Your mother can barely

boil water without burning the house down. What's it called, your restaurant?"

"Hayley's Kitchen."

He nodded appreciatively. "I like it. And you enjoy it? I know it must be a lot of work."

"It is. But I love it. I can't believe I waited so long to do something I feel like I was born to do."

"I'm so proud of you," Dwight whispered.

Hayley set the dish she was washing back down in the sink. "What are we doing here?"

Dwight looked at her, puzzled. "What do you mean?"

"I haven't seen you since I was a little girl," she said in a shaky voice. "And now here we are in this remote cabin making small talk. I wasn't prepared for this. It's a little overwhelming."

"I know, and I'm sorry about that. I've been thinking for a long time now about reaching out to you and your brother Randy. In fact, I was discussing it with Bubba and Elmer this weekend, how best to go about it, getting in touch again. And then, out of the blue, there you were, right in front of me. I'll admit, I was in a state of shock when I saw you too."

"My head is spinning, I have so many questions."

"I know you do. And honestly, I think I'm finally ready to answer them."

She returned her attention to washing the stack of dishes. Dwight lightly touched her arm. "Would you like to sit down by the fire, have a brandy? You can ask me anything you want."

She vigorously shook her head. "No, it's like a bomb exploded in here. I need to finish this." Hayley's own kitchen could be a mess, but she felt an innate need to keep herself busy, to concentrate on something, anything other than the fact that her long-lost father was standing mere inches from her.

"Okay," Dwight muttered.

There was another long silence, except for the running water and Hayley madly scrubbing a dish with the rough side of a sponge.

Dwight cleared his throat again, a habit Hayley remembered him always doing from when she was a little kid, knowing he was nervous about something, or wasn't sure what to say in a situation.

Finally, Dwight broke the silence again. "First off, I want to say I'm sorry."

"Sorry for what?"

Hayley wanted to hear him say it.

And to her surprise, he did.

"For deserting you, your mother, Randy. I was in a very bad place back then, but you three never should have had to pay for it."

Hayley placed the washed dish in a rack and picked up another, avoiding eye contact. "So why did you?"

"There were a lot of reasons. I was immature, I was dealing with some mental health issues, depression, your mother and I were having problems. Taking care of a family seemed like this huge, insurmountable challenge. I should've gotten help, but I was a coward. Instead, I ran."

"I heard you left because you were on the run from the FBI for reasons we still don't know about."

"I have made a lot of mistakes in my life, Hayley, things I regret more than you could ever know. And yes, I got mixed up in some schemes in my day that weren't exactly on the up-and-up—"

She cut him off. "You mean *illegal*!"

Dwight gave a slight nod. "But that is all in the past now. I live a simple, quiet, drama-free life in Albuquerque. You'd like Albuquerque. Maybe one day you could come for a visit."

She did not respond to the invitation.

She simply wasn't ready.

"I'm in my seventies now, and it's become painfully clear that I have more years behind me than ahead of me. I guess that's why I'm so eager to reconnect with my family, with you and Randy, your kids . . ."

"Gemma and Dustin."

"Right."

"Whom you have never even met."

"I know. But I want to try and make up for lost time. Get to know you again, get to know my grandkids. Maybe with time, be a part of your lives."

"You can't just show up out of the blue and expect us all to be one happy big family like *The Brady Bunch*!"

Stung, Dwight bowed his head. "I know. You're right. I just thought I am already here in Salmon Cove, it's so close to Bar Harbor. What is it, like a three-hour drive from here? And it's Christmas . . ."

"No! It's not the right time," Hayley said sharply.

Dwight raised the towel, waving it like a white flag of surrender. "You're right. I'm sorry. I overstepped."

"Mom is arriving in a couple of days."

"She's coming to Bar Harbor?"

"Yes, she'll be staying with me until after New

Year's with her boyfriend, Carl. So you can understand why I have to put my foot down."

"Yes, of course. I'm the last person in the world your mother wants to see. Maybe we can discuss at some point me coming during the summer. I can hide among those millions of tourists flocking into Acadia National Park."

"Maybe."

Another agonizing pause.

There was a tiny part of her that wanted to spend more time with him, to reintroduce him to Randy, who was barely old enough to even remember him. But that would be impossible. Not with Sheila blowing in to town. If she invited her estranged dad home for the holidays, her mother would never forgive her. No, the summer would be a much better time for him to visit. It would give her more time to lay the groundwork and be emotionally prepared.

That's just the way it had to be. It was a much better plan.

That's when an old joke suddenly popped into her head.

If you want to make God laugh, tell Him your plans.

Chapter 4

Hayley and Bruce could hardly miss Sheila descending on the escalator to baggage claim at the Bangor International Airport. Wearing a brightly colored seahorse-and-coral print tie-dyed blouse with rhinestone-embellished detail and canary-yellow capri pants and white sandals, a sparkly bag hanging off her shoulder, she lowered her huge, round sunglasses to maniacally wave at them and nearly knocked the toupee off the head of the man on the step in front of her. When she reached the bottom, she practically pushed the man aside, flinging her arms out, and scurried over to hug Bruce first.

"Mom, why are you dressed like you're still in Florida? It's not even thirty degrees outside!"

After smudging some lipstick on Bruce's left cheek, she released her grip on him and proceeded to grab Hayley by the arms, pulling her in for a brief hug. "Nice to see you too, dear!"

"I'm just worried you're going to catch cold and spend Christmas in bed."

"Don't worry, I packed the appropriate wardrobe for Maine's typical numbing cold weather. And Carl has my jacket with him."

Bruce looked around. "Where is Carl?"

Sheila reflexively rolled her eyes, annoyed. "Oh, he's coming. You know him. He always has to stop and chat with everyone! He got hung up flirting with one the flight attendants, who then introduced him to the captain, who then offered to take him on a tour of the cockpit after we landed. I swear I've lost years off my life waiting for that man to stop glad-handing every person he comes in contact with."

Hayley really liked her mother's boyfriend, Carl, a retired local man from Bar Harbor who rekindled a long-ago romance with Sheila on one of her past trips to Maine, and then moved down to Florida to be with her. Sheila bounded over to the baggage claim carousel listed for her flight, elbowing her way to the front so she had a clear view of her luggage when it came around.

With her mother momentarily distracted, Hayley quickly pivoted to Bruce and warned, "Now remember what I told you, Bruce. No mention of me running into my father in Salmon Cove."

"My lips are sealed, but did you tell Mona to keep her mouth shut? You know how loose-lipped she gets when she's had a few spiked eggnogs."

"I've sworn Mona to secrecy. She knows not to say a word. The last thing I need is for the news to get out that he was back in Maine, which will ruin Mom's whole holiday."

"Are you sure you're not overreacting? I mean, it's been what, almost forty years? Maybe your mom's gotten over it by now."

Hayley cocked an eyebrow. "Are you serious? Have you *met* my mother?"

"I'm just saying time heals all wounds."

"You can put that on a Hallmark card if you want, Bruce, but it simply does not apply here."

Bruce's eyes widened, but Hayley barely noticed. She was on a roll.

"If my mother were to find out that my father cooked me, Mona, Bubba, and Elmer a scrumptious five-course meal just a few days ago and told me in no uncertain terms that he wants to find a way back into my life— well, let's just say, the Chernobyl nuclear meltdown disaster would look like a minor power surge compared to Mom's reaction."

"Hayley . . ."

"So not a word, do you hear me?"

"Hayley . . ."

"What, Bruce?"

A booming voice filled the air directly behind her. "Did you just say your father is in Maine?"

Hayley's shoulders sank and her head drooped.

Bruce threw up his hands and shot her a look that seemed to say, *Hey, I tried to warn you*.

She slowly turned around to face her mother. "What are you doing back here? The luggage hasn't even been unloaded yet."

Sheila held out her sparkly bag. "I came back over to ask you to hold this. I'm going to need both hands for one of my bigger pieces."

Hayley didn't bother asking just how many pieces of luggage her mother had hauled up from Florida for a less than two-week stay.

"Are you saying you have been in touch with your father?"

"Yes," Hayley whispered.

"Well, that's just crazy. Your father is dead."

"No, he's not, Mom! He's very much alive. I just saw him two days ago. Whenever his name comes up, why do you always have to say, 'May he rest in peace'?"

"I'm being kind. Why speak ill of the dead?"

"He's not dead!"

"Well, he's dead to *me*!"

Hayley turned to Bruce. "I give up."

Sheila's eyes narrowed. "And did I hear you say you had a meal with him?"

"Mom, it's no big deal."

"No big deal? He deserted the family when you were a child, and now suddenly he's back in the picture, trying to bribe you with his cooking? Is he also going to be with us opening presents on Christmas morning? When were you going to tell me?"

Hayley spotted Carl saying goodbye to the entire flight crew before ambling over to them. He was more aptly dressed in a flannel shirt, jeans, and a puffy vest, carrying Sheila's baby-blue Sun Valley parka draped over one arm. "Hey, everybody! What'd I miss?"

"Turn right around, Carl, we're catching the next flight back to Florida!" Sheila exclaimed.

"Now hold on, Mom!" Hayley cried before quickly glancing over at Carl. "Merry Christmas, Carl, nice to see you!" Then she redirected her gaze straight back to her mother. "Now listen, Dad is not in Bar Harbor—repeat, *not* in Bar Harbor. This unexpected reunion happened in Salmon Cove when Mona and I made a quick trip to deliver Bubba his blood pressure meds. It turns out he and Bubba and Elmer have been meeting up for ice fishing weekends every December."

"*Every* December? Did you know about these weekends?" Sheila shrieked.

"No, of course not!" Hayley insisted.

"I can vouch for her, Sheila," Bruce piped in. "She was still in a state of shock when she got home the other day."

A buzzer rang and a red light began flashing, alerting the passengers that the flight's checked luggage was about to start pouring out onto the conveyor belt.

Sheila was clearly rattled by this latest news involving her ex-husband. "I don't want to see him, Hayley!"

"You won't have to! He's probably not even in Maine. As far as I know, he's already on his way back to New Mexico."

"How do you know that for sure?"

"Because he did try to talk his way into coming up for the holidays, but I dissuaded him. I told him it was not a good idea, at least right now, and he eventually agreed."

This seemed to assuage her slightly.

Carl, who looked like he had just walked into a buzz saw, spotted a pink suitcase rounding the bend on the conveyor belt. He mercifully took his leave, calling back, "That's one of ours!"

"I promise you, Mom, you're not going to see him. He's gone and we're going to have the perfect Christmas together."

That was a stretch, given their sometimes prickly relationship, but Hayley's main goal at the moment was keeping Sheila from getting on the next flight back to Melbourne.

Carl waddled over, carrying two large pink suitcases, a matching makeup case, and an army-issue duffel bag slung over his shoulder.

Bruce watched in awe. "Is that it?"

"Is that it?" Hayley repeated. "It looks like they're staying until Memorial Day."

Carl nodded. "I hope all of this fits in your car."

"We'll make it work," Bruce assured him.

"We're still missing a piece," Sheila said.

Hayley stared at her mother in disbelief. "There's something else?"

As if on cue, a baggage handler approached, carrying a midsize plastic crate, or more specifically, a pet carrier.

Hayley's mouth dropped open. "Mom, tell me you didn't."

"I did. I brought Blueberry."

Blueberry was an ornery, take-no-prisoners, plump Persian cat Hayley had adopted and brought home years ago, who spent the better part of a decade terrorizing Hayley's beleaguered shih tzu, Leroy, who now at an advanced age, was more ill-equipped than ever to handle this monster's sudden return to the scene of the crime. How would her poor dog handle him this time?

It was as if Sheila was reading her daughter's mind. "I know it's an imposition, Hayley, but I'm sure Leroy will adjust to having Blueberry around again. I had no choice. One of the pipes burst at the doggie hotel and flooded everything, so they had to close down until January, and my pet-sitter went to Brazil with her boyfriend, and all of my golfing buddies were either busy or out of town for the holidays, so I just couldn't leave my sweet boy behind on his own, now could I?"

"You could have at least given me a heads-up that you were bringing him!"

"I know, but I was afraid you might say no. Carl offered to stay behind and pet-sit, but I just couldn't have that," Sheila sighed. "I tried to bring him on the plane with me, but the bitchy flight attendant, the one Carl was shamelessly flirting with, refused! She said there wasn't enough space and I was going to have to check my baby like a piece of Samsonite."

"She was actually very nice," Carl interjected.

"Zip it, Carl!" Sheila snapped.

"I'm sure we can handle one cat," Bruce added optimistically, trying to restore a sense of calm.

Hayley glared at him. "Blueberry isn't just a cat. He's affectionately known as the Furball from Hell."

"No, he's a good boy, aren't you, Blueberry?" Sheila cooed, pursing her lips and making kissing sounds as she poked her finger against the steel mesh of the carrier.

They all heard an ominous low growl and some hissing and saw a pair of angry eyes peering out from the cage.

Carl let out a loud sneeze before fishing in his pocket for a handkerchief to wipe his nose.

"Bless you," Bruce said.

"Carl has developed a slight allergy to cats," Sheila explained.

"It's just a tiny burden to bear. But I love your mother, so it's worth it. Don't worry. I brought plenty of Benadryl."

"He pops those things like they were Tic Tacs," Sheila said.

Hayley suddenly noticed Bruce's eyes watering and his nose running. She turned to her mother and sighed. "Um, Mom, Bruce is also allergic to cats, in case you have forgotten, which was the whole reason I had you take Blueberry with you down to Florida in the first place."

"Oh, that's right! I must have plum forgot," Sheila laughed.

Then Carl startled everyone nearby with another loud sneeze. And then another one. And then another one. They all hoped his fit was finally over, but then he threw his head back, mouth open wide, and let out one more loud, honking sneeze, causing a baby in a stroller to start wailing from fright.

He reached into his vest pocket and pulled out his package of Benadryl, popping one out the foil backing and swallowing it.

Then it was Bruce's turn to rear back his head and let out a loud sneeze.

Once, twice, three times.

With a stuffy nose, Bruce asked Carl, "Hey, buddy, can you spare one of those Benadryl pills?"

Carl handed him the whole package. "Here, help yourself."

It was going to be a long car ride home.

And an even longer Christmas holiday.

Chapter 5

Sheila stared down her daughter in the kitchen at Hayley's house, her arms folded, waiting for Hayley to respond.

"My what?" Hayley asked.

"Your Christmas dinner menu. Do you have a copy for me to look at?"

"Mom, I don't have a Christmas menu."

"You don't? This close to Christmas and you still don't have a clue what you will be serving?"

"No, I know what I'm going to make, but I just didn't bother writing it down."

"I don't understand. You have printed menus at your restaurant," Sheila remarked.

"But that's my business. I don't have to be as organized at home. Don't worry. I'm planning a traditional Christmas dinner: roast turkey, stuffing, mashed potatoes, green beans, dinner rolls, cranberry sauce, a couple of pies."

"That's exactly the menu I served at my Thanksgiving dinner I hosted for Carl and some close friends in Florida just a few weeks ago."

"Well, Mom, Thanksgiving and Christmas dinners are typically pretty similar, so I'm not going to worry too much about it."

Sheila grimaced slightly. "That's fine for you, dear. But I am here to help. Maybe prepare a few vegan options, a couple of bland dishes because, as you know, Carl suffers from terrible acid reflux."

"No, I didn't know that," Hayley sighed.

"So you can see how a menu I could give a quick looksy-loo would be enormously helpful. That way, I would know what to expect and it would make my job a whole lot easier."

"You don't have a job. You're here to enjoy yourself, not take over the holiday planning. Let me talk to Carl. I'm sure I can come up with some side dishes that won't exacerbate his acid reflux. Would that be okay with you?"

"You don't have to get snippy, Hayley, I know how busy you are. I just wanted to take some of the pressure off you."

Hayley took a breath and recalibrated. "I appreciate that, Mom. But I've got this. Have some eggnog. Watch a Hallmark Christmas movie. Read a Danielle Steel novel. Wrap presents. The best Christmas gift you could give me is to just kick back and relax."

"If that's what you want, I will leave all the details to you," Sheila promised.

Bruce ambled into the kitchen to grab a couple more Budweisers from the fridge for Carl and himself, who were in the living room watching the New England

Patriots trounce the Buffalo Bills. Neither man wanted to be anywhere near the fireworks when Hayley and her mother started bickering, except for a quick in-and-out beer run to the kitchen.

"Have you started shopping for the food yet?" Sheila could not resist asking.

"No, Mom, it's been kind of busy, but I'll get to it, I swear to you," Hayley answered through gritted teeth.

"It's just that the best turkeys tend to go early and it's already mid-December. I just don't want you to get stuck with a paltry bird that will barely feed four people."

Bruce had started to sneak out of the kitchen with his two bottles of beer when Sheila called after him. "What have you asked Santa for Christmas this year, Bruce?"

Bruce stopped and spun around, a frozen smile on his face. "You really want to know?"

"Of course," Sheila said brightly.

"An Arctic Cat ZR 9000 Thundercat."

Sheila gave him a puzzled look. "A *what*?"

"It's a snowmobile," Hayley groaned. "And he's not getting one. They're too dangerous."

"I grew up riding snowmobiles. I know how to handle them, dear," Bruce said, stepping forward to buss Hayley's cheek before turning to Sheila. "And the Thundercat is state-of-the-art, a beautiful machine."

"And hugely expensive," Hayley added. "The restaurant had a good year, but not *that* good."

"Well, to be honest, Bruce, I agree with Hayley," Sheila said.

Hayley resisted the urge to peek out the window to see if any pigs were flying, or someone caught lightning in a bottle, or some other incredibly rare occurrence. Her mother had actually just agreed with her.

"You're too old to be riding one of those things. I can just picture you going too fast and hitting a tree branch or something and then winding up with a broken spine, bedridden for the rest of your miserable life," Sheila mused.

"Always taking a walk on the sunny side of the street, aren't you, Sheila?" Bruce cracked.

She ignored him and addressed her daughter. "Hayley, are you sure you don't want me to get a head start with the grocery shopping? Carl can drive me in your car to the Shop 'n Save."

"I told you, no, Mom, I've got everything under control." Then she pivoted toward Bruce. "And for the record, you are not getting a Thunderdome for Christmas!"

"Thundercat," Bruce muttered.

And speaking of cats, suddenly they heard a loud, hissing sound coming from the dining room. Blueberry had sussed out Leroy, who was hiding under the table, and was now slowly, methodically creeping toward him to terrorize him some more. Leroy let out a yelp, darted out from under the table, through the kitchen, down the hall and began scampering up the staircase to find shelter on the second floor from this marauding miscreant of a feline.

Satisfied with himself, Blueberry plopped down, back arched in the kitchen right next to Bruce's foot. It only took a few seconds before Bruce was once again suffering from a sneezing fit. "Hayley, where's the Benadryl?"

"Upstairs bathroom, left-hand drawer."

Wiping his nose, Bruce hurried out to give Carl his beer and bound upstairs to find some relief.

"I just have one more question," Sheila said.

"What, Mom?" Hayley asked, trying not to sound too irritated, but ultimately failing.

"Are you planning on serving Christmas Eve dinner on the early side so we're done in plenty of time for midnight Mass?"

"Bruce and I won't be going to midnight Mass."

"What? Why not?" Sheila gasped.

"Because we're not religious!"

"Neither am I, but it's Christmas. We should at least acknowledge the true meaning of the holiday."

"Not happening. But you and Carl are more than welcome to go and I will make sure we're finished with dessert in plenty of time for you to get to the church."

Sheila wisely chose to stay mum. She then walked into the utility room, emerging a few seconds later with a broom and dustpan.

"What are you doing?" Hayley asked.

"I thought I'd tackle some of those dust bunnies flying around your dining room floor."

Hayley peered into the dining room from the kitchen and for the life of her, could not spot any dust bunnies piling up, but she was not going to question her mother's critical eye or innate need to comment on Hayley's housekeeping skills.

She heard Carl sneezing in the living room.

She could visualize Blueberry jumping up on his lap in the recliner.

Suddenly the back door flew open and Mona hustled in, surprising her. She had an agitated look on her face that Hayley immediately picked up on.

"Mona, what's wrong? You look a little tense."

"I need to talk to you privately."

"What is it?"

Mona's eyes flicked to the dining room, where a curious Sheila was now moving her broom closer to the kitchen so she could eavesdrop on their conversation.

"Outside," Mona whispered, gesturing toward the door.

Hayley followed her out the back to the side porch. It was dark out and cold and spitting snow.

"Brace yourself," Mona warned. "I have some news."

Hayley did not like the sound of this. "Okay."

"It's about your dad."

Hayley tensed. "What about him?"

"He apparently changed his mind about not coming to Bar Harbor for the holidays."

Hayley's eyes widened. "*What*? No. He said he was going to make a plan to come next summer. I specifically told him now was not a good time for him to just show up."

"I know, I was there, but he obviously didn't listen to a word you said, because I was just over at my parents' house, and he was there making everyone a big prime rib dinner."

Hayley's heart dropped.

This was not good.

In fact, it was a mounting disaster.

Chapter 6

"I'm going out!" Hayley hollered as she burst through the back door into the kitchen, startling her mother, who had just finished sweeping dust bunnies and was now poking her nose in Hayley's cupboards.

"But you haven't even gotten dinner started yet," Sheila noted with just the right amount of judgement.

"I know, but the Christmas Shop is having a fifty-percent off sale on all stocking stuffers, so Mona and I want to race over there before all the best stuff is picked over."

Sheila stared at her, mouth agape. "You haven't even started shopping for stocking stuffers yet? It's so close to Christmas already."

"I know, I know, but as you're aware, I do have a business to run that's open year-round," Hayley explained calmly, desperately trying to resist the urge to roll her eyes.

Sheila crossed to the coatrack. "Fine. I always love a good sale. I'll come with you."

"No!" Hayley cried.

"Why not?"

"Um, because . . ." Hayley's mind raced. "There's no room in Mona's pickup truck. You'd have to sit in the back and you'll freeze to death."

"Why can't you sit in the back?"

Hayley didn't have an answer for that one. She just stared at her mother, not sure what to say next.

Sheila glanced out the kitchen window to see Mona in her truck, engine running, rubbing her hands together to keep warm, waiting for Hayley.

"No, I can bundle up. It's only, what, like a five-minute ride to the shop? There's no sense in you catching a cold with all you have left to do to prepare for Christmas."

"Mom!" Hayley blurted out.

Sheila stopped putting on her winter coat halfway. "What?"

"I really need your help."

Sheila's ears perked up.

These were words she always longed to hear coming out of her daughter's mouth, but rarely did.

"I haven't even thought about dinner yet, and Bruce and Carl are going to start complaining about being hungry soon, so if you could do me a favor, just this one time . . ."

"I'd be happy to make dinner!" Sheila practically squealed before adding, "I mean, your cupboards are completely bare, but I spotted enough ground beef and a package of pasta to possibly whip up my world-famous spaghetti beef Bolognese."

"I would be eternally grateful!"

Now assigned a mission, Sheila hung her coat back on the rack, and got busy opening the fridge and inspecting the contents of the vegetable crisper. "I think there might be enough lettuce and tomatoes to make a simple salad too. I don't see any dressing but, fingers crossed, there's enough mustard and balsamic vinegar here to make my own."

"Thanks, Mom!" Hayley chirped as she backed out of the kitchen and raced out the door to hop in Mona's truck. They sped down the back roads to Bubba and Jane's modest home just outside of town that was overly decorated with Christmas lights and tacky plastic Santa and Frosty the Snowman life-size figurines. Through the kitchen window, Hayley spotted her father, Dwight, with a big smile on his face and wearing an apron that said *Mr. Good Lookin' Is Cookin'* as he whipped a bowl of mashed potatoes with an electric whisk.

As Hayley and Mona jumped out of the truck, heading up the snow-covered walk to the front door, Dwight glanced out the window and caught sight of them approaching. His wide smile faltered a bit as he realized his presence in town was no longer a secret.

When Hayley and Mona barged into the house, they heard the classic 1957 album *A Jolly Christmas from Frank Sinatra* playing on Bubba's old stereo he kept in pristine condition. The crooner, backed up by the Ralph Brewster Singers, were in the middle of "Silent Night," which Hayley knew would not describe the night ahead. It was going to be anything but silent.

Mona caught her parents sitting in the living room,

sipping spiked eggnog and holding hands. "Can you two stop pawing each other for one lousy minute?"

"Yes, of course—you're right, Mona! How rude of us to show a little affection for each other in the privacy of our own home after nearly fifty years of marriage!" Jane barked.

Dwight came bounding in from the kitchen, wiping his hands on a dishrag. "Hayley! What a surprise seeing you here!"

He went in for a hug, but Hayley took a step back. "I'm the one who is truly surprised here, Dwight."

Dwight deflated, his shoulders sagging slightly. "You're right. I should explain." He turned to his hosts. "Bubba, Jane, would you mind if Hayley and I commandeer the game room out back? Prime rib's still in the oven. It's going to be another twenty minutes or so until we sit down to eat."

"*Mi casa, su casa!*" Bubba shouted proudly.

"One week on Duolingo and suddenly he thinks he speaks fluent Spanish," Jane joked.

Bubba leaned in and kissed her on the cheek, eliciting a quiet groan from Mona, who had never been comfortable with her parents showing any physical affection toward one other. Probably since it seemed like such a foreign concept after her long and ultimately disastrous marriage to her deadbeat husband, Dennis.

Dwight led Hayley through the living room into a family room that had been turned into a game room with a Ping-Pong table, a dartboard on the wall, stacks of board games like Trivial Pursuit and Yahtzee on a shelf, and a classic *Charlie's Angels* pinball machine

Bubba had bought for a steal when an arcade in Brewer went bankrupt in the early eighties.

Dwight stopped, slowly turning around to face his daughter. "I'm preparing an old prime rib family recipe. I'd be happy to pass it along to you. Maybe you can offer it as a special at your restaurant one of these days. Smells pretty good, doesn't it?"

He was stalling.

And Hayley was not having it.

She glared at him.

"Look, Hayley, I know I promised to stay away . . ."

"Well, I can see how well that plan worked out. What are you doing here?"

"I fully intended to drive back across country to New Mexico in time for Christmas, fingers crossed my rattletrap can even make it that far. But by the time I reached Ogunquit, a little voice inside my head told me to turn around."

"You don't always have to listen to those little voices inside your head. You can ignore them every once in a while."

"I know you're not happy with me right now."

"No, Dwight, I'm not. You said one thing and then you turned around and did the exact opposite."

"I understand. Just hear me out. I broke up with my girlfriend Jeannie in October and it's been really tough. Jeannie and I did everything together and I couldn't face the prospect of spending Christmas all alone in New Mexico. Jeannie was a real sweetheart, my whole world."

"Then why did you break up?"

Dwight hesitated, cleared his throat, and then spit

out under his breath, "It was a complete misunderstanding involving a cocktail waitress at the Dancing Eagle Casino, where we sometimes hang out and play blackjack. Jeannie could get awful jealous sometimes."

Hayley suspected Jeannie had every reason to be upset, but was not going to question her father's version of events because at this point it really did not matter to her.

She just wanted him gone.

"When I called Bubba and Jane and proposed I come up and spend Christmas with them here in Bar Harbor, well, they warmly opened their home and their hearts and made me feel so welcome, I offered to cook all the meals during my stay, including Christmas Day dinner with all the kids and grandchildren."

"That's a lot of people."

"I'm happy to do it. It's nice to be around a close, loving family for a change. Makes me feel nostalgic for my own family, shows me what could have been."

Hayley was not about to fall for this blatant attempt at playing on her heartstrings. "How long do you plan to stick around here?"

"Just until New Year's, then I'm gone. I'm heading straight back across the country. Next stop, Albuquerque! Swear to God!" He studied the worry lines on Hayley's forehead. "Hayley, I have no interest in opening old wounds. I will make it my personal mission to steer clear of your mother. Sheila will never ever know I was even in town. I promise!"

He had also promised to take her and Randy to Disney World the summer before he vanished and left them high and dry without a father. But she decided not to remind him of that one. She just shook her head in dismay. There was not much she could do, now that he was happily settled in at the Butler family home. All she could do was hope for the best that he would be true to his word and Dwight and Sheila's paths would never cross.

Famous last words.

Chapter 7

Hayley had never seen her brother Randy look so nervous as he stood behind the bar of his establishment, Drinks Like a Fish, sizing up a man who, up until this very moment, he had trouble even conceiving a mental picture of in his head since he had vanished from his life when he was still a young child.

Hayley glanced over at Dwight, who appeared equally apprehensive, but shot out a hand. "Good to see you, Randy."

Randy limply took his father's hand to shake it. Hayley had texted Randy to warn him that their father wanted to stop by the bar and say hello. Randy's hesitant reply suggested that perhaps he was not quite emotionally ready just yet to be reunited with his long-lost dad, but a few minutes later he had fired off another text throwing caution to the wind and told Hayley to bring him by. Dwight was beyond excited, and when they had strolled through the front door, and Dwight had spotted Randy hovering behind the bar

anxiously awaiting their arrival, tears pooled in his
eyes and he let out a barely audible gasp.

Hayley had not noticed before just how much her
brother physically resembled Dwight. The eyes. The
nose. The raucous, infectious laugh. The only difference between the two men seemed to be their fashion
sense, with Randy in a crisp, ironed blue-tonal checked
dress shirt with the sleeves rolled up and tight-fitting
khakis, and Dwight disheveled in a moth-attacked,
lint-covered ratty wool sweater and dirt-stained jeans.

Randy remained frozen in place behind the bar as if
finding comfort in the large barrier between them.
Hayley and Dwight saddled up on a couple of stools.
Randy nodded to Hayley. "Jack and Coke for you."
Then he turned to his father. "What can I get for you . . ."
He paused, thinking about how to finish the sentence
before settling on the less familial, "Dwight."

"Whatever's on tap, Randy, thank you," Dwight
replied in a scratchy voice before coughing and clearing his throat.

Randy set about getting their drinks, relieved to
have something to do while he processed all of this.
There was an uneasy silence after he handed Hayley
her cocktail and Dwight a mug of Miller Genuine
Draft.

After a few awkward sips and a longer stretch of silence, since the bar was mostly empty except for a
young couple canoodling at a table near the back,
Hayley finally took it upon herself to attempt to break
the ice. "When I first saw him at the cabin in Salmon
Cove, I recognized him right away because I thought I
was looking at you twenty years from now, Randy."

Randy studied his father's craggy, aged face and was having trouble seeing the resemblance.

Dwight took another sip of his beer, leaving some foam embedded in his mustache. "Do you still love comic books, Randy?"

"Not since I was in high school."

"I remember taking you down to the corner store every Thursday when the new comic books arrived and you'd start going through those boxes before the owner, Bill Carey, had even gotten a chance to put them on the magazine shelf," Dwight recalled, smiling at the memory. "You could barely read yet, but you sure did love the pictures. *Wonder Woman* was your favorite, if I'm not mistaken."

"Yeah, I thought she was so cool," he said, eyes downcast. "She had those awesome gold bracelets that deflected bullets and that amazing invisible plane. Plus, she kind of had a crush on Superman and so did I."

Dwight chuckled. "Remember that time I took you down to the athletic field because I wanted to teach you how to play baseball so you could someday try out for Little League?"

Randy nodded with a half grin. "I hated sports."

"How was I supposed to know? You never bothered to tell me," Dwight protested. "Instead, you just stood there on home plate with the bat raised as I pitched the ball and then you stepped right in front of it as it came at you, on purpose, so it hit you smack in the face."

"I knew if my nose started to bleed, you'd have to take me home, and it was Saturday morning—and not just any Saturday morning, but the fall premiere of all the new cartoons and I couldn't stand the idea of missing any of them, so I had no choice but to take direct action. There was no way in hell I was going to miss the very first episode of the *Adventures of the Gummi Bears*!"

"You're right! You're right! I should've known better!" Dwight cried. "What was I thinking?"

Hayley could take a guess.

He probably wanted Randy to be like all the other boys, sports minded, not TV obsessed. Maybe if he had stuck around longer he would have realized Randy was never going to be like most of the other boys in his class. He had his own path to forge.

Dwight was short on memories, since he had blown town so early on in their lives and so there was a noticeable lull in the conversation. Randy refilled Dwight's mug with more beer and then took the reins, his curiosity piqued. "After you, um, left, we heard a lot of crazy stories about you—secondhand, obviously—but I always wondered if they were true or just made up or embellished."

Dwight folded his arms on the bar. "Hit me."

"Okay," Randy said, ready to pepper him with questions about his sordid past. "Was it true that you worked on a dude ranch out west for a while as a cook and you spiked the cowboys' chili with Ex-Lax in order to keep them busy so you could slip away under the cover of darkness after you got caught pilfering one of the cowboys' gold-plated belt buckle in the bunkhouse?"

Dwight gave him a sly eye. "Who told you that one?"

Randy turned to Hayley. "She did."

"I think I heard Bubba tell that story one time when we were over at their house for a barbecue."

"I plead the Fifth on account that some of those boys are alive and out there and probably still on the hunt for me."

"What about the supposed knife fight you got into while working on the Alaskan pipeline?"

"Total hooey. Never happened. I've never even been to Alaska," Dwight confirmed.

"Okay, what about the supposed FBI chase through it's a small world at Disneyland?"

Dwight waffled a bit, not sure how to respond. "It wasn't it's a small world. It was Peter Pan's Flight. And it wasn't the FBI. It was a couple of security guys who thought I had shoplifted some mouse ears from the Disney store on Main Street. Not nearly as dramatic as a real-life FBI chase, but it did happen."

Randy suddenly got serious. "Were you ever on the run from the FBI?"

"I will admit, I have had a very colorful life," Dwight deflected. "But if half the stuff really happened that people say happened, there'd probably already be a movie made about me, hopefully starring Leonardo DiCaprio. But unfortunately, I'm not the badass some people like to make me out to be. Not by a long shot. In fact . . ." Dwight's voice was shaky. "It's turned out my life is kind of empty . . ."

He stared off into space, reflecting on a lifetime of bad choices. Hayley and Randy stared at him, not sure what to do. Then he quietly gathered himself and came back down to earth. "Especially with you two not a part of it. That's something I really want to change. I know it won't be easy, not after all the time that's passed, but I'm going to work hard and try, if you'll give me the chance."

Taken aback by this sudden emotional request, Hayley and Randy just looked at each other and nodded slightly, not wanting to dissuade him from trying to work his way back in their lives as if he never left, but still guarded enough that they were not about to trust him just yet.

Island Food & Spirits
By
HAYLEY POWELL

After an exhausting and trying day yesterday hosting my mother Sheila, her boyfriend Carl, and her beloved Persian cat Blueberry, who are visiting us over the holidays from Florida, at least I was able to enjoy a delicious dinner of spaghetti Bolognese prepared by my mother, one of her specialties, even though she's not Italian but Scottish Canadian from Nova Scotia.

Soon after her triumphant dinner, my mother announced that she and Carl were retiring for the evening.

I must admit I was a bit relieved to hear this because I had been nursing a massive headache all day that seemed to grow bigger and bigger by the minute as the day's events were finally catching up to me.

My mother and Carl headed upstairs and I glanced over at Bruce sitting on the couch with his red eyes and runny nose from his cat allergy and mouthed, "I'm sorry!"

Bruce, looking tired and miserable, just smiled and whispered, "We can get through this."

Boy, I love that man.

I decided it was definitely time to enjoy a nightcap. I turned to ask Bruce if he wanted one, but the poor guy was already stretched out on the couch and sound asleep, so I was on my own.

I poured myself a Jack and Coke and sank down in the recliner with a sigh. I closed my eyes and was about to drift off to sleep when I sensed movement in front of me and popped my eyes open. I had to stifle a scream and almost dropped my drink in fright.

My mother was standing in the doorway, her hair wrapped in a towel, bathrobe on, and cold cream smeared all over her face. She had come back downstairs to let me know that I did not have to be quiet on her and Carl's account, since Carl had his Benadryl and they both had taken a sleeping pill and she had also brought her white noise machine, which they had already turned on in their room.

"You can be as loud and raucous as you want. Whoop it up all night because you won't be bothering us!" she declared as she stared pointedly at the drink in my hand before turning around to head back upstairs.

Good lord, if turning on the TV and having a cocktail was whooping it up, then I must be some kind of party animal.

"Two weeks, it's only two weeks," I reminded myself under my breath.

"What's that, Hayley?" she called down from the top of the stairs "Did you say something?"

Good lord, that woman had the ears of a bat.

"No! I was just thinking out loud about making some gingerbread for tomorrow!"

"Yummy! Carl loves gingerbread!"

Great.

Now I was committed.

I pulled myself up out of the recliner, woke Bruce to send him upstairs to bed, and padded to the kitchen to start on the batter.

While mixing the ingredients for my gingerbread batter, I reminisced back to a simpler time in my life when I was sixteen and a newly licensed driver.

Every teen growing up on the island could not wait to get their license because it was a rite of passage and for most of us, a ticket to freedom. Whether you just drove around all the back roads, or you actually got to leave the island and drive the thirty minutes to Ellsworth to McDonald's with your friends or to the movies, it was that gateway to independence we all craved.

Looking back, it didn't take much to make us happy back in those days. Unfortunately, my mother did not share the same idea of me claiming my maturity and independence with a driver's license. We only had one car and she guarded it with her life. All of my begging and pleading to be allowed to take the car to Ellsworth for some fast food and a movie with a few responsible friends sadly fell on deaf ears.

Finally, after just being able to drive to the Shop 'n Save to pick up something on her grocery list she had forgotten, a miracle happened!

My mom informed me that she was going Christmas shopping in Ellsworth with her best friend, Jane, Mona's mother, for the day and needed me to deliver her six loaves of gingerbread that she had baked to the high school's Christmas bazaar and bake sale. I felt like heaven's gates had finally opened up, and I thought I could hear angels singing. I was actually going to be able to use the car for the whole day!

Then I heard her say in her usual sharp tone, "You go straight to the high school and back. No detours!"

I nodded yes, but my 16-year-old self, in the form of a little devil on my right shoulder, was whispering something else entirely.

After my mom left the house, I immediately jumped in the car, turned on the radio, blasting Hootie & the Blowfish, and drove straight over to Mona's house. After picking up Mona, we were off on our exciting adventure! It's amazing the places you can go on the island with the freedom of a driver's license. We started with a slice of pizza and soda at the Somesville General Store, and of course we ran into kids from school who were all doing the exact same thing, hanging out and driving around on a chilly, clear December day. To be fair, there isn't much else to do during the winter months on Mount Desert Island.

After that, we drove on to Southwest Harbor, and headed down to the waterfront where, of course, we ran into more friends from high school.

Next we were off to Northeast Harbor, then Town Hill, joyriding and feeling like we didn't have a care in the world. By the time we hit the head of the island where you cross the Trenton Bridge to the mainland, I suddenly realized we had been driving around for over four hours. I knew we had better get the car back before my mother returned home from Ellsworth. I did a quick U-turn and we sped back down Route Three towards Bar Harbor, feeling free as birds and singing to the radio at the top of our lungs.

That feeling was immediately squashed the moment I pulled into Mona's driveway, and we spotted Jane's car parked there.

Mona looked at me with a sense of dread.

I gulped. "Oh no, I'm dead!"

I knew my mother was already home.

Waiting for me to show up in her car.

I rushed home, my heart pounding, my brain straining to come up with every excuse I could think of to explain why I still had the car. As I rounded the corner, I could see my mother standing out on our front porch with her hands on her hips, her cheeks flushed with anger.

I wasn't even out of the driver's side when she came storming over and let me have it. Eventually, however, after all her yelling, my free-flowing tears, and both of us arguing back and forth, I must admit we had some kind of break-through, and much to my surprise, she agreed that I could earn privileges to use the car. I knew this was as good as I was going to get in this moment, and I was fine with this arrangement, as I happily headed upstairs to my room.

That's when I heard the phone ring and my mother answering the call and talking to someone on the other end. It did not take long to deduce the gist of the conversation. In all the excitement of having the car for the day, I had completely forgotten to take her gingerbread to the high school Christmas bazaar and bake sale that day. Then I heard her hang up the phone and bellow, "Hayley!"

Well, my newfound driving privileges had felt so good for the two whole minutes I had them.

If you're going to have gingerbread, you absolutely must have ginger coffee to go along with it. And for those of you who need an extra kick, be sure to pour in a splash of your favorite bourbon.

GINGER COFFEE

INGREDIENTS:
6 tablespoons ground coffee (not instant)
1 tablespoon crystallized ginger
½ teaspoon ground cinnamon
1 tablespoon orange zest
6 cups cold water
optional garnish: cinnamon stick, whipped
    cream

Combine your coffee, orange zest, ginger and cinnamon and place into a coffee filter. Pour the six cups of water into the coffee machine and brew.

Garnish with whipped cream and a cinnamon stick and enjoy.

For this week's recipe I think you know it's a classic gingerbread! Are you sensing a theme here? My suggestion is if you try this delicious recipe, then don't forget to put a dollop of whipped cream on top, whether it's homemade or from a tub. Either way, it's going to be delicious!

MOM'S GINGERBREAD

INGREDIENTS:
3 eggs
1 cup sugar
1 cup molasses
1½ teaspoon ginger
1½ teaspoon cinnamon
½ teaspoon cloves
1 cup vegetable oil
2 cups all-purpose flour
2 teaspoons baking powder
1 cup boiling water

Preheat oven to 350 degrees. Grease your 13x9 baking dish with baking spray.

In a stand mixer, mix your eggs, sugar, molasses, spices, oil, and boiling water until well combined. Mix your baking powder into the flour and add a little at a time to the batter mixture until it is all combined.

Pour the batter into your greased baking dish and place in preheated oven for 40 to 45 minutes or until a tooth-pick comes out clean.

Chapter 8

Hayley wasn't sure how she felt about Bruce guffawing over all of Dwight's colorful stories. She could see he had taken an instant liking to her father, the two men now ribbing and joking with each other like a pair of old friends. Hayley remained wary of falling too much for his charms, but her husband had no compunction about buddying up to the man and enjoying his company. Dwight also was friends with Bruce's father, Charlie, growing up in Bar Harbor back in the 1960s until Charlie went off to college in Vermont to study natural resources and conservation and Dwight stayed in town to marry Sheila and settle down while working at the Jackson Lab, a biomedical research facility employing dozens of locals, cleaning out mouse cages. By the time Charlie moved back to Maine with his wife and bouncing baby boy Brucie to accept a job as a park ranger for Acadia, Dwight was already long gone.

Dwight had just finished telling a story about how

he and Charlie had once stolen a school bus to go to
Dunkin' Donuts in Ellsworth to buy donuts for everyone during senior year and almost got expelled right
before graduation. Charlie valiantly took the blame,
claiming to have coerced Dwight, although it was clearly
the other way around. But because Charlie was valedic-
torian, they didn't dare boot him so late in the game, especially since he was already set to attend the University
of Vermont in the fall. Dwight skated by with Cs and Ds
but did manage to squeak through and get his diploma in
the end.

Bruce slapped his knee. "I remember Dad telling me
that story. He was so scared when you guys got caught.
He thought he was going to go to jail."

"No, it was a harmless senior prank," Dwight
laughed, waving it off.

"Um, you did steal a school bus," Hayley reminded
him, not as amused by the story as her husband.

Randy, sitting on the couch next to Hayley, just
stared at his father in awe. He never would have dared
pull such an audacious, outrageous stunt, not in a million years. Perhaps it was fortuitous that Dwight had
exited their lives so early on, saving them from his obviously bad influences.

Dwight clapped Bruce on the back. "You really scored
with this one, Hayley, I have to say. He's a keeper.
What took you so long to reel him in?"

"A long stretch of bad choices," Hayley said quietly,
not eager to broach the topic of her first husband,
Danny. She narrowed her eyes as she stared at her father. "But I finally got there. I'm sure you understand
all about bad choices, don't you, Dwight?"

He was not about to argue. He snickered without missing a beat. "You're right about that, Hayley. That should be the title of my autobiography, *A Life of Bad Choices*." He turned to Randy. "But enough about me. I've met Hayley's fella. When am I going to meet yours?"

"In about thirty seconds. I just heard him pull into the driveway," Randy said, jumping to his feet and crossing to the wet bar to mix Sergio a drink.

"So he's from Brazil, am I right? What's his name again, Sancho?"

"Sergio," Randy corrected him. "And yes, he's from São Paulo originally."

When Sergio breezed through the front door and shed his winter coat, he was still wearing his blue police uniform. At the sight of him entering the living room, Dwight's eyes nearly popped out of his head and he choked on his hot buttered rum.

Bruce placed a hand on his back. "You okay, Dwight?"

After a brief coughing fit, Dwight nodded and set his mug down on the coffee table as the blood slowly drained from his face. "Just swallowed the wrong way, that's all." But Hayley could see he was deeply disturbed by Sergio's uniform, not to mention the holstered gun strapped to his side.

Randy handed Sergio his drink and then took him by the arm and led him over to where Dwight was sitting next to Bruce by the crackling fireplace. "Sergio, I'd like you to meet Dwight, my . . . father."

Sergio stuck out his hand. "Pleased to meet you, Dwight."

"Same here," Dwight mumbled, shaking his hand

but avoiding eye contact. "Randy didn't mention you were in law enforcement."

"Sergio is the chief of police here in Bar Harbor," Randy touted proudly.

Dwight quickly withdrew his hand, eyes fixed on the floor. "Is that right?"

"Yes, I never thought when I was a young boy back in Brazil that I would wind up a law enforcement officer in the United States," Sergio said, ignoring the obvious chill coming from their suddenly disturbed guest.

"That's nice," Dwight said dismissively before checking his watch. "Well, I better get going. Bubba and Jane will be wondering where I am."

"But I thought you were going to stay for dinner," Randy sighed, disappointed.

"Another time. But it was a hoot hanging out, telling old war stories. We'll all have to do it again real soon."

Hayley noticed a pair of headlights sweeping across the window as a car pulled into the driveway. "You have company."

Dwight shot out of his chair and raced to the window as if he feared there might be more cops surrounding the house.

Randy turned to Sergio. "Are we expecting anyone?"

Sergio shrugged. "Not that I know of."

Dwight slowly turned away from the window and glanced nervously over at Hayley. "It's your mother."

Now it was Hayley's turn to shoot out of her seat.

"*What*? She's supposed to be in Ellsworth Christmas shopping with Carl!"

"Well, she's here now," Dwight croaked.

Hayley dashed to the window to see Sheila marching toward the front porch with Carl in tow, carrying some paper shopping bags.

"What is she doing here? She never said anything about dropping by tonight!" Randy cried.

Hayley, thinking fast, grabbed her father by the arm. "Come on, Bruce, let's slip him out the back."

"I can't leave," Bruce protested. "My car is parked outside. She already knows I'm here."

"Fine. We'll go and wait for you up on the corner of Main Street, then we can drive Dwight back to Bubba and Jane's."

The door flew open. Sheila never bothered to knock. Hayley could hear her mother's singsongy voice as she and Dwight escaped through the kitchen to the back door. "Hello! Hello! Everybody decent?"

"Mom! What a pleasant surprise!" Hayley could hear Randy chirp before adding more somberly, "You didn't call first."

"We just drove back from Ellsworth. I found the cutest little ornaments for your Christmas tree that I couldn't wait to give you. You're going to love them!"

Once outside in the bitter cold, Hayley donned her mittens and scarf as she and Dwight trudged through the snow across the lawn and then up the paved road to Main Street.

A few minutes passed until they saw a car approaching. They assumed it was Bruce, but it turned out to be

Sergio in his squad car. He stopped next to them and rolled down the window. "Bruce is right behind me. I just got a call. Another domestic disturbance over at the Flood house."

Hayley's heart skipped a beat. Carroll and Althea Flood were a long-married couple known for their knock-down, drag-out fights, many resulting in either Carroll or Althea or one of their neighbors calling the police. Althea also happened to be Bruce's first cousin. "We'll drop off Dwight and meet you there."

Sergio nodded, rolled the window back up, and peeled away just as Bruce's headlights came into view, heading straight for them.

Hayley had a sinking feeling it was going to be a very long night.

Chapter 9

When Hayley and Bruce pulled up behind Sergio's squad car after dropping Dwight off at the Butler house, they could see Sergio on the front lawn of the Flood house, trying to reason with a red-faced, fuming Carroll Flood, who was in a stained white tank top underneath an open winter coat, some sweatpants, and army green snow boots. Sergio had a comforting arm around Carroll, trying to calm him down. They could see his wife, Althea, lurking about in a second-floor bedroom window.

As Hayley and Bruce got out of the car and gingerly approached, they overheard Carroll blubbering, "Her temper's out of control, Sergio, I'm at my wit's end. I don't know how to handle her anymore!"

The upstairs window flew open and Althea tossed an armful of clothes and shoes and a leather belt out. It all came tumbling down, landing in a snowbank. She bellowed at the top of her lungs, "Here, go shack up someplace else! I'm sick of looking at you!"

Sergio had turned off the flashing blue light on top of his squad car, hoping not to draw too much attention, but Hayley could see the surrounding neighbors in their houses staring out the window, eager to witness what might happen next.

Sergio called up to Carroll's wife. "Althea, why don't you come down here so we can talk and work this out like adults!"

"That would require Carroll to *act* like an adult instead of a horny teenager on the prowl ready to flirt with any dog walker passing by with a double-D cup bra!"

Hayley was beginning to understand the root of the problem. Carroll Flood had always been a shameless flirt, and from what she knew about Althea, she was quite the jealous type.

"I just said hello like any friendly neighbor would, Althea! You don't have to start World War Three every time I speak to another woman!"

"You said you wanted to pet them!" Althea roared.

"I was talking about her twin beagles!"

"But you were *looking* at her breasts!"

Carroll threw up his hands. "See, Sergio, she's completely lost her mind! I can't even take a relaxing evening stroll around the neighborhood with my wife without it ending in someone calling the police!"

Bruce waved up at Althea. "Hey, cuz!"

Althea's angry demeanor dissipated and she lit up like a Christmas tree. "Hello, Bruce! How sweet of you and Hayley to stop by for a visit! Why don't you both come in for some hot cocoa and we can catch up!

I'll be finished ridding the house of all of Carroll's belongings in two shakes of a lamb's tail!"

"This isn't a social call. Hayley and I were with Sergio when the complaint came in. Are we talking about Pasty Fordham and her beagles?"

"Yes, I don't blame Patsy. She can't help that God gave her cleavage that would be picked up on satellite photos! It's Carroll! He's shameless! He makes it his life's mission to embarrass me!"

"Are you sure Carroll wasn't just talking about the dogs? I've seen them. They are really cute!" Hayley piped in.

"I'm not an idiot, Hayley! I saw what his eyes were really focused on!" Althea yelled down.

Sergio turned to Carroll. "Is she right, Carroll? Were you really looking at Patsy and not the dogs when you said you wanted to pet them?"

"Of course I was," Carroll mumbled. "I'm not blind. I mean, come on. Every red-blooded straight man in town wants an eyeful of Patsy whenever he's around her."

"Then just tell Althea you're sorry and let's end this, so we can all go home," Sergio pressed.

"And give her the satisfaction? No way!" Carroll snorted, scooping up some snow, forming a snowball, and hurling it up at Althea, who ducked. It hit the side of the house, missing her.

Sergio had seen enough. "Either you apologize, or I take you down to the precinct and book you for disturbing the peace and lock you up in the drunk tank for the night until I can put you before a judge in the morning."

"You would really do that?" Carroll asked, skeptically.

"I don't see any scenario where Althea would come and bail you out before an arraignment, do you?"

Carroll thought about this and then slowly turned, calling up to his wife, who was still hovering out the second-floor window. "Baby, I'm sorry. Yes, I admit, my eyes were on Patsy, but my heart, well, that beats only for you!"

Boy, is he smooth, Hayley thought to herself. No wonder with all their seemingly twice-weekly brawls, the couple always seemed to manage to eventually kiss and make up.

Hayley and Bruce could see Althea's steely gaze starting to crack.

"Come on, baby, let me in. We can snuggle up next to the fire and I can tell you how much I love you!"

"I'm going to have to think about it!" Althea sniffed.

"Honey pie, it's twenty degrees out here. I'm freezing my buns off and Sergio probably wants to go home to his husband! I tell you what: I will let you open one of the presents I got you early. Not to give anything away, but it fits in an envelope and you might have to get your passport renewed."

"An airline ticket! Omigod, where are you taking me?"

"You'll have to let me in to find out!"

Althea suddenly disappeared from the window, and in less than a minute the front door flew open and she beckoned her husband back inside the house.

Carroll patted Sergio on the back. "Thanks, Chief, I owe you one. Have a Merry Christmas."

"You too, Carroll." Sergio nodded.

"Night, Bruce. Night, Hayley. Merry Christmas!" Then Carroll bounded across the snow-covered lawn, enveloping his ecstatic wife in a bear hug before they withdrew inside the house and slammed the door so hard the wreath hanging on it fell off its hook and landed face down on the porch.

"Hopefully that's the end of the drama with those two for a while," Sergio said to Hayley and Bruce.

At the time, none of them had any idea just how wrong he would turn out to be.

Chapter 10

As Hayley weaved her way through the throng of party guests crushed into Liddy Crawford's living room for her annual Christmas soiree, she could not help but be impressed by the incredible lengths her BFF went every year to top herself. There was still the massive trees with all their tasteful ornaments and blinking lights—four in total, not including the decorated trees outside the house—the high-end caterer recently profiled in *Bon Appétit* magazine who served all the mouthwatering appetizers, and the three separate open bars strategically situated in all of the major first-floor rooms. But this year, as an added treat, instead of the usual high school choir hired to dress up and sing Christmas carols, she had invested in a professional piano player who regularly played at the Blue Note jazz club in Manhattan. He had flown all the way up from New York to Maine just to perform at Liddy's swanky party. Despite the notable upgrades this year that could have dampened the rowdy, freewheeling atmosphere, Liddy's Christmas party as always, was full of festive cheer.

Hayley maneuvered her way over to the hostess, who was wearing a Christmas tree camouflage blazer over a white top and black slacks, chatting up Liddy's father, Elmer, and his husband, the chiseled chinned, model gorgeous Italian Rocco, who was about two decades younger and looked like he had just stepped off the cover of an Abercrombie & Fitch catalogue cover. Elmer had met Rocco on a previous summer trip to Maine when he came to see Liddy when his ex-wife Celeste was, by design, out of town. Rocco was from Bangor, about an hour away, and was working as a waiter at the Wonder View restaurant for the summer where Elmer took Liddy for dinner one evening. The sparks were immediate, and Liddy, who had learned her father was gay shortly after her parents divorced, encouraged Elmer to ask the young man out on a date while he was still in town. It was a whirlwind courtship and by the end of Elmer's vacation, they were making plans for Rocco to come visit him in New York. That fateful trip occurred about a month later, and Rocco was packing for a permanent move to New York mere weeks later. Needless to say, Celeste's reaction to their relationship was far less supportive than her daughter's, and there had been bad blood between them ever since. So it was a stroke of luck that Celeste was out of town this evening, visiting her cousins in Presque Isle.

"Liddy, I love the piano player. How did you find him?" Hayley asked.

"It was all Dad and Rocco. He's a buddy of theirs in New York," Liddy replied.

"We've been going to the Blue Note to hear him play for years," Elmer said. "He was more than happy to do us this favor for my favorite daughter."

"I'm your *only* daughter," Liddy laughed.

The piano player was at the moment belting out Mariah Carey's "All I Want for Christmas Is You" and managing to hit all the high notes as a few drunken guests gathered around the piano, trying to sing along.

"Hayley, I must tell you, I never miss one of your columns. Elmer has the *Island Times* delivered to our New York apartment every day, and I just tried your summer corn casserole for a few friends we had over for dinner. It was to die for! Everybody loved it!"

Hayley lit up. "Why thank you, Rocco, I knew I always liked you!"

"Why weren't you at the cabin with Elmer, Bubba, and Dwight for this apparently annual super-secret ice fishing trip?" Hayley asked Rocco.

Rocco took a sip from the mug of spiced eggnog he was holding. "I was visiting my folks in Bangor. Besides, a remote cabin in the woods with no heat is not exactly my idea of a good time. I hate the cold weather, which is why I've been pestering Elmer to move to Palm Springs."

"I love Palm Springs!" Liddy cooed. "I would visit and probably never leave! I bet I could crush it as a Realtor out there. Gay men love me!"

Sheila, ashen-faced, approached the group. "Excuse me, Hayley, could I have a private word with you, please?"

"Sure, Mom," Hayley said, not liking the sound of

this one bit as Sheila took her firmly by the arm and led her over to a corner away from the crowd.

"Mom, you look sick to your stomach. What's wrong?"

"We have a situation."

"Okay, I'm sure it's not that bad. What are we talking about?"

"Jane and I had no idea that Elmer and Rocco were going to be here. Nobody ever bothered to mention it to us."

"Because Celeste is out of town, so I knew it would be fine for them to attend Liddy's party. I thought you and Jane liked Elmer and Rocco."

"We do, dear, they're both lovely, but Celeste? Not so much, as you can understand."

"But Celeste isn't here, which is why it shouldn't be a problem, right?"

"Wrong. Celeste called me two days ago and told me she was having a miserable time with her negative cousin who loves to criticize her all the time and decided to come home early."

Hayley's stomach dropped. "Oh no . . ."

"And when I told Jane, she said, Wouldn't it be a nice surprise if Celeste didn't tell Liddy she was back in town and just showed up at the party unannounced to surprise her?"

"Oh no!" Hayley moaned.

"And I said, Yes, that would be fun to see the look on her face when Celeste crashed the party!"

Hayley grabbed Sheila by the arm. "Mom, you have to call her right now and tell her not to come!"

"Yes, yes, that's what I'm going to do!" She began to pat herself down. "Now what did I do with my phone?"

"Mom, hurry!"

"I know I had it when Carl and I came in!" She turned to Carl, who was over by the biggest Christmas tree, chatting up Bruce and Mona's parents, Bubba and Jane. She screamed across the room over the din of the crowd and the piano player's crooning. "Carl, did I give you my phone?"

Carl, hearing his name, called out, "What?"

"My phone! My phone! Do you have my phone!" Sheila shouted, quickly losing patience.

The piano player finished Mariah Carey to rapturous applause. Then he stood up and waved Rocco over, encouraging him to fill in for him while he took a quick break. Rocco, a former singer and dancer from community theater, was thrilled at his sudden opportunity to perform. He plopped down on the bench and began banging out "Christmas (Baby Please Come Home)" as several party guests joined in.

Carl shot his hand up in the air, holding Sheila's phone.

She sighed, relieved. "Thank God! Hopefully I can reach Celeste in time!"

"Surprise, everyone!" a woman shrieked. At the sight of Liddy's mother, Celeste, trouncing through the front door, all dolled up in a classy red and green Christmas party dress, everyone in the house fell silent except for Rocco, who was oblivious, still belting out his favorite Christmas carol.

Celeste's eyes fell upon Rocco. Her mouth dropped open in shock. Elmer, who was just as stunned to see Celeste, managed to squeak out, "Celeste . . ."

Celeste's eyes darted from Rocco to Elmer, then narrowed as she began searching the crowd for her daughter.

Carl bounded up to Sheila, handing her the phone. "Here you go, honey."

Sheila swatted him away like a fly. "Never mind. I don't need it anymore."

As Celeste started to make a beeline for Elmer, Liddy bolted toward her, intercepting her just as she was passing Hayley, Sheila, and Carl.

"Well, it seems the surprise is on me!" Celeste hissed.

"Mother, please, don't make a scene. I had no idea you would be here. I thought you were up in Presque Isle."

"I came home early. Your Aunt Adelaide was a pill as usual and I couldn't stand staying with her and her creepy husband with the lazy eye a moment longer, even if it was the holidays. What is your father and— his *friend* doing here?"

"Rocco is Dad's husband, Mom. It's been ten years. You need to learn to accept it."

"I'm not his gatekeeper. Your father is free to do as he pleases. I just didn't expect to see him here in Maine. Isn't he too busy attending Christmas parties with all his fancy, rich New York friends to come all the way up here?"

"That's not fair. Dad's friends in Manhattan are wonderful. They're all very sweet and down-to-earth."

"I didn't know you were so chummy with his elite social circle," Celeste sniffed.

Elmer made a move to come over and say hello to his ex-wife, but Liddy shot him a warning look to stand down, at least for now.

"You know I don't just go to New York on shopping trips, Mother, I always make a point to see Dad and Rocco while I'm there. You can't begrudge me for wanting to have a relationship with my father, even though you two are no longer married."

"Of course I don't begrudge you. You're an adult. You can do whatever you want. I'd just like a little warning next time."

"I could say the same thing to you," Liddy replied, folding her arms.

Sheila stepped forward and hugged Celeste. "Give your mother a break, Liddy. I can commiserate with what she must be going through. It's not always easy when you're confronted by your painful past. I honestly wouldn't be as calm, cool, and collected as Celeste is right now if I ran into my awful ex-husband Dwight out of the blue."

"Ho-ho-ho! Merry Christmas!" Santa Claus bellowed as he marched in from the kitchen carrying a sack of gifts.

The sound of his voice was disconcertingly familiar to both Hayley and Sheila, who eyed Santa curiously as he dropped the sack and rubbed his big, protruding belly with his white-gloved hand.

Liddy cocked her head to the side, confused. "Wait, I asked Sal Moretti to play Santa Claus. That is definitely *not* Sal."

Hayley suddenly had a sinking feeling.

"Maybe it's the real Santa Claus!" Carl chimed in brightly.

"No, it can't be . . . ." Sheila muttered.

She propelled forward before Hayley could stop her, marched over to Santa Claus, grabbing a fistful of his white beard and yanking it down.

She was now staring into the scraggy, stubbled face of her own ex-husband, Dwight, whose eyes widened in bewilderment.

"Sheila, Jane told me you were going to be at Lucy Hollister's Christmas party tonight," Dwight whispered.

"Yes, I stopped by for a few minutes before coming here, and then from here I am going to drop by the Cooper residence for their event. It's what we call party-hopping."

"Oh," Dwight moaned. "Well, you can understand how I got my signals crossed. Anyway . . . Merry Christmas."

Sheila stood frozen in place.

It didn't help that they were both under the mistletoe and desperately trying to ignore that uncomfortable fact.

Hayley spun around and waved at Rocco to play something—anything—to cut the palpable tension. He started banging out a beloved classic, "Jingle Bells", encouraging everyone to sing along.

It didn't help.

Chapter 11

As Dwight and Sheila stared awkwardly at each other, neither knowing what to say, the front door to Liddy Crawford's packed home burst open yet again, and another Santa Claus barreled in carrying a sack of gifts over his shoulder. This was obviously the man originally recruited for the role, Hayley's former boss at the Island Times, corpulent Sal Moretti, who was the perfect casting choice with his naturally bulbous nose and ample gut. Sal stopped short at the sight of a second Santa Claus, who had obviously stolen his thunder.

"What the hell is going on here?" Sal roared, stepping out of his jolly ole Saint Nick character.

Liddy flew to his side to try and explain as Sheila suddenly turned her back on Dwight and stormed off. Dwight turned to Hayley, who was hovering behind him. "I swear, Hayley, I was told she wasn't going to be here."

"It's fine. She'll get over it," Hayley said, not believing one word she was saying, a feeling in her gut that the drama was only going to grow exponentially from this point forward. "Why are you dressed up as Santa Claus?"

Dwight shrugged. "I don't know. I saw the costume for rent at the Christmas Shop on Main Street and I thought, Why not? Might liven up the party."

"Look around, Dwight, this party does not need any more livening up, especially after the scene you just caused!"

"I can see that now," Dwight whispered, chastened. "Who knew another Santa Claus would show up?"

"I did! Liddy did! Everyone here did! Sal has played Santa at Liddy's last seven Christmas parties! You would have known too if you had just told me your plans!"

Hayley knew she was being hard on her father.

He was just trying to do something fun, but it had backfired spectacularly.

But she could not shake the guilt that she had assured her mother that Dwight was not going to be anywhere near Bar Harbor during her visit to Maine, and she had kept it a secret when she discovered he had gone back on his word to steer clear.

Was it an honest mistake?

Or was Dwight at this party to intentionally stir up trouble?

She just didn't know.

So much time had passed since he left the family.

She knew pretty much nothing about her father at all.

Or the kind of man he really was.

Spying Sheila stewing in a corner with Celeste and Jane, Hayley made a beeline for them to face this crisis head-on. As she approached, she could hear Jane apologizing.

"This is all my fault, Sheila, I should've said something earlier, but I didn't want to upset you!" Jane cried.

"I understand. You were just trying to protect me, Jane," Sheila said, her hand trembling as she touched Jane's arm.

"I told Dwight you were going to Lucy Hollister's party so he wouldn't show up there unannounced since he used to be friends with her husband, Stan, but he must have just assumed you wouldn't be coming to this party!"

Sheila turned to Celeste. "Did you know he was in town?"

"No! Absolutely not! And frankly, Jane, I am hurt you didn't confide in me. Do you think I can't keep a secret?"

Jane nodded. "Yes, Celeste, that's exactly what I think. There has never been a secret you have been able to keep!"

"Well, I never!" Celeste snapped, her cheeks reddening.

"Don't get upset, Celeste," Sheila urged. "Jane's right. You're a terrible gossip. But that's why we love you."

"I didn't tell anyone. Bubba, of course, knew because Dwight is crashing at our house on a futon. And then there is Mona and Hayley . . ."

Sheila's nostrils flared. "I beg your pardon?"

Jane suddenly realized her faux pas. "Well, Mona dropped by the other night. She never bothers to call and let us know she's coming, and when she saw Dwight having dinner with us, well, she called Hayley."

"So Hayley knew he was in town all along?" Sheila caught Hayley standing nearby, watching out of the corner of her eye. "Hayley, how could you hide this from me? Him randomly showing up here in a Santa suit caught me completely off-guard! I had no time to emotionally prepare! I must have looked like a complete fool in front of everyone! I've never been so embarrassed and humiliated in all my life!"

"Mom, please don't overreact. People hardly noticed," Hayley said weakly as Celeste and Jane gave her withering, skeptical looks. "Dwight swore to me that he was not going to come to Bar Harbor. I wasn't lying to you before. I was just as surprised as you were when I found out he was here. Yes, I chose not to tell you, because I thought it would be okay if you two never crossed paths, like Jane did. But wait—why does Jane get a free pass and I don't?"

"Because you're my daughter. It's your job to tell me everything! I have to get out of here. I'm having trouble breathing," Sheila gasped, clutching her chest.

"You just need some fresh air. It will be fine," Celeste assured her, taking Sheila by the arm and gradually leading her toward the back door off the kitchen.

Suddenly Sheila stopped in her tracks. "Dear lord, what is going on over there?"

Celeste glanced about. "Where?"

"Over in the corner, by the Christmas tree," Sheila

said in a squeaky voice, pointing with her right index finger.

They all followed Sheila's finger over to the tree, where Dwight, still dressed as Santa, had just told a joke to Carl, who was bent over guffawing.

"Well, look who's become bosom buddies already. This is a nightmare!" Sheila wailed as Jane rushed to take Sheila by the other arm and they led her away.

Sheila cranked her head around as she was shuffled off and called back to Hayley, "I'm calling the airline when we get home to see if I can change our return flight back to Florida for first thing tomorrow morning! I will not celebrate Christmas in the same town as that scheming, terrible excuse for a man!"

Hayley, resigned, just nodded. She knew she could probably talk her mother out of leaving early. Sheila just needed to cool down while Hayley formulated a plan to keep her mother and father as far apart as possible for the rest of the holiday season.

It would be a herculean task, given the amount of mutual friends involved, but it had to be done. And Hayley prayed Dwight would be cooperative, because she still was not 100 percent convinced that he did not show up at Liddy Crawford's annual Christmas party on purpose, knowing his embittered ex-wife would be in attendance, and causing such a spectacle.

Things could not get any worse, Hayley thought to herself.

And yet, they would.

Chapter 12

Carl rushed up to Hayley, who had now joined Sergio at the bar. She was going to need some stiff Christmas cheer to counteract the stress of all the family drama.

"We're leaving now," Carl said solemnly.

"Carl, please, talk to Mom. Convince her not to fly home before Christmas. She's been so looking forward to this trip."

"No, we're leaving the party. We're just calling it a night. I've managed to talk her into not changing our airline ticket."

Hayley felt a wave of relief wash over her. "Thank you, Carl. I owe you."

"On the one condition that she does not have to endure any more interaction with Dwight. I don't see what her problem is. He strikes me as a very charming, amiable guy."

"I think it would be wise of you not to share that

opinion with my mother, Carl," Hayley warned. "For all our sakes."

"Roger that." Carl nodded, seeing her point.

"Okay, good night, all. Sheila's waiting for me outside. Enjoy the rest of the party."

"Bye, Carl," Sergio said, handing Hayley a spiked eggnog. "Here, this is for you. I asked for a double shot of brandy."

Hayley took a sip and exhaled. "Merry Christmas."

"Merry Christmas, Hayley," Sergio said with a sympathetic smile. "Don't worry. New Year's will be here before you know it."

Carroll Flood hustled up to the bar and addressed the bartender. "Just a club soda with lime, Edwin."

"You got it," the bartender said, reaching for a plastic bottle and twisting off the cap.

Carroll noticed Sergio's surprised look. "Starting my New Year's resolution a little early, Chief. I've decided to cut down on my drinking. I think it's best for everyone."

"Congratulations, Carroll," Sergio said.

"Althea and I talked it out and we realized that I was avoiding my problems by getting lit every night, and that if I didn't stop, our whole marriage was going to fall apart. So I'm going to do my best to save it."

"That's very honorable of you. And smart. You don't want to lose Althea. She's a good egg," Sergio noted.

Carroll looked across the room to see Althea chatting up Celeste and Jane. "She is. She deserves better than me, but God love her, the saint is determined to stick by my side, for better or worse. I need to prove I'm worth it." He then turned back to Sergio and

Hayley with a rueful smile. "I guess my days of being the life of the party are finally over."

"Don't say that, Carroll, you'll always be the life of the party," Hayley insisted.

And it turned out he was. Within fifteen minutes, Carroll was belting out "I Saw Mommy Kissing Santa Claus" to the whole enraptured crowd as Rocco accompanied him on the piano. For the second refrain, he even hopped up on top of the piano, sprawling out like a torch singer played by Michelle Pfeiffer in *The Fabulous Baker Boys* to the delight of all of Liddy's guests. Hayley noticed a twinkle in Althea's eye as she watched her husband perform, happy in the knowledge that he was just as entertaining even when he was stone-cold sober.

When he finished, his audience erupted in thunderous applause. Carroll jumped down off the piano and took a deep bow before gesturing toward Rocco, who stood up from the piano bench and also bowed as the clapping continued.

Hayley wandered over to Mona, who was in a deep conversation with Dolly Halperin, who owned a local arts and crafts business and who also happened to be Carroll Flood's first wife, before he divorced her to marry Althea.

"He certainly wasn't this much fun when the two of us were married," Dolly scoffed as she folded her arms, watching Carroll soak in all the accolades from his rousing performance.

Dolly was an attractive woman with perhaps a skosh too much makeup, a full, curvy figure not unlike her namesake Dolly Parton, and a throwback bouffant of hair dyed brassy blond. She wore a large poinsettia pin on her tight green sweater, but it certainly did not hide the fact that she was braless on this cold Maine winter evening.

It had been ten years since Dolly and Carroll had split and it was pretty apparent she still had not gotten over it.

"Don't be bitter, Dolly, you're better off!" Mona said, clapping her on the back. "Everyone knows Carroll can be a handful, and now he's Althea's problem to handle."

"I know, you're right, Mona, but it still hurts sometimes. He and Althea have been together for so long now, and I thought by now I would have remarried, or at least be dating someone, but no, I've been having one long dry spell ever since I signed the divorce papers. I guess most of the single men in town aren't keen on buying damaged goods."

Hayley could not stand listening to Dolly's tale of woe any longer. "Dolly, don't put yourself down like that. You're a gorgeous woman with a big personality. You have a lot to offer. You'll definitely find someone. Just be patient."

"It's been ten years, Hayley, how long am I going to have to wait?"

Suddenly Liddy hurried up to the three women, nervously glancing over her shoulder. "Is he following me?"

Hayley looked behind her. "Who?"

"Albie Schooner. I've been avoiding him all night, but he cornered me in the kitchen, and I thought I would never get away."

"I think Albie is very sweet," Hayley agreed. "If

you don't like him, why did you invite him to your Christmas party?"

"I had no choice. I'm on the board of directors of the Criterion Theatre and he is technically one of our biggest draws with that stupid, boring classic movie night he hosts every week."

"I love Albie's movie nights," Dolly gushed. "Especially his introductions before the screening. He knows everything about the golden age of Hollywood, the stars and directors, and all the juicy behind-the-scenes stories."

"How nice for you, Dolly, but if I have to listen to Albie explain the key differences between the Janet Gaynor *A Star Is Born* and the Judy Garland *A Star Is Born* and the Barbra Streisand *A Star Is Born* and the Lady Gaga *A Star Is Born*, well, I'm going to hang myself next to the mistletoe!"

Hayley chuckled. "I'm actually interested in hearing what he has to say about that."

"Do you have a couple of hours? He never stops!" Liddy snapped.

Mona vigorously shook her head. "I'm going to have to agree with Liddy on this one. Sounds superboring to me."

"I can't believe Mona Barnes actually agrees with something *I* said." Liddy spun around to search her throng of guests, spotting Albie talking a mile a minute to Bruce, who appeared mildly interested in hearing what the movie buff had to say. "Just warn me if you see him heading in this direction. He is so obnoxious."

"I like him!" Hayley said.

"Me too," Dolly whispered. "I mean, I don't really

know him, we've never officially met, but I do enjoy attending his special movie nights. He's doing classic Hitchcock the whole month of December."

A light bulb suddenly went off in Hayley's brain. "Hold on now, Dolly. You're single. Albie's single. Have you ever thought of asking him out?"

Dolly's eyes widened. "On a date? No! I wouldn't dare! I mean, what if he said no?"

"Albie hasn't been with a woman since the sixth grade when he pretended the school nurse was his girlfriend after she warmed the stethoscope by blowing on it before checking to see if he had a chest cold. Trust me, he's not going to say no!" Mona laughed.

Hayley studied Albie chatting with Bruce. He definitely had a geriatric Sheldon vibe from *The Big Bang Theory*, but he was handsome in an odd sort of way. She also found his fountain of film knowledge endearing. Dolly, though younger, was obviously fun-loving and interested. This could definitely be a good match.

"Excuse me," a man said, tapping Liddy on the shoulder.

It was Carroll Flood.

He did not notice his ex-wife among the group at first.

"Where are you hiding those delicious gumdrops you put out every year?"

"They're right over there in a bowl on the coffee table," Liddy said, pointing him in the right direction.

"Still scarfing down gumdrops every chance you get, I see," Dolly said, folding her arms.

Carroll finally noticed her. "Um, oh, hello, Dolly. Happy holidays."

"Same to you, Carroll," Dolly seethed, still not over him.

Hayley was more determined than ever now to help Dolly move on by fixing her up with Albie Schooner.

There was a long, awkward silence.

Finally, Carroll slowly started to back away. "Well, I'm going to get me some of those gumdrops. Coffee table, you said?" He turned around but stopped in his tracks, his eyes falling upon Dwight in his Santa suit with no beard, who was mingling with Bubba, Elmer, and Rocco near the dessert table. "What the hell is *he* doing here?"

"Who?" Mona asked.

"Dwight Jordan! I thought he was dead!" Carroll snarled. "Or at least I hoped he was!"

Carroll took off like a shot, barreling through the crowd to get across the room to Dwight, who was oblivious to the impending onslaught.

"Oh no," Hayley moaned, chasing after Carroll.

By the time Carroll reached him, Dwight had sensed a whirling dervish was bearing down on him and turned around to face a tomato–red-faced Carroll Flood with spittle on the sides of his mouth.

"Talk about a blast from the past. How have you been, buddy?" Dwight asked calmly, ignoring Carroll's rage.

"How dare you show your face around here after what you did to me! I ought to punch your lights out!"

"Which would be a huge mistake with the chief of police standing right behind you," Bubba sternly reminded him.

On cue, Sergio stepped forward. "Do we have a problem here, Carroll?"

"You're damn right we do!" He pointed a crooked finger in Dwight's face. "This man ruined my life!"

Dwight never even blinked.

It was as if he had been expecting this kind of attack.

Hayley had no idea what any of this was about, but she did not have to wait to find out because Carroll wanted everyone at Liddy Crawford's Christmas party to know the whole story.

"You all know when I was younger I had big plans to be a professional baker!" Carroll shouted to the crowd.

Everyone, of course, knew about Carroll's baking talent. He had won every baking contest he had ever entered, except for one time when he was felled by the flu and had to bow out of the Historical Society's annual gingerbread house contest in 2009.

"Well, I'm not just a baker, I consider myself a decent cook as well, and back in the 1980s I was working at the same dude ranch as Dwight out in Arizona! You've all heard the story! Dwight here spiked the chili with Ex-Lax in order to distract the cowboys while he made off with a belt buckle worth its weight in gold!"

"It was a long time ago, Carroll," Dwight said in a soothing voice. "I admit I made mistakes in my life."

"But your mistakes in life cost me dearly! I got swept up in your shenanigans! Everyone at the ranch thought I was in on it since I was head cook and you worked for me. Word got around. My reputation never recovered. I couldn't find work anywhere after that incident! And it's all *your* fault!"

Hayley detected a slight hint of guilt on Dwight's face as he stood in front of Carroll, calmly listening.

"I had no other option but to move back to Maine and get a job at the town dump with the help of my father! Who knows where I would be now if you hadn't sabotaged me!"

Dwight bowed his head. "You're right, Carroll. I'm sorry. But you've done all right. You have a nice home, a beautiful wife . . ."

Hayley saw Dolly cringing.

Dwight was obviously referring to his second wife, Althea.

Carroll put a hand up in front of Dwight's face to silence him. "Stop! Just stop! I don't want to hear your limp apology! You don't get to talk about my life now!"

Dwight took a step back. "You're right, Carroll. So I'm going to do everyone here a favor and just say good night."

Dwight turned to go, but Carroll lunged forward, grabbing him by the arm. "No! You don't get to just walk out of here! You and I have unfinished business!"

Everyone braced themselves for Carroll to take a roundhouse swing at Dwight.

Even Dwight winced.

But Carroll didn't hit him.

Instead, he peacefully let go of his arm.

"We're going to settle this once and for all."

Dwight stared at him, confused. "Are you challenging me to a duel, Carroll? Because I'm not going to fight you."

"Yes, a duel of sorts. But instead of fists or guns or knives, we battle with baked goods!"

Dwight arched an eyebrow. "Baked goods?"

"You always considered yourself better than me when it came to our individual culinary skills. You constantly looked down on me when we were younger! Even on that dude ranch in Arizona when I was the boss and you were working for me, you kept belittling me, criticizing my food, telling me how you would have made it better! I was going to fire you, but then you ran off into the night and I never got the chance! Well, now I can finally prove to you that I'm the master chef, not you!"

Mona raised a hand, curious. "How are you going to do that?"

Ignoring Mona, Carroll kept his gaze fixed on a surprisingly unfazed Dwight. "I challenge you to enter the Bar Harbor Historical Society's gingerbread house competition and we'll see who has the *real* talent!"

Dwight did not miss a beat. "You're on."

"Good! And may the best man win!" Carroll roared.

Chapter 13

Hayley gasped at the state of her kitchen when she and Mona breezed through the back door. One could assume a bomb had gone off and sent dishes and cutlery and pots and pans flying everywhere. The counters and floor were covered in flour; mixing bowls and cooking pans were piled high in the sink. Blueberry played with a wad of dough that had dropped to the floor like it was catnip, batting it around with his sharp-clawed paws. Leroy was hiding under the kitchen table nervously watching Blueberry's every move, anticipating a sudden surprise attack at any moment. Sheila and Jane stood in front of the stove, inspecting pieces of baked gingerbread fresh from the oven while Celeste sat at the table behind them, legs crossed, her nose buried in one of Hayley's cookbooks.

"'According to the recipe, the most important part is making sure we have a sturdy base,'" Celeste read from the recipe.

Jane poked at a piece of hardened gingerbread. "It still feels a little soft to me. I'm worried it won't support the walls of the cottage."

"It's harder than the last three we tried," Sheila said, breaking off a piece and popping it into her mouth. "But let's try again, one more time."

"What's happening here?" Hayley asked, although a part of her really did not want to know.

"The three of us have decided to enter the Historical Society's gingerbread house contest," Sheila answered matter-of-factly, waving Hayley away. "And we still have to make the royal icing, so if you two could give us some space, we would certainly appreciate it."

Hayley's jaw dropped. "Are you seriously shooing me out of my own kitchen?"

"It's a tiny kitchen! We can barely move about without bumping into each other, but if you insist on staying, I suppose we could use an extra pair of hands. But Mona, I'm afraid you would be one too many."

"Don't worry, I'm happy to sit this one out!" Mona exclaimed.

"I don't understand. Why are you entering this contest? First of all, you made a very big deal about not having any interaction with Dwight while you're here, and everyone in town knows he is the one to beat in the gingerbread house contest, thanks to Carroll Flood's challenge."

"I'm fully aware I will be competing with your father, but I certainly do not have to speak to him or even look at him in order to whoop his butt and scoop first prize right out from under him!"

"Which leads me to my second point. You don't

bake! Every cookie you ever served me when I was a child was store-bought."

"I'm sure that's not true," Sheila sniffed.

"Yes, it is!" Hayley cried.

Sheila looked to her BFFs, Jane and Celeste, who avoided eye contact with her because it was painfully clear they could not in good conscience come to her defense.

"Well, people change," Sheila said dismissively.

"Really? So when did you take up baking?" Hayley asked, folding her arms.

Jane checked her watch. "About an hour ago."

"Is this some kind of revenge strategy? Is it your mission to show up Dwight by beating him in the contest? Mom, that's a fool's errand. You know what a talented baker he is."

"Somebody needs to try and take him down a peg or two. I'm sick of that smug look on his face all the time!" Sheila sighed before picking up a spoon and scooping some icing out of a bowl. "Besides, Jane is our secret weapon. She bakes desserts for her grandkids all the time!" She stuck the spoon in her mouth to taste the icing. Her smile slowly faded. She chewed and chewed, a distasteful look on her face, before spitting it out in the sink. "Jane, it's gritty and chunky. The icing needs to be smooth and silky. How long did you knead it?"

"That was Celeste's job!" Jane said accusingly.

Celeste shrugged. "I got bored."

"We need to work together if we're going to win this!" Sheila insisted.

Celeste put down the cookbook, not noticing her

daughter Liddy coming in quietly through the back door behind Hayley and Mona.

"Look, I know a professional baker from Boston I can call who is visiting his family in Southwest Harbor for the holidays. I'm sure he would be happy to make the perfect gingerbread house for us while we go out for cocktails!" Celeste suggested.

"That's cheating!" Hayley wailed.

"Who's going to know?" Celeste scoffed.

"I will!"

They all turned as Hayley and Mona parted to reveal Liddy angrily glaring at her mother.

"Liddy, sweetie, darling, I didn't see you come in," Celeste said, her face frozen.

"And as one of the Historical Society's esteemed celebrity judges, I won't hesitate to disqualify you, not for a second, if I even get a whiff of proof that you three did not bake and construct your entry all on your own from scratch!"

Sheila stepped forward, wiping her hands on the stained apron she was wearing. "Liddy, I promise you, we will stick to playing by the rules. I want to win this fair and square." She picked up a piece of one of the discarded gingerbread walls and broke off a piece, holding it out for Liddy to try. A small piece fell to the floor where Blueberry wandered over, took one sniff and a quick lick, and then recoiled, tail in the air and strutted away past Leroy, who was still hiding under the table, shrinking back, hoping to make himself invisible.

They all stared at the untouched piece on the floor.

Liddy shook her head. "No, thanks. I'm going to wait until the actual contest to taste test anything."

"Good call," Mona joked.

Liddy turned to Hayley and Mona. "Why don't we clear out and let them do their thing? We can have some fried clams and cosmos at Drinks Like a Fish. My treat!"

Liddy did not have to ask twice.

A trashed kitchen was worth not having to watch the train wreck unfolding in front of them. "Good luck, Mom! I won't be late!"

As Hayley, Liddy, and Mona hustled out the door, they heard Sheila declare like a drill sergeant, "Okay, ladies, back to work!"

Chapter 14

Albie Schooner stood confidently in front of the large cardboard poster of Alfred Hitchcock's *Rope* set up on an easel that was situated to the left of the concession stand at the Criterion Theatre as Dwight waited patiently for Albie to answer the question he had just asked.

Albie repeated Dwight's question out loud. "What are the other Hitchcock movies starring Jimmy Stewart besides *Rope*?"

"That's right." Dwight nodded. "There are three more."

"Jeez, Dwight, that's such a softball question," Albie scoffed before breaking into a wide smile and rattling off, "*Rope* was his first in 1948, followed by *Rear Window* in 1954, *The Man Who Knew Too Much* in 1956, and of course, *Vertigo* in 1958."

"That's correct," Dwight said, impressed.

Albie looked at the group of people in Dwight's

party, eager for more. "What else have you got? Hit me! I'm a master of Hitchcock film facts!"

"Who was Hitchcock's favorite actor to work with?" Hayley piped in, flanked by Bruce and Dolly, who they had invited to tag along with them to Albie's classic movie night.

"That's an easy one. Cary Grant," Albie responded, pleased with himself.

Dwight clapped Albie on the back. "It's really good to see you again, Albie. It's been a long time."

"You're looking good, Dwight. Nice to finally see you back in town."

Hayley, who had invited Dolly in the hopes of formally introducing her to Albie with the hope for a possible love connection despite Bruce's warning to stay out of the matchmaking game, could not resist giving it the old college try. "Dolly, it's your turn to try and stump the film wizard here." Then, feigning ignorance, Hayley turned to Albie. "Oh, do you two know each other?"

Albie acknowledged Dolly with a nervous nod. "I've seen you around at the grocery store and post office but we've never formally met." He stuck out his hand. "Albie Schooner."

With a coquettish giggle that was disconcerting for a woman her age, Dolly took his hand. "Dolly Flood. Well, I like to go by my maiden name these days, Dolly Halperin."

Albie gave her a wink. "Pleasure to finally meet you face-to-pretty-face, Dolly."

Hayley found herself getting excited.

She saw an immediate spark between them.

But when she glanced over at Bruce, he just rolled his eyes and shook his head.

Albie rubbed his hands. "Go on. What have you got for me, Dolly?"

She reared back, confused. "I beg your pardon?"

"Test me! Throw me a question! Hit me with your best shot! I'm ready!"

"Oh, right!" Dolly laughed, her mind obviously elsewhere, mulling over what she personally had for Albie, to whom she was obviously attracted. "Um, how many Hitchcock movies did that blond actress star in, I forget her name . . ."

Dwight, anxious to compete, jumped in. "Grace Kelly? Two. *Rear Window* and *To Catch a Thief*!"

Albie made a buzzer sound. "Wrong! Grace Kelly was in three movies directed by Alfred Hitchcock. You're forgetting *Dial M for Murder*!"

Dwight pounded his fist into the palm of his other hand. "That's right! That one completely slipped my mind. Maybe I should just cut my losses and buy everyone some popcorn."

"She wasn't who I was thinking of," Dolly said, racking her brain, trying to come up with a name.

Albie tried helping her out. "Kim Novak? One. *Vertigo*. Janet Leigh? One. *Psycho*. Hitch loved blondes!"

Dolly scratched her head. "Who was Melanie Griffith's mother?"

Albie slapped his forehead. "Tippi Hedren! Of course! Two films. *The Birds* and *Marnie*!"

Bruce could no longer hold his tongue. He was

dying to get into this trivia game. "Okay, smart guy, which actress appeared in the most Hitchcock films?"

"That's a trick question," Albie shot back.

"No, it's not. It's Ingrid Bergman."

"And you would be wrong, Bruce. Ingrid Bergman was in three, just like Grace Kelly. *Spellbound*, *Notorious*, and *Under Capricorn*. The actress who appeared in the most films is Bess Flowers."

Bruce arched an eyebrow. "Who?"

"Exactly! That's why it's a trick question. You asked me which actress appeared in the most films, not starred in, and that would be Bess Flowers. She had uncredited roles in seven Hitchcock films."

"I got to say, Albie, you're very good," Bruce conceded.

"I better get up to the projection booth. I'll see you out front in a bit. I'm going to give a little presentation before the film on the making of the picture, a few fun facts, and when to look for Hitchcock's typical cameo appearance!" He spun around to head up the staircase to the balcony, but turned back around, blushing a little. "It was awfully nice to meet you, Dolly."

"Same here, Albie," Dolly whispered, matching the blush in his cheeks.

"Enjoy the show!" Albie waved and then bounded up the steps, pretty impressively for a man in his seventies. "I believe this is one of Hitchcock's most underrated films!"

Hayley had seen *Rope* when she was around twelve years old one afternoon on a local TV station. She remembered thinking Farley Granger was dreamy with

his wavy dark hair and bedroom eyes, ignoring the fact
that his character strangled a former classmate while
trying to pull off the perfect murder with his hinted-at
lover John Dall in the 1948 psychological crime
thriller. But a lot of the nuances and complexities were
lost on her prepubescent brain at the time, so she was
looking forward to giving the film another look with
fresh eyes as an adult.

Hayley noticed Dwight was at the front of the line at
the concession stand, ordering snacks from the pimply
faced teenager behind the register. She sidled up next
to him. "No butter on my popcorn, Dwight, thanks."

"I remember," he said softly.

Once the concession worker scooped out four bags
of popcorn, three sodas, a bottled water, and some
Junior Mints, and rang it all up, Dwight tried to pay
with a credit card, which the nervous teenager had to
inform him had been declined when he tried swiping it
through the machine. Dwight made an excuse about
the credit card company not receiving his last payment
for some reason, and Bruce tried to diffuse the tension
that was ratcheting up by offering to pay with his own
card. But Dwight adamantly refused and had just
enough cash in his wallet to cover the expense. As they
all grabbed their snacks and turned to head into the
theater, Dwight found himself face-to-face with an
older local couple whom Hayley knew well, Marlene
and Tucker Shaw, who were standing directly behind
them in line.

Dwight's mouth dropped open in surprise. "Marlene . . ."

Marlene was noticeably flustered, reacting as if she

had just seen a ghost. "Dwight, I—Well, this is a—What are you doing back in town?"

"I came to spend the holidays with my family," Dwight said, glancing over at Hayley before redirecting his gaze back to Marlene. "You're looking well."

Marlene was in her late sixties, very well put together, and a retired bank loan manager. Her handsome husband Tucker still worked as an accountant serving the local community. They had been married going on thirty-five years.

"Thank you, that's nice of you to say . . . Um, you too. I mean you're looking good as well . . ." Marlene was fumbling around in desperate need of being rescued, so her husband Tucker finally decided to bail her out by shaking Dwight's hand. "Tucker Shaw. I'm the husband."

"Good meeting you, Tucker," Dwight said as they firmly pumped hands, perhaps for a few seconds longer than necessary in some weird sort of who was more manly moment.

There was an unbearably long pause.

Marlene could not stand the awkwardness a moment longer. "Well, we should order our popcorn."

Dwight finally stepped aside and allowed them to move up to the concession stand to order from the increasingly impatient pimply teenager.

"Oh, by the way, can you fill in for me on Saturday, Marlene?" Dolly asked, clasping her hands in prayer, hoping.

"Of course. I'm available whenever you need me!" Marlene replied.

Since Marlene was retired and looking for things to

keep her busy, Dolly had offered her a part-time job at her arts and crafts shop, running the register whenever Dolly had appointments to keep or errands to run during her store's business hours.

As Hayley, Bruce, Dwight, and Dolly headed down the aisle of the theater and filed into an empty row, Hayley sat down in a seat between Bruce and Dwight and looked at her father, who was lost in thought, munching on his popcorn.

"Everything all right?"

Dwight spoke with his mouth full. "Of course. Why?"

"You seemed a little tense after running into Marlene Shaw."

"Marlene? Well, I knew her as Marlene Young back in the day when she was still single. But no, I'm not tense at all. It was really nice seeing her again after all these years."

Dwight's left eye twitched slightly, indicating to Hayley that he might not be telling her the whole truth.

"It just struck me as a strained exchange between the two of you, like you had some sort of history together."

"Don't be paranoid, Hayley. I don't ever remember a bad word that was ever said between me and Marlene. We're just old friends," he said, tossing a handful of popcorn in his mouth before adding, "Trust me."

And then she noticed his eye twitch again.

Chapter 15

When Hayley arrived at the receptionist desk of the *Island Times* newspaper office, there was no one there to greet her. Hayley nostalgically stared at the desk where she had sat for over fifteen years of her life, serving as office manager for editor in chief Sal Moretti. Although she still contributed her food and cocktails column, she was no longer ordering office supplies, taking down ads over the phone, and planning all the holiday parties. She had once been the engine that kept the office running and was proud of her time spent there. But now she was enjoying a new chapter in her life, running her own restaurant, Hayley's Kitchen. She had swung by the office because Bruce had dropped off his car at the shop for new tires that morning and needed a ride home from work.

The office was unusually quiet even for the end of a workday. Hayley waited a few minutes for the new office manager to return to her desk, but she never came. Perhaps she had left early today.

Hayley wandered into the back bullpen, which appeared deserted. She continued on down the row of offices, passing her old boss Sal's office. The door was closed. Either he was in a meeting or he had also already left to go home. Bruce's office was located right next to Sal's. The door was open a crack and when Hayley swung it open, she found Bruce standing next to the wall he shared with Sal, his ear pressed against it.

"Bruce, what are you doing?"

Startled, Bruce jumped back and then, annoyed, put a finger to his lips. "Shhhh. Keep your voice down." Then he was back against the wall, ear smudged against it, straining to hear the muffled voices on the other side.

Hayley brought down the volume of her own voice to a whisper. Instead of scolding her husband for eavesdropping on an apparently private conversation, she was dying to find out the details herself. "Who's in there with Sal?"

Bruce answered in a hushed tone, "Carroll Flood."

"Why is he here?"

Bruce listened a few more moments, then cranked his head around toward his wife. "He came in about fifteen minutes ago wanting to pitch Sal a story for the paper. From what I can gather so far, it's about Dwight."

"What?" Hayley cried.

Bruce threw her an admonishing look. "Quiet!"

Hayley rushed over to join Bruce at the wall and pressed her own ear against it, trying to pick up pieces of the conversation happening on the other side. Although the voices were barely audible, she did manage to hear Carroll announce a possible headline for the article he wanted published.

"'The Many Crimes of Dwight Jordan.' How does that strike you, Sal?"

"Very provocative, Carroll, but I'm going to need more than just your suspicions and a lot of hearsay. I need facts and evidence before I go rushing in to indict a man who has a long history in this town."

Carroll's voice grew louder. "You have a duty to this community to expose Dwight for the man he truly is, Sal: a wanted criminal. Don't be nervous about pulling the trigger on this just because you have a personal relationship with his daughter."

Me, Hayley thought. *He's talking about me!*

Sal spoke in a measured tone. "Let me do a little digging on my own, Carroll, and see what comes up. If I do manage to get my hands on some irrefutable proof of your claims, then by all means I'll write a story!"

"You're humoring me, I can sense it. You're not going to follow up on any of this."

"I said I will, Carroll, and I will."

"Man of your word, huh?" Carroll scoffed.

"Yes, I am!" Sal protested.

"You journalists are all the same! You don't think twice taking down someone whose politics you don't agree with, or rich, entitled fat cats you don't like, but the minute you get a tip on someone you like or feel sorry for, then it gets swept right under the carpet."

"You have no idea what you're talking about, Carroll! This paper prides itself on its objectivity. We don't play favorites. And if I find actual evidence tying Dwight Jordan to a crime that hasn't expired due to the statute of limitations, then I promise you, I *will* follow up on it."

Hayley could picture the dubious expression on Carroll's face. "Then I guess we're done here." She heard a chair being pushed back and the door to the next office open. Hayley and Bruce hurried over to the door of his office to listen as Carroll was leaving.

"Mark my words, if you fumble this, I'm going to call a tip into the FBI and let them handle it. I will not rest until they lock that menace to society up and throw away the key!"

"You're free to do whatever you want, Carroll, but if I were you, I would hold off on contacting the FBI, at least until I had a shred of evidence to back up your incendiary claims."

"You're right, Sal. You're *not* me. Have a Merry Christmas!"

And then they heard Carroll stomping out of the bullpen and out the front door of the *Island Times*, slamming it so hard behind him the windows rattled.

"I need a drink!" Sal muttered to himself as they heard him clomp back to his desk and open a bottom drawer where Hayley knew he kept a bottle of his favorite bourbon.

Hayley then dashed over to the phone on Bruce's desk, scooped it up, and punched in a number she knew by heart.

"Hello?" a woman answered.

"Hi, Jane, it's Hayley. Is Dwight there?"

"Yes, he's in the kitchen making a seafood scampi for us tonight and it smells delicious!"

"Can I talk to him for a moment, please?"

"Of course, dear. Hold on just a sec!"

She heard Jane calling for Dwight and after a few moments, he was on the phone.

"Hey there, do you and Bruce want to come by for dinner? You're going to love this scampi recipe!"

"As tempting as that sounds, we can't tonight. I'm just calling to give you a heads-up."

There was a distinct note of concern in Dwight's voice. "Okay, what's up?"

"I just stopped by the *Island Times* to pick up Bruce from work, and we overheard Carroll Flood pressuring the editor Sal into pursuing a story . . . about you."

"About *me*?"

"Yes, and as you can probably guess, it's not going to be a flattering puff piece about all your good deeds. No, he is waging a one-man campaign to bring you down!"

There was a long pause as Dwight took all of this in.

And then he burst out laughing.

"Dwight, I'm serious. He says he has a lot of incriminating stories that will undoubtedly lead to your arrest."

Dwight finally managed to tamp down his hysterics. "I'm sorry, Hayley, I sure do appreciate you alerting me to this, but Carroll's got nothing on me. They're just stories. Nothing more than that. I swear, if he had half the dirt he probably claims to have, I'd be writing you from an eight-by-ten jail cell by now. But the old coot's bluffing. He just has a personal grudge against me. I'm sorry about that, for sure, but there's not much I can do. I say, bring it on."

"So you're not the least bit worried about this?"

"Hell, no! Carroll Flood just likes stirring up trouble, especially when he's been drinking. Just ask his poor wife. You've seen what he can be like."

He was right.

She had seen Carroll at his worst.

Recently, in fact.

But he certainly did not appear to be drunk now.

In fact, according to him, he was on the wagon.

Dwight was remarkably calm and composed, and that went a long way to assuaging her fears. At least for now, anyway. But she also had to wonder if Dwight's serene facade was merely a pretense? Was he actually in a complete state of turmoil on the inside and just a very good actor at hiding his true emotions?

The only thing she knew for certain at this point was that she really did not know her father at all.

Chapter 16

The Neuschwanstein fairy tale castle located in the town of Hohenschwangau in Bavaria was built by order of King Ludwig II in the late nineteenth century, and was years ago the inspiration for Walt Disney's Cinderella castle, evoking the romanticism of medieval castles with its towering spires, turrets, and elaborate ornamentation. And today, at the Bar Harbor Historical Society, the castle served as the inspiration for Dwight Jordan's entry in the annual gingerbread house contest. A crowd of onlookers were gathered around Dwight's table, gaping in awe at the intricacy of detail in the piece, full of color and made with hundreds of pieces of gingerbread, modeling chocolate, rolled fondant, and royal icing.

"How on earth did you manage to make something so fantastical, Dwight?" one of the judges marveled.

"My secret ingredient," Dwight said, winking. "A sprinkling of magical pixie dust."

Hayley could plainly see Carroll Flood stewing from across the room as he presented his own elaborate creation, a replica of Hogwarts from the Harry Potter movies. It was objectively just as impressive as Dwight's amazing effort, especially his creative touches, like using Cocoa Puffs to build the exterior walls, but the crowd clearly preferred Dwight's gingerbread castle. Hayley spotted Carroll's wife, Althea, hovering near her husband, a look of dread on her face as she watched her husband grow increasing agitated by the rapturous reception Dwight was receiving as he stood all alone next to his own creation. The only person to stop at his table was a six-year-old boy who tried yanking off a couple of Cocoa Puffs to eat before Carroll shooed him away.

Carroll Flood was nervous.

He had won this contest every year for the last six years due to his exceptional baking skills. But this year, Dwight was giving him a real run for his money.

And at this point, Carroll could see his chances of a seven-year streak slowly slipping away.

And he was not happy about it.

The contest was being held at the Historical Society's museum, which was housed in the La Rochelle, a waterfront mansion built in 1902, one of the few remaining from northern New England's gilded age. The museum closed for the season every October, but the Historical Society opened its doors for the locals to attend their popular gingerbread house contest every holiday season.

As the judges showered him with praise, Dwight was quick to share the credit with his two helpers who assisted him in the construction of the piece, Bubba Butler and Elmer Crawford. But both men insisted Dwight had done most of the heavy lifting.

Hayley could hear Carroll loudly complaining to Althea that it didn't seem fair that Dwight had enlisted outside help. After all, he attached every Cocoa Puff to his Hogwarts castle on his own, but alas, there was no rule on how many people were allowed to work on a gingerbread house.

Meanwhile, on the opposite end of the main hall, in what could best be described as the losers section, stood the last-minute entrants, Sheila, Jane, and Celeste, with their less-than-stellar drooping gingerbread cottage, which was sadly dwarfed by both Dwight and Carroll's herculean efforts. Hayley could tell her mother was miffed that no one was even stopping by to even say hello, let alone offer a compliment or encouraging word. So Hayley casually crossed the room at the same moment as Albie Schooner sidled up to the table to take a look at their cottage just as the roof caved in and the whole house collapsed into a pile, making it look like an accident at a frosting factory.

"Oh no!" Celeste cried.

Albie took a step back. "I swear I didn't touch it!"

"I made doubly sure the gingerbread pieces were hard, so they wouldn't do this! What on earth happened?" Sheila lamented.

"The roof couldn't handle the weight of the sweet treats you put on the rooftop and it just caved in," Hayley interjected.

"How much can a few gumdrops weigh?" Sheila sighed.

"Quite a lot, when you use five bags of them," Jane muttered.

"There goes our chance of winning!" Sheila huffed.

Hayley held her tongue. Even if their gingerbread cottage had remained standing, this trio did not have a snowball's chance in hell of placing, even fifth runner-up. But she was not about to goad her mother into an argument.

"Well, let's just hope Dwight doesn't win!" Sheila blurted out loud. "I mean, his entry is nice, but it certainly doesn't dazzle."

At this point, Sheila had to be in denial.

Dwight's castle was a masterpiece.

Hayley turned to Albie, who had surreptitiously scooped up some stray frosting from Sheila, Jane, and Celeste's gingerbread disaster and was sticking it in his mouth. "By the way, Albie, what did you think of Dolly?"

Albie blushed. "She seems nice."

"Did you two have a chance to talk after the movie?"

"A little bit."

He squirmed a little, embarrassed.

Hayley thought it was adorable.

"Are you going to ask her out?"

Albie giggled. "Maybe. I don't know."

"Well, don't wait too long. Dolly's a catch. Some-one's bound to scoop her up sooner rather than later."

He seemed to take her words to heart. Then he used his wet finger to dip for more frosting from the pile of gingerbread rubble. "I think they're about to announce the winner!" Albie squeaked as he self-consciously wandered away to join the crowd.

Hayley smiled, feeling a sense of satisfaction for possibly orchestrating this budding love connection.

Liddy stepped up to a small podium set up in front of the main hall and spoke into the microphone. "Good afternoon, everyone and welcome to the Bar Harbor Historical Society's annual gingerbread house contest!"

Warm applause from the attendees.

"I am pleased to announce that the five judges have deliberated and selected our winners, but before we begin handing out prizes, I should tell you we have received a complaint from one of our contestants."

The room fell silent.

"Apparently, someone does not believe that I can be an impartial judge, since I have a connection to one of the competitors. My father, Elmer, has contributed to Dwight Jordan's entry, not to mention that my mother is also a contestant." She stared daggers at Carroll Flood so everyone in the room knew exactly who she was talking about. "I strongly disagree with this opinion. I consider myself a very fair and open-minded person!"

Hayley detected a few snickers from the crowd.

"But since the issue has been raised, I will recuse myself just so there is not a whiff of perceived favoritism." She glared at Carroll. "Happy?"

Carroll, red-faced, wisely kept his mouth shut.

"But just so you all know, even without my vote, the judges unanimously agreed on all the winners. So without further ado, our fifth runner-up is . . ."

Hayley saw her mother holding her breath, still

fooling herself into believing that she actually stood a chance of placing.

"Belinda Hall's Tootsie Roll gingerbread house!"

Hayley heard Belinda squeal with delight as Sheila shook her head in disbelief.

The next three prizes—second, third, and fourth runner-ups—were hastily presented, and Sheila continued to be amazed whenever her name was not called, although Jane and Celeste were more resigned to their fate of going home empty-handed, especially since they had already dumped their entry into a nearby trash can.

Hayley watched Carroll clench his fists, steaming, as Liddy announced the first runner-up, second place. "The winner of a one-hundred-dollar gift certificate to the Reading Room Restaurant at the Bar Harbor Motor Inn—Carroll Flood!"

Everyone cheered him on, but Carroll was having none of it. He just stood beside his Hogwarts castle, eyes blazing, steam practically coming out of all his pores. He did not even bother to go up and accept his prize from Liddy. Althea had to do it for him.

Liddy relished his indignation. "And now, the winner of the Bar Harbor Historical Society gingerbread house contest, and a check for fifteen hundred dollars is—bippety-boppety-boo!—Dwight Jordan and company's Cinderella Castle!"

The crowd went wild.

Dwight bounded up to the podium and did a little victory dance before grabbing Liddy in a hug and waving to his fans.

Carroll wasted no time in marching right up to Dwight, in front of everyone, and sticking his big, bulbous nose in his face. "This is outrageous! The whole thing must be rigged! Who did you bribe to win this thing?"

"No one," Liddy sniffed. "They won fair and square."

Bubba and Elmer moved in on them, prepared to intervene if Carroll, whose short, violent temper was legendary, suddenly got physical.

Someone from the crowd yelled, "Sore loser! Sit down!"

Carroll whipped around, full of rage. "Who said that?"

No one stepped forward.

Althea, mortified by her husband's public spectacle, shuffled over to him, her head down, and tugged at his plaid shirtsleeve. "Carroll, let's just go home. Second prize isn't too shabby. You should still be proud."

"No!" He shook her off. "I want to hear from all the judges! Tell me to my face that my Hogwarts isn't better than his clichéd Cinderella Castle!"

But before the judges could be individually polled, Carroll Flood suddenly and without warning collapsed face down on the floor. Some droplets of blood splattered when his giant nose smashed against the hardwood, causing it to bleed. Althea dropped down beside him, shaking him, trying to revive him. "Carroll? Carroll? What's the matter? Wake up! Please, wake up!"

Hayley was already on her phone calling 911.

Island Food & Spirits
BY
HAYLEY POWELL

Peering out the window at the falling snow that was now coming down harder and faster than just one hour before, I thought back to those winter months when my kids were small and still in grade school. Whenever the local meteorologist on WABI TV, the CBS affiliate in Bangor, predicted a snowstorm on a school night, the kids would jump up and down excitedly, beside themselves over the possibility of school being canceled the following morning due to inclement weather and hazardous road conditions. This happened without fail, much to my chagrin, because it was like they were high on sugar when the snow started to fall, and I was focused on getting them ready for bed and making sure their homework was done.

Our town of Bar Harbor has had a loud whistle based at the fire station that is fed with air from an air compressor for many decades, blowing every day promptly at noon and at 9 PM. The fire department also blows it year-round to alert the town of a fire, and of course, also during the winter very early in the morning whenever there is a snowstorm large enough to trigger officials to cancel school for the day out of safety concerns.

It has always amazed me that every morning during the other seasons, I had to fight tooth and nail to drag the kids out of bed and force them to get ready for school, but on a snowstorm morning, when that whistle blew, I didn't have to lift a finger. They were up and out of bed like a shot, racing downstairs to gobble down some breakfast, don their cold-buster snowsuits, and race out the door to start erecting a snow fort, or building a snowman, or grabbing their sleds to ride down the small hill in the back of our house.

This, mind you, was all before 8 AM. By 8:30, they would come barreling back inside the house, their cheeks red, their mittens wet, and would inevitably complain about how they were freezing as they began stripping off their outer layers and laying them out to dry on the radiators. Then they would turn to me and whine about how they were hungry and how there was nothing to do but watch television since I had so cruelly forced them to finish all their homework the night before.

This is where I employed the same tactic that my mother had during my own childhood, just as her mother had, and so on and so on. I told them if they were going to stay inside, they could use their time wisely and clean their rooms. Never have I ever seen two kids struggle to get their snowsuits back on so fast and flee outside with fresh ideas and a fierce determination to keep busy until at least lunchtime.

My BFFs Mona and Liddy were exactly the same as me when we were kids. We hardly relished the thought of having to stay stuck inside cleaning our rooms on a rare day off from school, so we met up warmly bundled in our snow clothes, ready to have fun.

One memorable day off from school due to a snowstorm was when we were in the sixth grade. We eagerly headed out to see what trouble we could get into, and ended up near the town garage, where the snowplows had been piling up giant mounds of snow since early dawn.

We weren't the only kids who had the idea of making a snow fort in the mountain of snow, because there were about a half-dozen other kids who showed up with the same thought. We all decided to band together and work as a team. We began digging out tunnels to form our own cave inside the giant pile of snow so we could build our dream snow fort.

The only problem was, the workers at the town garage frowned upon us digging through their mountain of snow because they deemed it too dangerous. Please! What a bunch of worrywarts. Always worst-case scenario! Luckily, they were too busy plowing that day so they weren't around to yell at us. We had the whole place to ourselves!

That was, until a small group of older kids, eighth graders, came by and decided that they wanted to drive us out of our snow cave and claim it as their own. Well, a big snowball war began to save our cave, and in the end our group of eleven-year-old warriors won out with cheers and laughter, standing on top of our mountain of snow, waving goodbye to the retreating bigger kids. We felt like the Scottish warriors from Braveheart.

The noon whistle blew and everyone started heading home to eat lunch and to warm up. Liddy, Mona, and I were climbing down the snowbank when Liddy suddenly remembered she had left her favorite scarf and hat her grandmother had knitted for her inside the snow cave. She didn't want to go back inside to get it alone, so after the rest of the kids had gone, Mona and I followed Liddy through the tunnel and into the cave.

What we didn't know was the group of older kids saw everyone leave, but not knowing that we had gone back inside the cave, they decided a little payback was called for, and they kicked in the opening of the tunnel and packed it with snow for good measure, then ran away laughing, not realizing Liddy, Mona, and I were now trapped inside!

We had heard the commotion coming from the tunnel, so after retrieving Liddy's hat and scarf, we rushed to the opening, only to realize it had been caved in. We frantically started digging to remove the snow, but then the ceiling started giving away. The more we dug with our little hands, the more the top of the fort began to collapse. Freaking out, we yelled as loud as we could for help, but no one could hear us. Finally, our voices hoarse, we crawled backwards deeper into our cave to regroup and think.

When you're eleven years old, there actually isn't a lot of regrouping and thinking to do. Mostly it's a lot of panicking and trying not to cry. We were getting really scared, not to mention hungry and freezing cold, but we were also furious with those rotten kids that vandalized the front of our tunnel, and started planning our revenge on them when, or if, we ever got out of this jam.

As the hours passed, none of us could stop thinking about food. I wished I had eaten pancakes for breakfast instead of plain old cereal for my last meal. Liddy promptly burst into tears, sobbing that she too wished she had eaten pancakes instead of yogurt. Mona chimed in, admitting she did have pancakes for breakfast, but wished she had eaten the sausage links her mother had served with them. With no sustenance, we were surely going to perish: death by starvation! This frightening realization prompted a fresh flood of tears!

We huddled and hugged and cried and wondered when our parents would notice us missing and send out a search party, or if we would be stuck here until someone discovered our bodies after the spring thaw.

There was more wailing and crying.

But then, Mona raised a mitten. "Shhh."

We could hear what sounded like footsteps and muffled voices.

We started yelling for help, but then stopped, straining to listen, and yes, we definitely heard voices. We crawled on our hands and knees as quickly as we could through the tunnel, and that's when we distinctly heard someone digging. Suddenly the tunnel cleared, and one of our sixth-grade friends from the morning, Tommy, poked his head in and asked, "What happened?"

The three of us knocked him down into a snowbank when we climbed out and attacked him with a group hug. We quickly brought Tommy up to speed on our life-altering survival story, how the older kids had buried us alive, how the three of us had faced death head-on. It was all very dramatic and the three of us fully expected a book to be written about our ordeal, and maybe someday a movie to be made starring Drew Barrymore, Brooke Shields, and Alyssa Milano playing the three of us. Maybe Kirk Cameron could play Tommy. He liked that idea.

Anyway, the priority now was food. It would be dark soon and time for dinner. Tommy gave us a puzzled look. "Dinner? It's only twelve-thirty."

"No, it can't be!" Mona insisted. "We've been stuck in there for hours!"

"No, you haven't," Tommy insisted. "I went home at eleven-forty-five for lunch and came right back here. You were in there less than forty-five minutes."

Our dreams of a major motion picture based on our lives quickly evaporated and we swore Tommy to secrecy. He was not to breathe a word about what he knew. He happily agreed in exchange for one of my mother's amazing gingerbread milkshakes. Deal!

We all strolled back to my house, and when the four of us sauntered into the kitchen, the delicious smell of gingerbread was wafting through the air. My brother Randy was seated at the kitchen table with a plateful of gingerbread pancakes topped with whipped cream and honey.

My mom turned to us and said, "There you are! You're late for lunch. You're welcome to stay too, Tommy. Now, all of you get out of those damp clothes and come get some of these pancakes before they get cold."

We quickly shed our wet jackets and boots and sat down, digging into those mouthwatering warm gingerbread pancakes like we had not had a thing to eat for days.

GINGERBREAD MILKSHAKE

INGREDIENTS:
3 or 4 ginger snap cookies
3 cups favorite vanilla ice cream
1 cup milk
½ teaspoon ground ginger
1 teaspoon cinnamon

In a blender place your cookies and blend until very crumbled.

Add your vanilla ice cream, milk, ground ginger, and cinnamon and blend until smooth.

Pour into a glass and top with whipped cream if desired.

For an adult treat, add an ounce or more of your favorite bourbon or rum. You won't regret it!

GINGERBREAD PANCAKES

INGREDIENTS:

DRY INGREDIENTS:
2¼ cups flour
2 teaspoons cinnamon
½ teaspoon ground nutmeg
½ teaspoon ground ginger
½ teaspoon pumpkin pie spice
2 teaspoons baking powder
½ cup brown sugar
½ teaspoon salt

WET INGREDIENTS:
1¼ cups milk
⅓ cup molasses
2 large eggs
3 tablespoons vegetable oil

In a stand mixer, add all of your dry ingredients and give them a mix.

In a bowl, mix together all of your wet ingredients until combined.

Add your wet ingredients to your dry and mix until just combined.

Grease your griddle with cooking spray, butter, or oil, then heat it up.

Using a ¼ cup measuring cup pour your pancake batter onto the griddle and cook until you see bubbles forming on the pancake, then flip and cook for a couple of minutes until pancakes are done.

Remove and serve on a plate with syrup, honey, and whipped cream if you desire.

Enjoy!

Chapter 17

As Hayley returned from the hospital cafeteria and delivered two paper cups of coffee to Bruce and Althea Flood, who were sitting side by side, Bruce's arm around his cousin, comforting her, Hayley noticed Nurse Tilly had returned to the nurses' station and was chatting to someone on the phone.

Althea, sobbing quietly, acknowledged Hayley with a nod and slurped her coffee before bowing her head back down again and resting it on Bruce's shoulder. There was still no word on Carroll's condition and the waiting was pure agony for all of them.

Hayley felt helpless.

She felt she had to do something, but she had no idea what.

She made a beeline for the nurses' station, where Nurse Tilly was still on the phone.

"Don't try denying it, Donnie, I was there and I'm not blind. You were shamelessly flirting with Michelle at Drinks Like a Fish." Nurse Tilly's eyes blazed with fury. "You did *not* just say 'so what'!" She listened, nostrils flaring. "Well, I'm sorry to disagree, but it *is* a big deal. You were straight-up disrespecting me and I will not stand for it!" She sighed loudly. "No, I'm not breaking up with you, but you are on notice, Donnie: You need to shape up or I *will* dump you, and maybe ask Sergeant Earl out."

She finally looked up and noticed Hayley hovering around the nurses' station, waiting to speak to her. She raised a finger, signaling her to hold on for a second. "I don't care that you outrank him, I don't want to date a title—I want to date a man who treats me right and Earl has always been a gentleman whenever I pop by the station with my homemade brownies."

Nurse Tilly and Chief Sergio's second-in-command, Lieutenant Donnie, had been an item for a few years now, but were constantly hitting relationship turbulence. Hayley had seen them bickering at her restaurant, in the hospital parking lot, and even at the police station. Still, apparently the couple could not quit each other, because they were still together.

"I have to go, Donnie, I'm still working my shift. We will discuss this when I get home. No, the gym can wait. You better be there when I walk through that door!" She slammed down the phone and warily glanced up at Hayley. "Yes, Hayley, what can I do for you?"

"I was just checking to see if there is any word on—"

Nurse Tilly sighed. "No, nothing since the last time you asked . . ." She checked her watch. "Ten minutes ago. The doctor will be out when he has some news. So please, just sit down over there and wait. I'm very busy here."

Not too busy to chat on the phone with her live-in boyfriend, but Hayley decided not to make an issue of it. As she turned to head back to the waiting area and join Bruce and Althea, she spotted Dr. Cormack, her general practitioner and resident heart specialist, walk through the swinging metal doors that led back to the operating rooms. He was in scrubs and lowered a face mask. Hayley instantly noticed the grave look on his face.

Nurse Tilly piped up. "See, you just had to be patient."

Hayley ignored Tilly's comment and dashed over to Dr. Cormack, who slowly approached Bruce and Althea. They both slowly stood up to greet him.

Althea clutched Bruce's hand tightly as she stared at the doctor expectantly.

Dr. Cormack grimaced. "I'm so sorry, Althea, we did everything we could."

Althea's knees buckled and she pitched forward, but Bruce caught her and kept her up on her feet with his arm across the back of her waist for support.

"No! No!" Althea wailed.

Bruce gently kissed the top of her head. "I'm so, so sorry, cousin."

"How?" Hayley managed to choke out.

"I suspect he suffered a massive coronary, but until the coroner conducts a thorough autopsy, I can't be one hundred percent certain," Dr. Cormack answered solemnly. "Still, all signs seem to point to a seismic cardiac event."

"I don't understand. He was perfectly fine. I never

heard him complain about any chest pains. Aren't there supposed to be symptoms?"

"Not always," Dr. Cormack replied. "But he could have brushed them off and not mentioned them to you. Again, my deepest condolences, Althea. Carroll was a good man."

There was an awkward pause as Althea clutched Bruce's shirt and buried her face in his chest, wailing. Dr. Cormack had never been known for his empathetic bedside manner. He clearly was anxious to return to his other patients.

"Well, if you will excuse me," he muttered.

"Thank you, Doctor," Bruce said with a weak smile.

Dr. Cormack turned and skedaddled back through the swinging doors just as the elevator doors opened and Dwight sauntered out. Hayley's stomach dropped. The last person who needed to be here right now was her father, who had been feuding with the deceased.

Before anyone could stop him, Dwight slapped on his most concerned-looking face and barreled over to the group. "What's the good word?"

Althea slowly raised her head up to confront him and said in a low growl, "What are *you* doing here?"

"I was worried about Carroll and I thought I would come by and check up on him," Dwight said as innocently as he could.

"Well, you don't have to worry anymore because he's *dead*!" Althea snapped.

Dwight reacted with genuine surprise. "What?"

"That's right! And you *killed* him!"

Bruce patted Althea's back. "Now, now, Althea,

there's no point in laying blame right now. For all we know, Carroll died of natural causes."

But Althea pointed a finger directly in Dwight's face. "No! Dwight Jordan is definitely the cause and there is nothing natural about that man! He's a heartless scammer and his ruthless behavior was responsible for my poor Carroll's death!"

Dwight appeared confused. "I'm sorry, what is she saying?"

"She believes you purposely caused the stress that triggered Carroll's fatal heart attack," Hayley muttered.

Dwight shook his head. "No. I mean Carroll and I had our differences, but I held no ill will toward him. In fact, I took great pleasure in his competitive spirit. I thought we were just having fun, engaging in a healthy and friendly contest."

Althea gasped. She reared her hand back to slap Dwight hard across the face, but Bruce anticipated the move and grabbed ahold of her wrist, stopping her at the last second.

Hayley could see her father was not helping the situation. "Dwight, why don't you just go? I will call you later."

Dwight tried reaching out to touch Althea's arm. "Althea, please, I never meant—"

"Dwight, go! Please!" Hayley said curtly.

He finally got the message.

He nodded sadly, then turned on his heel and skulked away.

Althea snatched a tissue from her purse and began wiping her runny nose, her eyes still wet from tears. "I know our marriage could be rocky, but I really did love the big ole sloppy lug!"

She had already forgotten about Dwight's unwanted presence.

Bruce rubbed her back. "I know. And so did he."

Althea broke down again and Bruce hugged her as Hayley watched her father shuffle slowly onto the elevator. As the doors closed she could see him staring at the floor with a tinge of sadness. But she could not tell if his melancholic demeanor was related to the passing of an old friend or to the fact that if it turned out Carroll Flood did not die of natural causes, he might find himself in the crosshairs of an epic scandal.

Only time would tell.

Chapter 18

"**M**erry Christmas!" Sabrina Merryweather crowed at Hayley's front door while holding something wrapped in tinfoil. She handed it to Hayley.

"Let me guess. Your mother's world-famous Christmas fruitcake," Hayley said, covering her sense of dread.

"I know how much you and Bruce love it!"

This was a blatant lie.

They detested fruitcake.

Especially Sabrina's mother's annual effort, which was always too dense and dry, the candied fruits too cloyingly sweet and the dried fruits too chewy. Even worse, unlike most fruitcakes, her mother, a deeply religious woman who never touched a drop of alcohol, refused to soak her fruitcakes in spirits or liquor to make it more palatable.

Which was why Sabrina, the unwilling recipient every year of about a dozen of her mother's fruitcakes, chose to regift them to all her friends so she would not have to keep any of them in her own home. Hayley, without fail, was one of the lucky ones on the receiving end of this unwanted tradition. In addition to being the county coroner, Sabrina was also one of Hayley's frenemies from high school. That might explain Sabrina's streak of cruelty in force-feeding her this awful monstrosity every year.

Hayley was not about to take this assault lying down. "Sabrina, this is so generous of you. Hey, why don't you come in and have a piece with us?"

Sabrina reared back, her eyes bulging as her mind raced to come up with an excuse to pass. "Oh gosh, I'd love to, Hayley, but I can't. I still have about nine more to deliver around town tonight."

"I insist," Hayley pressed, eyes narrowing, daring Sabrina. "I'll put some coffee on. Your mother's fruitcakes are so delicious, it would be a shame not to share it. You can report back to her how much we all loved it."

Sabrina opened her mouth to protest, but knew she had been backed into a corner. "Well, all right. There's something I wanted to talk to you about anyway, so maybe I'll just stay a few minutes, but then I really need to be on my way."

Hayley opened the door wider, ushering her inside as she called back to the living room, "Bruce, we have company!"

When Hayley handed Bruce the fruitcake and asked him to cut three pieces while she brewed some coffee, the weight of it caught him off guard and he nearly dropped it because it was as heavy as a large stone.

"Do we have any whipped cream in the fridge that

might help cover the taste?" Bruce asked under his breath.

"Bottom shelf," Hayley said as she followed him to the kitchen and grabbed three coffee mugs from the cupboard. When she and Bruce returned to the living room with fruitcake and coffee, they found Sabrina poking around their Christmas tree, examining all the wrapped gifts.

She plucked one small package nestled on a bottom branch and covered in tinsel and shook it, detecting a jangling sound. "Sounds like expensive jewelry." She glanced at the tag. It was to Hayley from Bruce. "Definitely jewelry."

Bruce cleared his throat.

He did not appreciate her spoiling any surprises.

Sabrina then plopped down in the middle of the couch as Hayley set the plate of fruitcake, which was drowning in whipped cream, and dessert fork on the coffee table in front of her and handed her a cup of coffee, black, just the way she liked it.

Bruce dropped down in his recliner with his own piece and Hayley perched on the edge of a chair across from Sabrina. They all stared distastefully at the fruitcake, wondering which of them would be brave enough to dive in first.

Hayley had no compunction about not playing fair. "Go for it, Bruce. Take a bite and let Sabrina know if it is as tasty as it was last year."

Bruce glared at his wife, unamused. "Don't rush me. It's not like it's ever going to go bad." He then cut a small piece off with his tiny fork and raised it to his lips, sniffing it. Finally, he closed his eyes and popped it in, chewing and chewing and chewing, trying his best to maintain a neutral expression.

Sabrina decided her best course of action to avoid eating the fruitcake was to ignore it altogether. "So, I have an ulterior motive for dropping by unannounced bearing fruitcake. I knew you two would want to hear what I learned today after getting Carroll Flood's toxicology report back from the lab."

Hayley practically threw her dessert plate down on a side table, where it clattered, the fork bouncing up and falling to the floor. "What?"

"Pentobarbital."

Hayley and Bruce exchanged confused looks before Bruce replied, "Never heard of it."

"It's a fast-acting poison, and I'm not kidding when I say *fast*. It can cause death between fifteen and thirty minutes."

"Is it like cyanide?" Hayley asked.

"No, it's a euthanasia drug. Very powerful stuff. As little as two grams can be a lethal dose. It's most commonly used in veterinary practices for anesthesia and euthanasia, as well as assisted suicide due to its rapid onset of coma and perception of a peaceful death."

Bruce scratched his stubble. "How did Carroll get ahold of something like that?"

"It's easier to obtain than you might think. Anyone can order it off the internet from a jurisdiction with little to no regulation," Sabrina sighed. "It's become very popular with people who want to end their lives."

"Are you suggesting Carroll committed suicide?" Bruce scoffed. "I don't buy that for a second. He was so determined to win the gingerbread house contest, I don't see him deciding to end it all right then and there in front of half the town just because he came in second."

"Which means someone poisoned him," Hayley concluded before turning back to Sabrina. "But how?"

"Pentobarbital comes in powder form. He would have had to have somehow ingested it. Think back to that day. Do you remember him eating or drinking anything?"

Bruce shook his head. "No. But maybe someone put powder on his gingerbread house!"

"But he never ate any of his gingerbread house," Hayley reminded him. "And he wouldn't have allowed anyone to even touch it before the judges made their decision."

Bruce slapped his knee. "Maybe he breathed it in!"

"No, that wouldn't have been enough to kill him," Sabrina said. "It had to be on something he ate or drank."

A light bulb suddenly went off in Hayley's head. "Gumdrops!"

Bruce raised an eyebrow. "What?"

"Gumdrops! Carroll loved gumdrops! I remember that day he was on a mission to find some."

Bruce suddenly sat up straight. "Maybe someone who knew Carroll loved gumdrops coated them with the poison and made sure he found them."

"The crime scene investigators found some gumdrops in the pocket of Carroll's pants and bagged them as evidence. I can test them to see if they have traces of any poison."

Eyeing her untouched piece of her mother's fruitcake, Sabrina finally had her out. She jumped to her feet. "I should go straight back to my office without delay and find out for certain! I'm so sorry I can't stay and enjoy the fruitcake with you!"

And with that, Sabrina fled out the door.

Bruce, with a crooked smile, scraped all three pieces of fruitcake onto one plate, marched into the kitchen, and dumped them all in the garbage can.

They were free.

Free at last.

And by noon the next day, Sabrina had made the official announcement that traces of the lethal drug pentobarbital had indeed been found on the gumdrops in Carroll's pants pocket. Less than a half hour later, Chief Sergio had reclassified Carroll Flood's death as a homicide.

Chapter 19

Hayley stepped outside on the side deck of her house in the bitter cold while clamping her phone to her ear, so she could talk to her brother in private without her mother, Sheila, who was preparing a sumptuous pot roast dinner, overhearing. "You can't be serious, Randy."

"Hayley, come on. It's Christmas Eve."

"I thought you were going to host him at your house tonight," Hayley said with a heavy sigh.

"We were. But Michelle called in sick, I know she's faking—she just wants to hang out with her boyfriend—but it doesn't matter. Someone has to fill in to keep the bar open."

"Why not just close for the night?"

"Because I've been advertising Christmas Eve at Drinks Like a Fish for weeks. We have holiday drink specials, I've got hot hors d'oeuvres, customers are bringing wrapped gifts for the toy drive. I can't cancel now!"

"What about Sergio?"

"He's knee-deep in the Carroll Flood murder investigation ever since Sabrina dropped the bomb about him being poisoned. If Dad comes over to my house, he'll be sitting there by himself, staring at the Christmas tree lights all night."

"Okay, what about Bubba and Jane? Can't he just spend the evening with them? I mean, he's already staying in their guest room. It seems like the perfect solution."

"They're going over to Mona's house and you know what a full house she's got with all her kids and grandkids. There is literally no room at the table. Plus, he told me he doesn't want to intrude on their family gathering, so that's definitely not happening. You're my last hope, Hayley. I can't bear the thought of him being alone on Christmas Eve."

"Randy, I can't . . ."

"Please!"

"Mom will never go for it. The one condition she had for not scooting home to Florida once she found out Dwight was in Bar Harbor was that she would never have to be in the same room with him for as long as she's here."

"I know, but maybe once you tell her the circumstances—"

"She despises him with every fiber of her being!"

"What's the harm in asking?"

Hayley dropped her head.

Her brother was not going to give up on this.

"Fine! I'll ask! But I'm putting you on speaker so

you can hear what she says so there will be no confusion later."

Hayley marched back into the kitchen where Sheila was braising the beef with red wine, while Bruce set the dining room table. Carl was sitting at the kitchen table nursing a bottle of beer while doomscrolling the news on his phone. Leroy was curled up underneath the table, his head resting on Carl's left shoe, while Blueberry washed himself in a corner, keeping an eye on any food scraps that might accidentally fall to the floor.

"Mom, Randy's on the phone," Hayley announced.

"Merry Christmas Eve, darling!" Sheila cooed. "I've outdone myself tonight. This is going to be the most tender and moist pot roast I have ever prepared! Are you sure you and Sergio can't join us? There's plenty to go around."

"Sorry, I have to work. But we'll be over tomorrow morning for breakfast," Randy answered.

"Mom, Randy has something to ask you."

There was a long pause on the other end of the phone.

Randy had thought Hayley was going to do all the dirty work, but she had no intention so this was quite an unexpected curveball.

"What?" Randy croaked.

"Go on, ask her."

Another interminable silence.

"That's okay. You go ahead, Hayley."

"No, you," she growled through gritted teeth.

Sheila slid the large tin pan with the pot roast into

the oven and shut the door. "Well, somebody ask me soon. I'm not getting any younger."

Hayley waited for Randy, but the coward was keeping his mouth shut out of self-preservation. Finally, he whispered, "Dad has nowhere to go for Christmas Eve."

Sheila crinkled her nose. "That's not a question."

"And . . ." Hayley drew out the word.

Sheila tapped her foot impatiently. "And what?"

Randy's voice crackled through the phone. "And Hayley wants to know if you would mind if she invited him to spend Christmas Eve at her house with you all."

Carl raised his eyes from his phone, suddenly intrigued.

Even Blueberry stopped washing himself, sensing the tension building in the kitchen.

Sheila locked eyes with Hayley. "Absolutely not."

Hayley spoke into her phone. "Well, we tried."

"Mom, have a heart! The poor man is all alone in the world!" Randy protested.

"How on earth is that my problem?" Sheila sniffed. "Your father deserted this family. That was his choice and his choice alone. He's made his bed and now he has to lie in it. And I'm sure, given his history, he's never been alone for too long!"

Carl stood up from the table, disturbing a snoozing Leroy, who had to move his head from Carl's shoe. He walked up behind Sheila and put his hands on her shoulders. "Come on, Sheila, where's your holiday spirit?"

"You want to talk spirits? How about the evil spirit that inhabits the body of that good-for-nothing, soulless, rotten ex-husband of mine!"

"Oh, come on. He's not all that bad," Carl said.

Hayley braced herself.

Carl was playing with fire at this point.

Sheila spun around to confront him. "You don't know half the story. That man nearly destroyed me. Left me on my own to raise two children. He never sent a dime in child support. He just vanished from our lives forever. Until now."

"I understand. I'm not asking you to forget what he did to you, to the kids. I'm just saying it's the Christmas season and people tend to be in a forgiving mood around the holidays, and maybe it would be a magnanimous gesture to at least not leave a fellow human being, despite his massive flaws, standing out in the cold on Christmas Eve."

"The Butlers have a very reliable heat pump in their house. I'm fairly certain Dwight's not going to freeze to death!" Sheila barked.

Carl glanced down at the pot of freshly mashed potatoes and tray of roasted carrots on the stove and the giant pot roast cooking in the oven and a half-dozen plates of pies, cookies, and other Christmas sweets lining the kitchen counter. "Looks like we have enough food to feed the entire town."

"Dwight, please, don't make me do this," Sheila begged.

"I won't. I promise. But I know you, Sheila. I know what kind of woman you are. And I know you can't help but do the right thing in the end." He kissed her gently on the forehead. "That's why I love you." He paused before continuing. "But this is entirely *your* decision."

Checkmate.

Now she would look like Scrooge if she stuck to her guns.

Man, was he good.

"Wow . . ." Randy whispered through the speaker on Hayley's phone. Carl was a master of manipulation. Or maybe he just knew their mother better than either of them did.

Sheila slowly turned to Hayley. "Call your father. Tell him he can come over for dinner if he wants."

"Thank you, Mom!" Randy crowed.

"But he is *not* to talk to me, or look at me, or address me in any way, except to compliment my pot roast."

"Deal!" Hayley agreed.

Two hour later, Hayley returned to the house after picking up Dwight at the Butler house. Bruce greeted him with a hearty handshake, but Carl, who seemed to be growing fond of Dwight, grabbed him in a warm bear hug, welcoming him. Dwight shed his winter coat and draped it over a kitchen chair as Bruce handed him a bourbon on the rocks. Sheila kept her back to them all, standing at the stove, continuing to mash her potatoes even though they had been done for a while now.

"Merry Christmas, Sheila," Dwight said after a sip of his bourbon. He was already ignoring Hayley's instruction not to engage with his ex-wife.

They could all see Sheila's body stiffen before muttering under her breath, "Merry Christmas."

After that initial strained interaction, the two of them kept a safe distance with Bruce, Carl, and Dwight retiring to the living room with their drinks and Hayley hanging back in the kitchen to assist her mother in getting the elaborate meal on the table. The pot roast was now cooling and the homemade popovers were rising in the oven. They would be ready to sit down to dinner soon. Hayley noticed that the plate of gingerbread cookies with red and green icing in the shape of Christmas trees that had been sitting on the kitchen counter was now nothing but crumbs.

"Mom, if you eat all the cookies, you won't have room for your delicious dinner."

Sheila spun around. "What are you talking about? I haven't had one cookie all day despite desperately craving them."

Hayley sighed. "Bruce, did you eat all the Christmas tree cookies?"

"Never touched 'em!"

"Me neither!" Carl piped in.

"I didn't even see them!" Dwight called out.

Hayley spotted Leroy still hiding under the kitchen table. "Leroy couldn't have gotten up on the counter, so that leaves . . ."

Their eyes fell upon Blueberry, whose massive belly seemed more rounder than ever. Hayley deduced the probable sequence of events. When Hayley had gone into the living room with more drinks for everyone and Sheila's back was turned and she was facing the stove, Blueberry had had the opportunity to jump up on an empty chair, then climb up onto the kitchen table, and make a small leap to the kitchen counter where he could easily feast on the plate of frosted gingerbread cookies, only to jump back down when he was done.

"Blueberry!"

The corpulent Persian cat just stared at Hayley. She would have seen the guilt in Leroy's eyes, but Blueberry—that was a cat with no conscience, no shame, a total lack of remorse. He actually looked proud that he had gotten away with it.

And then he started heaving.

"Hayley, I think he's going to be sick!"

"Of course he is! He ate a half-dozen cookies!"

"Maybe you should take him outside."

Hayley watched in horror as Blueberry stood heaving over Dwight's winter coat that had slid off one of the kitchen chairs, no doubt when Blueberry jumped up on it and was now lying on the floor. Hayley shot out an arm to grab the sleeve and pull it out of harm's way, but she just wasn't fast enough.

Blueberry vomited all over it.

"Oh no!" Hayley wailed.

Feeling much butter, Blueberry shot his tail up in the air and traipsed out of the kitchen toward the living room.

Hayley checked the tag inside Dwight's coat. "It's machine washable. I'm going to toss it in for a cycle while we eat."

"Don't forget to check the pockets first," Sheila suggested.

Hayley fished through the pockets, pulling out a pack of gum, a set of keys presumably to the Butler house to use while he was staying there, some tissues, loose change, and finally, one last item that shook her to the core.

Hayley held a small lab vial in the palm of her hand that was about a third full of white powder.

Her heart sank.

Powder.

Could it possibly be pentobarbital?

The poison used to kill Carroll Flood?

And if it was, what was it doing in Dwight Jordan's coat pocket?

Chapter 20

Bruce immediately sensed something was wrong when he ambled into the kitchen for another drink. Sheila was humming "Oh Christmas Tree" while standing at the stove, her back to them, tending to her dinner. As Hayley stood frozen in place, a shocked look on her face, Bruce mouthed "What?" Hayley silently indicated they should step outside and so he followed her out the door.

"Be right back, Mom," Hayley croaked.

"All right, but don't be long. Dinner's just about ready."

Hurrying out the back door onto the side deck, the cold drilling into her bones causing her to shiver, Hayley held up the vial in front of Bruce's face.

"What is that?"

"I found it in Dwight's coat pocket."

"Is it some kind of medication?"

"No, I think it might be—" Hayley swallowed hard

before continuing. "The poison that killed Carroll Flood."

Bruce's eyes widened in surprise. "What? How can you be sure? There's no label on it. And why would Dwight just carry that around in his coat pocket? If he did use that to take out Carroll, then he'd be stupid not to get rid of it by now."

"I don't know, Bruce, I just have a really bad feeling. What are we going to do?"

"We should ask him."

"Ask him if he murdered Carroll Flood? It's Christmas Eve!"

Bruce turned around and marched back inside the house, returning a few moments later with Dwight, who was now sipping some hot cocoa and got some whipped cream caught in his scraggly beard. He had a twinkle in his eye and he offered Hayley a wide smile. "What's up, buttercup?"

She hated ruining his festive mood.

But she had little choice.

Hayley showed him the vial in her hand. "Can you tell me what this is?"

"It's one of those tiny test tubes they use when they draw your blood at the doctor's office, right?"

"Yes, but what is that powdery substance inside the vial?"

Dwight studied it for a moment and then shrugged. "Beats me. Looks like plain old baking flour to me. Where'd you get it?"

"Your coat pocket!" Hayley cried before quickly lowering her voice. "What were you doing with this?"

Dwight reared back and shook his head. "I have no idea, but that certainly isn't mine!"

"Then how did it get there? It didn't just magically appear all by itself."

"Someone must have put it there," Dwight calmly explained.

"Who?"

Dwight shrugged again. "If I knew, Hayley, I would tell you. But what's the big deal? If it's just flour—"

"I highly suspect this is *not* flour! I believe this might be pentobarbital."

Dwight scratched his head, confused. "Penti-barbie-what?"

"The poison used to kill Carroll Flood, the man you feuded with at the Historical Society, the man whose death has been ruled a homicide, his life snuffed out by a powdery poison that looks suspiciously like *this*!" She thrust the vial in front of his face, almost touching his nose to make her point.

"Someone must be trying to frame me," Dwight mumbled.

"That's what pretty much every murderer says when he gets caught with evidence tying him to the crime!" Hayley sighed.

A pallor spread across Dwight's face. "Hayley, do you honestly believe that I am capable of taking another man's life?"

"I don't know, Dwight! Because I don't know you! You've been gone since I was a little kid, only to reappear in all our lives now, right before one of your long-time enemies dropped dead in front of half the town! I really don't know what to believe at this point!"

Dwight bowed his head, wounded by her sharp words. "I'm sorry you feel that way, but you have to trust me, I did not kill Carroll Flood! I would never hurt anyone."

She assumed he meant physically. The emotional damage left in Dwight Jordan's wake was practically incalculable.

Bruce glanced nervously at his wife. "What do we do now?"

"We need to hand this over to Sergio so he can get it tested," Hayley explained.

Dwight's whole body stiffened. "You're not serious."

"Of course I am. It's the only way to prove this isn't the same poison that was used to kill Carroll."

"Hayley, you can't!" Dwight begged. "Given my, um, checkered history, if that stuff turns out to be penti-barbie-doll—"

"Pentobarbital," Hayley corrected.

"Whatever! He's going to arrest me and throw me in jail! I've been to jail before—"

"Let me put on my big surprise face," Hayley sighed.

"And I can't do it. I can't go through that ever again."

"If we hide this potential evidence, then both Bruce and I will be complicit in the crime and we could get arrested too!"

"She's right, Dwight."

Hayley stopped suddenly.

That wasn't Bruce's voice.

That voice, with its heavy Brazilian accent, definitely belonged to someone else.

They all spun around to see Sergio standing in the doorway that led back to the kitchen. He was still in his police uniform.

"Sergio, what are you doing here?" Hayley managed to choke out.

"I stopped by the Butler place to question Dwight about what he might have seen at the Historical Society before Carroll collapsed, and caught Jane and Bubba as they were leaving for Mona's house. She told me you were over here tonight. Sheila let me in the front door and told me you were all outside on the side deck."

They all stood, staring at him, looking incredibly guilty.

"How much did you hear?" Hayley asked with a sense of dread.

Sergio stepped forward and plucked the vial out of Dwight's hand with his gloved hand. "Enough. I think it would be wise if you came with me down to the station, Dwight."

"But it's Christmas Eve!" he protested.

Sadly, that was not going to be enough to stop the chief of police from pushing forward with his murder investigation.

Dwight's only hope was for that powder to turn out to be a harmless substance, perhaps someone's idea of a sick joke.

But Hayley was not going to hold her breath for a miracle.

Because things were definitely not looking good for her estranged father.

Chapter 21

"Sergio, please, I'm begging you, don't arrest me. I'm an innocent man. I didn't kill anyone!" Dwight wailed as they all headed inside to bring Sheila and Carl up to speed.

"No one's arresting you, Dwight," Sergio assured him before adding solemnly, "yet."

Hayley could feel the panic rising in her father.

Sheila stopped carving her fully cooked pot roast and turned to face everyone. "Good lord. What's he done now?"

"Hayley found a vial of what could be the poison that killed Carroll Flood in Dwight's coat pocket!" Bruce couldn't help blurting out.

"But we don't know for sure how it got there. Dwight is claiming he's never seen it," Hayley quickly added.

"Of course he is," Sheila scoffed.

"Mom, not helping!" Hayley scolded.

"Sergio, will you be staying for dinner?" Sheila asked.

"Uh, no, I'm on duty. And don't count on Dwight either. He's coming with me."

"Don't worry about that. I haven't counted on Dwight for anything in decades," Sheila sneered. Noticing Hayley's annoyed look, Sheila made a dismissive shoulder movement. "What? It's the truth."

Carl ambled in from the living room. "What's going on?"

"Dwight's being arrested for murder," Sheila quickly responded.

"He's not being arrested!" Hayley cried.

"Yet," Bruce quietly added.

Sheila made a move toward Dwight, who shrank back, his eyes fixed on the carving knife in her hand. Realizing how menacing she looked, especially given her ill will toward her ex-husband, Sheila gently put the knife down on the counter before approaching him. "Dwight, I can tell when you're scared. You've got the same look you had when you got caught writing bad checks at the Shop 'n Save when I was pregnant with Hayley."

"We were broke and we needed baby food and diapers and your parents refused to help because they didn't want you to marry me!"

"In hindsight, they had a good reason to worry!" Sheila barked. "But in this case, if you truly are innocent, then do the right thing for once in your life and cooperate with the police."

"She's right, Dwight," Bruce interjected. "Sergio is

family. He doesn't want to see you go to jail. And he's a fair man. I promise you he will respect your innocence . . . until proven guilty."

"That's right," Sergio said before turning to Hayley. "Do you have a plastic bag I can borrow?"

Hayley crossed to the top cupboard drawer and opened it, plucking out a plastic bag, which she handed to him. He dropped the vial of powder in the bag and sealed it shut.

Dwight's knees nearly buckled. Despite everyone assuring him that Sergio was not out to get him, he was at this very moment gathering evidence to build a case against him.

And Sheila was not above pointing out the obvious. "Let's face it. That vial of poison in his coat pocket is pretty damning."

Carl placed a hand on her shoulder and squeezed gently, trying to signal her to back off.

Dwight bowed his head, defeated. "You're right, Bruce, I have nothing to fear. I trust Sergio to find the real killer." He glanced nervously over at the chief. "Let me just get my coat and we can go."

"It's in the washing machine," Hayley said, pointing to the utility room off the kitchen.

"I'll toss it in the dryer for a bit and then we can go," Dwight said and then scooted out the back door to the utility room. Sheila waited until he was gone before she burst out with, "He definitely did it!"

"Mom, please, at least wait until he leaves before you start pointing fingers!" Hayley hissed.

"I don't know. I've gotten to know the guy a little

bit, and I can't see him committing such a cold-blooded act," Carl was quick to point out.

Sheila glared at him. "I didn't realize you two had become such bosom buddies! The man spent half his life a wanted criminal! You have no idea what he's really like!"

"Mom!"

Sergio suddenly tensed. "What could be taking him so long to put his coat in the dryer?"

Hayley felt a sense of dread. "Oh no—"

Sergio bounded across the kitchen and swung open the back door that led to the utility room. He poked his head in and then whipped it back around toward the group in the kitchen. "He must have slipped out the back door!"

"See! Nobody would listen to me! He's on the run again!" Sheila reminded everyone within earshot.

The doorbell at the front door rang.

Bruce shot down the hallway to answer it.

When he flung open the door, there was a uniformed Sergeant Earl gripping the arm of a moping Dwight shivering in the cold without his jacket. "I caught him sneaking around the side of the house trying to get away, Chief. I know you told me to stay put in the squad car, but I figured you wouldn't want him on the loose."

"Good work, Earl," Sergio said with a smile before grabbing Dwight's arm and taking custody of him from the sergeant.

"I just panicked!" Dwight whimpered. "I just needed to get away and think."

"You tried skipping town, Dwight! That's not going to look good to the jury at your murder trial," Sheila was more than happy to point out.

Hayley was dying to stifle her mother, but nothing short of stuffing a Christmas cookie into her mouth was going to keep her from speaking her mind. And Blueberry had already devoured every cookie in the house.

Sergio unhooked a pair of handcuffs from his belt and was about to snap them on Dwight's wrists.

"Are you really going to lock him up in jail on Christmas Eve?" Carl asked sympathetically.

Sergio was torn. Dwight was, after all, his father-in-law but he also had a job to do. After rolling it over in his mind for a few moments, he slowly hooked the handcuffs back on his belt, still gripping Dwight by the arm. "Here is what's going to happen, Dwight. Are you listening?"

Chastened, Dwight nodded.

"I'm not going to let you stay with the Butlers, where I can't keep an eye on you, but if you move in with me and Randy until we figure all this out, then I won't have to lock you up over Christmas."

Hayley knew her house was out of the equation. Sheila would never agree to staying under the same roof as her ex.

Sergio gripped his arm tighter. "But if you try anything, if you even attempt to use the toilet without telling me, I will snap an ankle bracelet on you quicker than you can blink so I can keep track of you, do you hear me?"

Dwight nodded again.

"I don't think we have one of those down at the station, Chief," Earl said.

Sergio glanced at him, confused. "What?"

"An ankle bracelet. We'd have to call the state police to get our hands on one of those contraptions. And nobody really knows how to operate one. I mean, who does the monitoring? Do we take turns?"

"It was just a warning, Earl! Now keep your mouth shut!" Sergio snapped.

"Yes, sir," Earl muttered.

Dwight patted Sergio's arm with his free hand. "Sergio, you don't have to worry. I won't try to flee again, you have my word."

"And his word is as good as gold," Sheila cracked sarcastically. "Fool's gold, maybe!" She cackled, amused by her own joke, but no one else joined in laughing.

"You'll be very comfortable at Randy and Sergio's house, Dwight," Hayley said, stepping forward and giving him a quick hug.

Dwight leaned in and whispered in her ear. "Hayley, I know he's your brother's husband, but he's also a cop, and I have learned through my own personal experiences that cops can't be trusted."

"I don't believe that's true, Dwight, not if you follow the law and—"

He cut Hayley off. "They like to close cases quickly, even if they have to railroad someone! Please, you gotta help me clear my name before I wind up in prison for something I didn't do!"

Sergio urged him out the door. "Let's go, Dwight."

Dwight cranked his head around, calling back to Hayley. "Hayley, please! Help me!"

Sergio opened the back door of the police cruiser and placed a hand on Dwight's head, lowering him inside before slamming the door shut and circling around to the driver's side as Earl slid in the passenger seat.

Hayley could picture her father's desperate face staring at her from the blacked-out back seat window. Although her mother was ready to convict him, she knew there had to be more to the story. And she was willing to give Dwight the benefit of the doubt.

Which meant finding the person responsible for cruelly snuffing out the life of poor Carroll Flood.

Island Food & Spirits
BY
HAYLEY POWELL

A few weeks ago, at one of our girls' weekly catch-up on all the gossip dinner and cocktail evenings, my besties Liddy and Mona and I were chowing down on bowls of ginger chicken soup that Liddy had seen in a magazine and decided to give it a try. Much to our surprise, this recipe had quickly become one of our wintertime favorites.

Liddy, who is not exactly known for her cooking skills, had been gifted a Crock-Pot last Christmas from her "married cousin" Louise. When Liddy had called her cousin to thank her for the lovely gift, Louise had made a few snide comments that this slow cooker might help to improve her cooking, which she surmised, might go a long way in helping Liddy to finally catch a man. Liddy had laughed it off, explaining that she had no interest in being tied down, and how she relished her independence, unlike Louise, who was married to Seth, the human sloth. Every time Liddy paid them a visit, Seth was planted on the couch in front of the TV, playing some war game on his PlayStation, rudely ignoring everyone in the room. Poor Louise literally had to physically stand in front of the television screen blocking his view in order to get his attention. No way did Liddy need that in her life! But in the spirit of Christmas, Liddy had held her tongue and just thanked Louise again for the Crock-Pot before happily ending the conversation and hanging up.

Later, upon reflection, however, Liddy did decide that Louise had a point, and Liddy was never one to shy away from a challenge, so she made the decision to up her cooking game, and she would start with her newly gifted Crock-Pot.

As the new year approached, Liddy embarked on her quest for delicious slow cooker meals by buying a cookbook at Sherman's Bookstore in town and selecting a few delicious-sounding recipes to try out. If it just happened to win over a possible future husband, so be it. But Liddy was quick to explain that this was not her primary goal. She was a forward-thinking, modern woman who did not need to be defined by a man. Mona and I just nodded obediently.

Liddy's first attempts, unfortunately, did not come without a few mishaps, which Mona described as "the good, bad, and the ugly" as we were drafted to be her guinea pigs for her weekly taste tests.

Eventually, Liddy's experiments slowly improved throughout the year. Practice makes perfect, as they say. But Liddy remained adamant that she did not want to cook for a man she did not feel connected to. It was her goal to cook for someone who she was truly interested in, a kind-hearted, decent man, who she deemed good marriage material. Apparently, Liddy had forgotten her "modern woman not needing to be defined by a man" speech, but Mona and I, in the interest of peace, kept our mouths shut and continued our habit of just nodding obediently.

Around early December, Liddy met a sweet man named Fred, who was another local Realtor out of Ellsworth. Liddy had been dealing with him often through their prospective buyers and sellers and they had run into each other at a few local Realtor gatherings. Eventually they took notice of each other, and after much convincing from Mona and me, Liddy took the giant step of inviting Fred to dinner at her home, which would be her first time cooking for anyone outside of me and Mona and a few brave family members.

Liddy decided to make her Crock-Pot ginger chicken soup, which we all agreed was her best meal to date. We suggested she pair it with some fresh baked bread, which I heartily agreed to bake for her, and Mona provided her with a homemade blueberry pie. If Fred did not enjoy this mouthwatering meal, then this guy was definitely not husband material.

On the evening of the big date, Liddy promised to call us as soon as it was over to let us know how it went. Bruce, Mona, and I decided to head over to Drinks Like a Fish to visit with

Randy, who was tending bar, and have a couple of cocktails as well as Randy's famous chicken wings.

I knew Bruce was happy because he loved hanging out with his brother-in-law and he loved Randy's chicken wings even more, so it was a win-win situation.

Just as Randy placed a heaping plate of crispy hot wings on the table for us to dive into, my phone rang. Glancing at the screen, I saw it was Liddy calling, which confused me because her date had only started about an hour ago. I had a sinking feeling, so I thought I had better answer her call.

Before I even had a chance to speak, Liddy was crying and babbling and I could not make out anything she was saying.

"Liddy, slow down! I can't hear you! What's wrong?"

I could only make out a few words here and there.

"Killed him!"

"Ambulance!"

"Emergency room!"

I got the gist of the situation.

Something had gone horribly wrong on her date.

I yelled into the phone to stay put and hung up and told Mona we had to rush right over to the Bar Harbor Hospital. We jumped off our stools and raced for the door before I realized Bruce was still at the bar, happily munching on the chicken wings, his face slathered in barbecue sauce.

"Bruce, come on! We have to go! Liddy's in trouble!" I cried.

Bruce, his mouth open, ready to devour another wing, hesitated.

He clearly did not want to leave.

"For god's sake, Bruce! She may have killed someone! You're a crime reporter! This is an emergency!"

After staring longingly at the chicken wing in his hand, he dropped it back on the plate, grabbed his coat, and hurried toward us, muttering under his breath something about how it was always an emergency with us.

I ignored that unnecessary crack for the time being, and we all ran out of the bar to Bruce's car and sped across town to the hospital.

Arriving at the emergency room, Mona and I flew inside with Bruce trailing behind us. We found Liddy sitting in a chair in the waiting room, sobbing uncontrollably as Nurse Tilly patted her on her back, speaking to her softly, desperately trying to calm her down.

I knelt down in front of Liddy and asked her to explain exactly what happened. Through her tears and sobs and pauses to catch her breath, Liddy managed to tell us that while they were eating dinner, all of a sudden poor Fred began looking splotchy and sweaty, then he clutched his throat because he was having trouble breathing. He managed to choke out something about having an allergy, but wasn't able to finish because at that point he tipped over sideways and fell off his chair and onto the floor, flat on his back. Liddy had started screaming, frantically trying to wake him up, but he did not move, so she quickly called for an ambulance. When it pulled up to her house, lights flashing and sirens wailing, the paramedics barged in and lifted Fred up and set him down on the gurney before strapping him in. Liddy followed them out, jumping in the back of the ambulance with her unconscious date, and now she was here at the hospital. Then she collapsed in a fresh wave of tears.

We all just looked at each other, not knowing what to do, but thankfully the doctor on call, who saw to poor Fred, finally came out and Bruce, always the voice of calm and reason, walked up to him and asked what was happening.

The doctor told us that thankfully Fred was going to be all right. He had suffered an allergic reaction to the coconut milk in Liddy's soup, but Liddy's quick thinking and fast reaction had probably saved his life.

Bruce winked at Liddy and joked, "Darn, Liddy, if the date wasn't going good, you could have just asked him to leave. You didn't have to try and kill him!" Bruce guffawed and the doctor had to suppress a smile. Bruce clammed up once I gave him a sharp jab with my elbow and Liddy threw him a scathing look. The doctor told Liddy that Fred would like to see her. She was sure he was going to tell her he never wanted to see her ever again, but on a happy note, Fred did not break up with Liddy, and they have been quietly dating now for a few weeks. Also, after some serious convincing, Liddy actually got back on the horse and made a few more Crock-Pot meals for Fred after consulting and confirming with him that he had absolutely no more allergies that she didn't know about. I'm hopeful that they will continue to see each other and I'm excited to see what the New Year may bring for this adorable new couple.

This week, with Liddy's permission, I'm sharing her ginger chicken soup recipe and I'm sure you will love it on a cold and snowy Maine winter night. But first try my ginger vodka cocktail because I promise you it will take the chill out of the air.

Ginger Vodka Cocktail

Ingredients:
2 ounces vodka
1 ounce ginger syrup
½ ounce lime juice
splash club soda
wedge of lime for garnish

In a cocktail shaker, add vodka, ginger syrup, and lime juice and fill with ice.

Shake well to mix.

Strain into a rocks glass over ice and garnish with a wedge of lime.

LIDDY'S CROCK-POT GINGER CHICKEN SOUP

INGREDIENTS:
2 tablespoons olive oil
1 small onion, diced
3 stalks celery, diced
3 cloves garlic, minced
1 tablespoon fresh grated ginger
2 medium sweet potatoes cut into one-inch
    cubes
2 pounds boneless skinless chicken breast
5 cups chicken broth
1 teaspoon fresh thyme, chopped
½ teaspoon kosher salt
½ teaspoon ground pepper
1 bay leaf
2 teaspoon ground turmeric
1 cup coconut milk
1 head kale, chopped
juice of one lemon

Melt your butter in a large pot over medium heat. Add your chicken and cook on each side for 3 minutes or until browned, remove from pan and set aside.

Add your onion and celery to the pot and cook for five to six minutes until translucent, add your garlic and ginger and sauté for about one minute.

Transfer this and all of your ingredients except coconut milk and kale to your Crock-Pot and cook on low for 6 to 8 hours until chicken can be easily shredded.

Remove your chicken and shred with two forks, add chicken back to Crock-Pot and now add your coconut milk and kale, stirring until kale is wilted.

Add more salt and pepper to taste and serve in bowl and enjoy!

Chapter 22

As the tangerine light of dawn snuck through the curtains, Hayley's eyes fluttered open and she stretched her creaky body underneath the comforter before slowly turning over to see the recognizable lump of her husband still snoring softly.

It was Christmas morning.

She could smell the coffee brewing and morning pastries bubbling in the oven—something savory, no doubt, with cheese melted on top. That was her mother's favorite. After slaving away preparing a feast the night before, Sheila was already up making breakfast. Hayley checked her phone on the night table for the time. It was only a quarter past seven. She closed her eyes, hoping to drift off to sleep again for a few more minutes when a loud crash from downstairs made Hayley jump and startled Bruce awake.

Bruce shot up in the bed. "What was that?"

"I don't know. But it doesn't sound good."

They heard someone stomping down the hall into the living room, followed by Sheila shouting, "Oh no!"

"Definitely not good," Bruce agreed, grabbing his T-shirt he had discarded the night before and pulling it on over his head. Hayley grabbed her burgundy robe, tying it around her waist, and the two of them shuffled down the stairs to find a disaster scene in the living room.

The Christmas tree had toppled over on its side, burying some presents. Sheila, in a silk robe and plushy slippers, was shooing Leroy and Blueberry out of the room. "Go! Get out! Bad dog! Bad dog!"

Leroy, unable to speak and defend himself, scooted out of the room to the kitchen, presumably to hide under the table again, while Blueberry, with a bored, disinterested look on his face, sauntered out behind him heading to his milk bowl next to the fridge.

Bruce surveyed the damage. "What happened?"

"Isn't it obvious?" Sheila sniffed. "Leroy was clearly chasing poor Blueberry around and knocked over the tree!"

Hayley chortled incredulously. "Is that what you think happened? Blueberry has been stalking and terrorizing Leroy ever since he got here. I hardly think this is Leroy's fault!"

"What kind of dog is afraid of a sweet, innocent cat? Historically, dogs are the aggressors," Sheila said. "Watch your step, Bruce. There are broken ornaments everywhere and I don't want you cutting your foot."

"Where's Carl?" Bruce asked.

"We needed more milk for the coffee, so I sent him to the convenience store since the Shop 'n Save is closed today."

Hayley noticed some light blue wrapping paper with little white kittens on it had been chewed on and a little bow ripped free on the floor. She bent down and examined the evidence. "This is the same wrapping paper I used to wrap Blueberry's present."

Sheila began picking up broken shards of the ornaments and putting them on the coffee table. "So?"

"So I know what happened. It was catnip. Blueberry must have smelled it, tore it open, and batted it around a while before setting his sights on Leroy."

"I have seen enough true crime shows to know all of that is speculative. You have no witnesses to prove anything. Good luck getting that past a jury!" Sheila insisted.

That woman is so stubborn, Hayley thought to herself.

Which was probably where she got it from.

After slipping on some sneakers to protect his bare feet, Bruce went about lifting the tree back up on its stand and gathering the ornaments that had not smashed to pieces and placing them on the bare branches. Carl returned a few minutes later, and except for Blueberry hissing once at Leroy—who scrambled out of the kitchen for another hiding place—there were no further incidents.

They all sat down to a delicious breakfast of scrambled eggs, sausage, waffles, pastries, and coffee. Sheila suggested a round of mimosas, but everyone declined. They had all consumed enough alcohol the night before. Once the plates were cleared and more coffee poured, Sheila was beside herself with excitement. "Are we ready to open presents?"

"We should wait for Randy," Hayley said.

"It's going on nine o'clock. Your brother is always late. We shouldn't reward his tardiness by waiting for him. Besides, I'm going to burst if I don't open that giant gift from Carl over there in the corner." She pointed to a large rectangular box wrapped in pink cellophane and red bows. Hayley would have guessed by its size that it was one of those electric piano keyboards if her mother had shown a modicum of musical talent, which she never had.

Sheila eagerly tore into the box, pulling out a smaller box from the large one, and then an even smaller one from the next box until she was down to the last box, still rectangular but a fraction of the size of the original box. Sheila's eyes sparkled and she broke into a wide smile when she opened it and picked up a gorgeous pearl necklace.

"Oh, Carl," she cooed, swooning.

"I saw you eyeing it at the jewelry store in Vero Beach a few months ago," Carl said as she bussed his cheek.

Hayley was certain her mother had dropped enough hints where he would have been in trouble if he had not doubled back to buy it for her.

"How did I get so lucky to find such a handsome, romantic devil?"

Hayley and Bruce endured a few more uncomfortable moments of Sheila and Carl pawing and kissing each other before Bruce, unable to take anymore, grabbed a present that had not been crushed by the tree and handed it to Hayley. She tore it open with gusto, surprised and happy to find a blouse she had casually but strategically showed Bruce in a mail-order catalogue around Thanksgiving. She knew he would come through.

Hayley stopped herself.

She was more like her mother than she cared to admit.

Sheila set about lining up four gifts for Carl numbered in order, which turned out to be a new suit, shirt, tie, and finally dress shoes. Happily retired in Florida, Hayley wondered on what occasion Carl might have use for a brand-new suit, but she was not going to bring that up.

When all was said and done, everyone had a pile of gifts around them, except for Bruce. He sat on the couch empty-handed, trying not to draw any attention to the fact. But Hayley could tell he was confused and a little disappointed. Even Sheila and Carl had failed to give him anything, not even an ugly, ill-fitting Christmas sweater like she had shipped to him last year.

Sheila glanced at Hayley with a conspiratorial wink. "Oh, Bruce, I forgot. I have one more gift for Carl. I was afraid of him snooping around so I put it in the garage. Would you be a dear and go get it for me?"

"Sure," Bruce said, climbing to his feet and padding out of the living room, down the hall, through the kitchen, and out the back door.

Hayley grinned. "Should be any second now. In five . . . four . . . three . . . two . . ."

They suddenly heard Bruce outside screaming at the top of his lungs.

"One."

They all hustled out to see Bruce marveling at the brand-new snowmobile Hayley had purchased for him for Christmas with the help of her mother and Carl and Randy and Sergio. It was a group effort. Everyone had pitched in.

And it was not just any snowmobile.

It was the Arctic Cat ZR 9000 Thundercat, the one Bruce had been coveting for years.

Bruce was already astride the impressive machine and was pretending to be riding it through the snow. He gazed at Hayley lovingly. "I can't believe you went ahead and got me this!"

"It's from all of us. The whole family," Hayley said.

"Thank you, Sheila, thank you, Carl, this is so awesome!"

He started to get emotional.

Leave it to Bruce to remain dry-eyed during a Hallmark Christmas movie, but release a torrent of waterworks over an expensive snowmobile. Hayley had to restrain Bruce from immediately loading his new toy onto his truck's flatbed and heading out to the park to test-drive it. There would be plenty of time for that later.

Twenty minutes later, Randy arrived solo, explaining that he and Sergio had decided one of them should remain behind and keep an eye on Dwight.

After kisses from Sheila and opening his gifts from Hayley and Bruce, including new boots and a sharp-looking winter jacket from L.L. Bean, Sheila made a big production of gathering everyone in the living room for one final surprise.

"I know how difficult it is finding the perfect Christmas gifts for my two children, since they tend to buy everything they want before I even have a chance. It's always about instant gratification with these two!"

"Like mother, like son," Hayley whispered.

"Pot, kettle," Randy retorted.

"But this year, I decided to try something different. Get them something they might not think to get for themselves." She pulled out two purple envelopes from the pocket of her bathrobe and handed one to each of them. "So here you go. I hope you like it. Merry Christmas from Mom!"

Exchanging wary looks, Hayley and Randy opened the envelopes at the same time and pulled out two cards. They both had puzzled looks on their faces.

"I got you DNA tests!" Sheila squealed with delight. "Now you can trace back our family history!"

"How?"

"The last time I was here, I nonchalantly took some spit samples from the two of you; Hayley when you were brushing your teeth and Randy at the bar, when he had a cold and spit into the sink. Anyway, I sent them away. All you have to do now is log onto the website and read your results."

"I must say, I thought maybe it was a Walmart gift card, but I was not expecting this," Randy laughed.

"I had mine done last year and I have a smidgen of Native American blood in me," Sheila boasted proudly. "But mostly I'm Irish and Scottish, which I expect you two will be as well. But you never know. Life is full of surprises. Bruce, where's your laptop? I'm sure they're dying to know."

Hayley knew her mother would not rest until she and Randy poured over the DNA results. After logging onto Bruce's computer, they accessed the website, typed in the ID number, and brought up Hayley's results first.

Sheila had been right.

Eighty-nine percent Irish and Scottish.

A negligible amount of southern Europe.

Less than a percent of indigenous DNA.

Identified in the family tree predictably was Sheila and Dwight, both sets of grandparents, great-grandparents, great-great-grandparents, relatives dating all the way back to the eighteenth century.

Something suddenly caught Hayley's eye.

An anonymous profile with no photo.

According to the test, this person, a female, shared 50 percent of Hayley's DNA, which would make her a half-sibling.

"Mom, what's this?" Hayley asked, pointing to the profile.

Sheila crinkled up her nose. "I have absolutely no idea. It must be some kind of mistake."

They quickly typed in Randy's ID number to bring up his results and the mystery person was there as well.

A half sister they never even knew about.

"Mom!" Randy wailed.

"I knew nothing about this! I wasn't allowed to peek at the results. They're for your eyes only until you choose to share them!"

"We have a *sister*?" Hayley cried.

Sheila's bottom lip was now quivering. "Believe me, I would know if I gave birth to another child. And

I can assure you I did not! Having you two nearly wrecked my insides! This has to be your father's doing! Lord knows what he was up to before he deserted us and skipped town, not to mention after!"

There was a long, interminable silence.

Finally, Bruce spoke up. "Merry Christmas, everyone."

Chapter 23

Sergio, in a T-shirt and sweatpants, sat at the kitchen table in his and Randy's sprawling seaside home devouring a heaping portion of Dwight's homemade gingerbread French toast casserole, gnawing on a side of bacon, picking at a plate of fresh fruit, and sipping a yummy pumpkin latte. It was, as the saying goes, a feast fit for a king. Dwight, dressed in a flannel shirt and faded jeans, stood by the stove, eyeing Sergio expectantly, waiting for his final verdict as Hayley and Randy arrived at the house and wandered into the kitchen.

"This might be the best breakfast casserole I have ever tasted," Sergio moaned, scooping up another piece and popping it into his mouth as his eyes closed and he took the time to savor it.

"It's easy to make. I find it's best to refrigerate the soaked bread mixture overnight."

"Well, whatever your secret is, Dwight, it works!" Sergio said. "I need to send this recipe back to my mother in Brazil. She will love it." He glanced up at Hayley and Randy hovering in the doorway to the kitchen. "You two have to try this."

"There's plenty to go around," Dwight said, beaming.

"Maybe later," Randy said solemnly.

Sergio immediately picked up on the somber mood. "What's wrong? Did somebody make Santa's naughty list and not get what they wanted for Christmas?"

Randy shook his head. "Oh, we got something all right, didn't we, Hayley?"

"Yes, but I wouldn't say it was something we wanted per se."

Sergio gave them a curious look. "Well, don't keep us in suspense—what?"

"A sister, Sergio! We got a sister!" Randy cried.

Sergio dropped his fork. "A what?"

Randy thrust the card with the genealogy and DNA information in front of Dwight. "Here."

Dwight reluctantly took the card and started to read it. "What is this?"

"Apparently proof that Hayley and I have a half sister we never knew anything about!"

There was silence as Dwight read the report, his lips moving along as he scanned the card. "I—I don't understand. How could you have—?"

"It would be pretty hard for Mom to cover up a nine-month pregnancy without anyone in town noticing, so the only other possibility is that you're the one responsible for all this!"

Sergio slowly stood up from the table. "Dwight, what haven't you told them?"

"Nothing! I swear! I knew nothing about this! I'm as surprised as you are."

Hayley scoffed. "Oh, please, Dwight. You seem to have a lifelong problem with telling the truth."

"No, I—" He stopped in his tracks, his mind racing. "Wait a minute."

"I knew it!" Randy pounded his fist into the palm of his other hand. "I knew you were hiding something!"

"I never hid anything. She never told me she got pregnant all those years ago," Dwight murmured.

"Who, Dwight?" Hayley demanded to know.

"Before I left Bar Harbor, your mother and I were fighting as usual and I went out to the Thirsty Whale to blow off some steam, and there was a waitress working there at the time, and she was so easy to talk to, and I remember she was awfully pretty back then—"

"And one thing led to another!" Hayley snapped.

Dwight nodded guiltily. "Yes. But it was just the one time and I left town shortly after that. I never knew. She never said anything to me."

"Probably because nobody knew where you went. You were impossible to find," Hayley said, scowling.

"I can't believe this. All these years I've had another kid and I didn't have an inkling," Dwight whispered in disbelief.

Randy stepped forward and got right up in his father's face. "Who was the woman, Dwight?"

Dwight shook his head. "You probably don't even know her."

"We know everybody in this town. Who is it?"

Dwight nervously scratched the back of his neck and muttered almost inaudibly, "Marlene."

Hayley and Randy both gasped and cried in unison, "Marlene Shaw?"

Dwight gave a slight nod. "Yeah, but she wasn't Shaw at the time. Her maiden name was Young."

"We know who Marlene is, Dwight!" Randy wailed. "We've known her our whole lives!"

Hayley covered her mouth. "No wonder she was so upset when she saw you in the concession line at the Criterion Theatre! She never thought she would run into her baby daddy over thirty years later!"

Randy turned to his sister. "Do you know what this means? Marlene Shaw only has one child. And she would be around the right age when Dwight skipped town."

"Betsy? The cashier at the Shop 'n Save?" Hayley said in a hushed tone, completely taken aback.

"I've been in her checkout line with my groceries hundreds of times over the years and had no idea she was my *sister*!" Randy cried. "This is insane!"

Hayley studied Dwight's piercing hazel eyes. "Omigod, it's been right in front of us this whole time."

Randy spun around toward her. "What?"

"The eyes. They're exactly the same. Everyone calls Betsy 'Bright Eyes' because of her big, beautiful eyes. It's so obvious to me now. She inherited them from her birth father!"

Dwight shifted uncomfortably, desperate to change the subject. "You still hungry, Sergio? I can fry you up some more bacon, extra-crispy, just the way you like it?"

"Uh, no thanks, Dwight, I'm good."

Hayley and Randy stood in the kitchen, speechless. This was an unexpected Christmas surprise for the ages, one they never anticipated nor desired.

What was going to happen now?

Chapter 24

"I know what you're up to," Randy whispered in Hayley's ear as she pushed a shopping cart down the produce section at the Shop 'n Save.

"I'm sure I don't know what you're talking about!" Hayley insisted, stopping to inspect some heads of lettuce.

"Dragging me out of bed so early, making sure we got here early enough on a Sunday morning before the church crowd descends on this place and it's a madhouse."

"I just didn't want to have to fight the weekend crowd, so I thought we'd get the grocery shopping for the party done early when we'd have the store mostly to ourselves."

"Uh-huh," Randy said in a skeptical tone. "Hayley, your New Year's Eve party is still six days away. You never shop this early. You've always been more of a last-minute kind of gal."

"Yeah, well, is it a crime to want to shake things up? Get a head start for once?"

"But why?" Randy picked up a wilting head of lettuce. "Why not wait until closer to the date when the food will be fresher?"

She snatched the lettuce out of his hand and tossed it back on the pile before moving on to the tomatoes. "Randy, just what are you trying to get at?"

"You can't fool me. I know why we're here. Betsy Shaw has worked the early Sunday morning shift for how many decades now? You knew she would be here. What are you planning to say? You can't just come out and tell her she's got two siblings she never knew about and voilà! Here we are!"

"Of course I'm not going to say anything to Betsy. At least not yet."

"Then what are we doing here? We're the only ones in the whole store besides Betsy and Doobie Cunningham the bag boy."

"I just want to scope out the situation. Get a closer look at Betsy to see if there is any more of a family resemblance. I mean, this could all be one big mistake."

"But Dwight admitted having an affair with Betsy's mother, Marlene. The DNA results don't lie. It *has* to be her!"

"Or Dwight could be hiding another affair from us. He hasn't exactly been the paragon of transparency when it comes to his personal life. There could be a whole bunch of half-siblings out there wandering the earth we still don't know about and the Ancestry website just happened to catch one of them!"

Hayley ripped a plastic bag off the roll and started filling it with fresh tomatoes.

By the time Hayley and Randy finished filling their cart with food for the party, more shoppers were arriving at the store to do their weekly grocery shopping. Hayley grabbed a package of frozen peas from a freezer in the frozen food section and placed it in the overflowing cart. She checked her list twice and confirmed that they had everything they needed. When they pushed the cart toward Betsy's checkout lane, Abby Savage, a retired schoolteacher and another early bird from Northeast Harbor who had just turned eighty, saw them approaching and swerved her cart sharply to the left to get in line ahead of them.

"Good morning, Abby!" Betsy said, smiling brightly.

"Hello, Betsy," Abby replied, unloading her items from her cart. "Don't ring up my total until I can give you my coupons. They're in my purse."

Randy turned to Hayley. "Did you see how she saw us coming and cut right in front of us? So rude!"

"She's eighty and she only has something like ten items. She's allowed," Hayley said.

Randy began tapping his foot impatiently as Abby took her time picking the grocery items out of her cart and carefully placing them on the conveyor belt. At this rate, it would be noon before Betsy could complete the transaction.

Hayley leaned in to her brother and whispered in his ear, "Relax, we're next in line."

Randy couldn't take it anymore. He stepped forward with a friendly smile. "Here, Mrs. Savage, let me help you."

He reached down and quickly began grabbing her items and hurling them down on the belt.

"Oh, thank you, dear, that's very kind of you," Abby said as she snapped open her purse to retrieve her coupons. She then handed them to Betsy, who was ringing up the rest of her items as Doobie, a slow-witted boy with a hangdog face, shuffled up.

"Paper or plastic?"

"I have my own bags, Doobie," Abby said.

Doobie stared at the empty cart. "Where are they?"

Abby glanced back. "Oh no, I must have left him in my car. Doobie, would you mind running out there and getting them? They're in the back seat. The car is unlocked."

Doobie wanted to protest, but he retreated before any words came out of his mouth, lumbering out the sliding glass door to the parking lot.

Randy sighed loudly at the delay and Hayley elbowed him in the ribs, urging him to knock it off.

Betsy studied the coupons as she sifted through them all. "Mrs. Savage, I'm afraid these have all expired."

Abby's eyes widened. "What?"

She snatched them back from Betsy to inspect them, but squinted trying to read them. "Hold on. Let me get my glasses from my purse." She began rummaging for her reading glasses as Randy covered his face with his hands. Finally, she pulled a case out and opened it, plucking out her bifocals and sliding them up the bridge of her nose. She examined every coupon one at a time. It was taking a maddeningly long time.

Suddenly, Judy Baker, another longtime cashier at

the Shop 'n Save, emerged from the break room to start her shift. She took her place at her station, punching her employee code into the register and turning on the light, indicating her lane was open. "Hayley, I can take you over here!"

Hayley stood frozen in place.

Judy assumed she had not heard her. "Hayley, I'm wide open! Let's do this!"

Hayley did not know what to do.

"That's okay, Judy, we'll wait for Betsy!" Randy chirped.

Judy did not look hurt or slighted by the snub, just confused.

Abby had just completed her thorough examination of her expired coupons. "You're right, Betsy. Now I'm not sure I have enough money to pay for my groceries. I may have to put a couple of items back."

"Wait, we have some digital coupons that will give you a discount. Do you have our app on your phone?"

Abby stared at her, dumbfounded. "Your app?"

Betsy, trying her best to help, grabbed her own phone. "Here, I will use mine."

Doobie sauntered back to the register. "They weren't there."

"They're in the back seat."

"I looked. They weren't there."

Abby thought about this a few moments. "Oh. They must be in the trunk." She fished through her purse and extracted a set of keys. "Here, Doobie, take these. The bottom button on the left—press that one, I think."

"I know how to open the trunk of a car," Doobie moaned, shuffling off again.

Judy folded her arms and grinned. "You sure I can't ring you up, Hayley? I'm just standing around, bored. Who knows? You may get out of here by Tuesday."

Hayley was about to give up when Lisa Springer, a local beautician, mercifully arrived and pushed her cart filled with groceries into Judy's lane and began unloading.

"You go ahead and take Lisa. We'll tough it out over here," Hayley said with a quick wave to Lisa, who smiled and waved back.

Finally, after another seven minutes of bringing down Abby's total with digital coupons and Doobie finally returning with two recyclable bags he used to pack her groceries, Abby was finally through the checkout process and on her way to her car with Doobie carrying her bags, praying there was enough change left for a small tip.

"Good morning, Hayley, Randy," Betsy chirped as they began unloading the overflowing cart.

Hayley could not help but stare at Betsy, who quickly noticed and became self-conscious. "Everything all right, Hayley?"

Hayley snapped out of her reverie. "Yes, fine. Just spacey this morning. I'm a little out of it. I've been hosting my mother this Christmas."

No, she was not above blaming her mother for her odd behavior.

"At least you can ship her back to Florida, I'm stuck with my mother all year long!" Betsy joked, cracking herself up.

Randy laughed too, and in a jaw-droppingly obvious moment, Hayley suddenly realized that her brother

Randy and Betsy had the exact same laugh. Randy stopped suddenly as it hit him too, but Betsy did not seem to pick up on the shocking similarity.

Betsy finished running all the groceries through. "Do you have any coupons today?"

Hayley shook her head, still stunned by the identical laughs. She nervously began chewing her nails before she caught herself and stopped.

"I'm just like you!" Betsy declared.

"What?" Hayley muttered as she handed Betsy her credit card.

"Always chewing my nails. For as long as I remember. My mother was always yelling at me, 'Betsy! Stop that! It's a nasty habit! You must get it from your father!'"

Doobie returned from helping Abby Savage with her groceries. "Paper or plastic?"

Neither Hayley nor Randy could speak.

Doobie cleared his throat and tried again. "Paper or plastic?"

Randy reached into the basket of the cart and grabbed two bags, his hand shaking. "We, uh, we brought our own."

Randy just stood there, staring at an increasingly uncomfortable Betsy, not handing the bags to Doobie. Finally, Doobie came around to the lane and gently took them out of Randy's extended hand. Then he started packing their groceries.

As the receipt began spooling out of the register, Betsy ripped it off and handed it to Hayley, who had gone from biting her nails to now absentmindedly twirling her hair.

"Gosh, I do that too," Betsy marveled.

Hayley jolted back to reality. "I'm sorry, what?"

"Twirl my hair. I do it all the time. Bite my nails and twirl my hair. It drives my mother crazy! Huh. I love cooking too, just like you. We must have been separated at birth!" Betsy cackled.

"Have a good day, Betsy," Hayley said robotically the moment Doobie finished bagging their groceries and placing them in the cart as Randy followed close on her heels, both their minds reeling.

"You too!" Betsy cooed, having no clue she had most likely just been conversing with her older brother and sister.

Chapter 25

Bruce pulled his truck up in front of the entrance to Mount Desert Island High School, where the annual local Christmas craft fair was being held in the gymnasium.

Hayley, sitting in the passenger seat, turned to her husband. "I don't understand why you refuse to come in with me."

"Because, honey, you'll have a much better chance of getting Dolly to open up without me standing there reminding her that her ex-husband cheated on her with my cousin Althea and then divorced Dolly to marry her."

He made sense.

But Hayley still did not like the idea of Bruce getting out of accompanying her inside. She knew he detested craft fairs and this was just a lucky excuse to stay in the car and kick back and listen to some eighties rock tunes on the radio.

Hayley opened the door and jumped out of the

truck, spinning around and saying to Bruce, "This won't take long. You better be here when I get back."

"Where am I going to go?"

She gestured to the brand-new snowmobile tied down in the flatbed of his truck. "I can see you taking your new toy out for a spin in the woods around here."

Bruce opened his mouth to protest, but stopped short because he knew she was right.

"No joyriding while I'm gone!"

"Yes, dear," Bruce snickered.

Hayley zipped up her winter jacket in the freezing cold and trudged up the icy walk to the front door of the school. Inside, the gymnasium was buzzing with locals in the gym, wandering around and checking out the artisan arts and crafts at all the vendors who had set up to sell their wares. It did not take long for Hayley to pinpoint Dolly Halperin's location. She knew Dolly's craft specialty was balloon wreaths. She would blow up balloons in holiday colors like red, pink, and minty green and zip-tie the green ones to wreath wire, pushing them together as she went along before adding other colors as the ornaments, using balloon tape. Then she would attach to the top a colorful ribbon made out of poster board and tied with a piece of fishing line through the back loop. People went nuts for these clever balloon wreaths and Dolly, without fail, sold out her inventory every year. As Hayley approached Dolly's table, she could see that Dolly had expanded her repertoire this year by adding homemade paper bird ornaments, Christmas characters made of foam including Santa, various elves, a reindeer, a penguin, a gingerbread man, and Frosty the Snowman. She also had a pile of knitted scarves and sweaters and even a few boxes of baked goods.

"I'll have one of everything!" Hayley gushed as she perused all of Dolly's items, impressed. "You've really outdone yourself this year, Dolly."

"Thank you, Hayley," Dolly cooed, beaming. "I have samples of my gingerbread cookies if you'd like to try one before buying a box."

Hayley knew this impromptu interrogation was going to cost her. She was prepared to have to dole out some cash in order to get Dolly to talk. She plucked a cookie from the sample plate and took a bite. "Oh, that's delicious. I'll take a box. And of course, it wouldn't be Christmas if I didn't buy one of your balloon wreaths. My kids loved them so much growing up."

Hayley failed to mention her kids loved taking bobby pins and popping the balloons in order to scare the living daylights out of their mother, more than the artistry of the craft.

Dolly reached down in a large box and extracted a balloon wreath exactly like the one displayed behind her. "There you go. Anything else?"

Hayley selected a couple of the foam characters, including the reindeer and the penguin. "They'll be perfect for the mantle above my fireplace."

Dolly began adding up the sale in her head. "Now let's see: forty dollars for the wreath, twenty each for the ornaments, fifteen for the box of cookies . . ." She picked up a foam elf and tossed it on the pile. "How about I add this elf for an even hundred?"

It was the ugliest elf of the bunch. Dolly obviously was anxious just to get rid of it. But Hayley did not say a word. She smiled tightly and swallowed hard. Bruce would not be happy when she came out with a hundred dollars' worth of Christmas merchandise and it was already after Christmas. The balloons would no doubt deflate by Valentine's Day.

"You can find the best bargains here in the days just after Christmas. That's why we stay open until New Year's Eve. It's like a giant clearance sale!" Dolly gushed as she snatched the pair of fifty-dollar bills out of Hayley's hand before she could change her mind. She shoved them in her small metal cashbox and firmly closed the lid and locked it.

"Would you like a bag for all this?" Dolly asked.

"Yes, please," Hayley answered, watching Dolly open a light blue holiday gift bag with white snowflakes printed on it and begin filling it with Hayley's purchases. "By the way, Dolly, have you and Albie made a date to go out yet?"

Dolly's eyes betrayed a slight panic. "Uh, no, not yet. Why do you ask?"

"No reason. I just thought you two might hit it off, and it would make a wonderful New Year's resolution for you to actually go out on a date."

Just the mention of the word *date* caused Dolly to flush red with embarrassment. She then tried stuffing the balloon wreath into the bag, but it wouldn't fit. She was shoving it in so hard and the squeaking sounds were so loud, Hayley feared the balloons might start popping. She gently took the wreath from Dolly. "That's okay, Dolly, I can carry this separately."

Dolly handed the bag to Hayley and said shyly while avoiding eye contact, "I'm really not the type to take charge. I was hoping Albie might make the first move."

"Well, then, I'm sure you won't have to wait long. I really believe Albie is interested in going out with you."

Dolly wanted to change the subject more than anything. She picked up one of her paper bird ornaments. "These have been selling like hotcakes."

Hayley decided to oblige her. "I know you two weren't exactly on the best of terms, but it's still very sad about Carroll."

"Is it?" Dolly sneered under her breath.

Well, Dolly Halperin wasn't so meek and mild as she liked to project. Still, she caught herself and quickly shifted gears back to her shy, soft-spoken self. "No, you're right. Despite how he treated me, I only wished the best for him . . . and that woman."

"Althea," Hayley said.

Dolly's eyes rolled back in her head. "Yeah. Her."

"Were you there at the Historical Society when it happened? I don't recall seeing you."

"That's because I was out of town."

"Oh. Where?"

Dolly raised her eyes, finally making eye contact with Hayley. "I took my crafts to a Christmas fair in Bucksport, where my sister lives. I knew I couldn't compete with Carroll in the gingerbread house contest—he always wins—so instead I decided to visit my sister for the weekend and make some money on the side. I can give you her phone number if you don't believe me."

Hayley reared back, feigning surprise. "No! Dolly, I never meant to imply—"

"Yes, you did. And you're not the first. Do you know how many people have come by my table today, peppering me with questions about my ex-husband? They all think I had something to do with it. Look, why don't you call your brother-in-law, the police chief, so he can get in touch with the dozens of eyewitnesses who saw me up in Bucksport that day. They will no doubt corroborate my story so all these people will know I have an airtight alibi and this unrelenting cloud of suspicion can finally be lifted!"

Hayley felt sorry for her.

She glanced around and could see people staring at Dolly as if she was some homicidal woman scorned.

In fact, she felt so guilty, she reached into her pocket and dropped another twenty-dollar bill, buying up four paper bird ornaments for her Christmas tree, which would be coming down in just a few days.

Oh, well. There was always next year.

Chapter 26

The Long Pond winter carnival drew a devoted crowd, nearly half the island population, when it was held every year the week between Christmas and New Year. The festival featured a lobster feed cookout on the frozen pond, a snowman building contest, lots of games and sledding, and even an outdoor crafts fair as long as it wasn't snowing too hard. Dolly Halperin sat front and center, selling her wares at a table close to the lobster feed. A smart businesswoman, she knew everyone would have to pass by her after piling their plates with boiled lobsters, buttered corn on the cob, and various side dishes. Dolly always had plenty of embroidered napkins ready for purchase by the dozens of messy eaters.

This year, Bruce offered rides to the local kids on his brand-spanking-new Arctic Cat ZR 9000 Thunder-cat snowmobile, and much to Hayley's surprise, there was a waiting line that stretched all the way from the lobster feed to the gaming vendors. Hayley tallied at

least twenty-five enthusiastic red-cheeked children waiting for a complimentary joyride around the pond. She
smiled as Bruce handed one excited boy a tiny helmet
to strap on before he eagerly climbed on the back of
the snowmobile, grabbed the sides of Bruce's down
jacket with his tiny fists, and yelled at the top of his
lungs, "Hit the gas! And don't spare the horsepower!"

Bruce chuckled and revved the engine before shooting off into the snow, the boy screaming with delight.

Hayley watched them speeding off, and then wandered across the ice, stepping carefully so as not to
slip, making her way to a clearing on land with a snow-
packed hill that sloped up to the top of a ridge, where a
group of people with sleds and toboggans waited for
their turn to fly down. A gaggle of teenagers piled on
top of each other on one long toboggan tried riding all
the way down, but a few fell off and the toboggan
veered to the left, rolling over and sending the rest of
the teens sprawling in the snow, as they all laughed
hysterically.

Up at the top, Hayley spotted just who she had been
looking for—Betsy Shaw and her longtime boyfriend,
Hank, a sweet guy a few years younger than her who
worked for a local contractor, Ben Holmes. His boss
was going to be ready to retire soon and it was no secret Hank was itching to take over the business, since
Ben's only child, Cameron, was focused on studying
dance in New York City and had zero interest in running the family company.

Hank set his sled down and climbed on, urging
Betsy to sit down in front of him. She hesitated a moment, not sure she was up for it, but at Hank's urging,

she finally plopped down, her back pressed against his wide chest as he wrapped his arms around her and signaled a teenager behind them to give them a good shove. The boy obliged and the sled shot down the hill at lightning speed with Betsy screaming all the way. When they reached the bottom, they sledded about ten feet, stopping right in front of where Hayley was standing.

Betsy rolled off the sled, face planted in the snow, arms and legs splayed like she was about to make a snow angel. Hank crawled to his feet, picked up the sled, then went to check on Betsy.

"You okay, hon?"

"I'm just kissing the ground, happy to still be alive."

Hank chortled. "Ready to go again?"

Betsy slowly turned over onto her back and looked up at him. "Not if you still want that foot massage later!"

"Okay, I'll brave it alone!" Hank said, laughing as he trudged back up the hill.

Hayley stepped forward, extending a hand. "Can I help you up, Betsy?"

"Oh, hi, Hayley. I didn't see you standing there. Probably because my head's still spinning and my brain is processing the trauma."

"I take it you won't be bobsledding at the next Winter Olympics," Hayley joked, gripping Betsy's mittens and hauling her to her feet.

"That would be a safe bet," Betsy replied, brushing the snow off her retro rainbow ski suit.

"Hank's such a nice guy. How long have you two been dating?"

"Gosh, let me think," Betsy said, tilting her head to one side.

Hayley tried not to react, but was stunned. Bruce was always commenting on how Hayley tilted her head to one side when she was lost in thought. Betsy had the exact same habit.

"Almost three years, I think. Yes, it will be three years in March." Betsy stopped, noticing Hayley's dumbfounded look. "Is anything the matter, Hayley? You look like you've seen a ghost!"

Hayley snapped out of it. "What? No, it's nothing. Really. It's just the way you do this—" Hayley tilted her head to the side. "I just find it funny. I mean, not ha-ha funny, just weird."

"Why?"

"Because I do it too. All the time. Without thinking. I just find it strange that we both do it. Like we're related." Hayley quickly put the brakes on her babbling. "But of course, I know we're not. I mean, that's ridiculous, right?"

Betsy stared at her, not quite sure how to respond, which just caused Hayley to get more nervous and jittery and to blather on some more. "If it was the only thing, I'd say it's just a wild coincidence, but at the store the other day, you and Randy . . ."

Betsy's eyes narrowed. "Me and Randy what?"

Hayley wanted to kick herself for starting this whole excruciating conversation. "Nothing. Forget it."

"No, tell me." Betsy crossed her arms, waiting.

"When we were checking out, you and Randy both laughed at the same time, and it was the exact same laugh. I mean, it was like I was hearing it in surround sound. What are the odds that two people, totally unrelated, would do that? It's kind of spooky."

There was an agonizingly long pause.

Finally, Betsy unfolded her arms and spoke quietly. "I know, Hayley."

A shiver shot up Hayley's spine. "Um, you know what, Betsy?"

"I know Dwight is my father."

Hayley gulped. "You do?"

"I've known for a long time. Ever since I was fourteen years old."

Hayley's mouth dropped open, floored. "Did Marlene tell you?"

"Oh, gosh, no. My mother never tells me anything. If we didn't install cable when I was twelve, I still wouldn't even know about the birds and the bees. She's always trying to protect me, which is stupid because you can never hide the truth forever. Someone's always going to find out. When I was a freshman in high school, I was forced to clean the attic one Sunday afternoon and I came across some letters Dwight had sent Mom apologizing for skipping town and leaving her to raise me alone. He said he couldn't handle the pressure of raising another kid."

Hayley scoffed at that poor, cowardly excuse. Dwight Jordan couldn't even handle raising the two kids he had already fathered, let alone a third totally unexpected one.

And sadly, she was not surprised that Dwight had lied, pretending he didn't know Marlene was pregnant when he left.

"Betsy, I don't understand. You knew all this time and you never once said anything to us?"

"I wanted to respect everyone's privacy," Betsy said with a shrug. "Besides, there was a lot of bad blood between my mother and Dwight. When I showed Mom the letters, she grabbed them from me and burned them in the fireplace and told me never to bring that man up again. Ever. I didn't want to keep pushing her buttons, so I let it go. If she found out I ever went straight to you and told you, she would have freaked. I was basically a kid who didn't want to upset my mother and cause more family drama, so I just kept my mouth shut."

"So you never thought about tracking Dwight down?"

"Oh, all the time, but I never did. Not even when I became an adult and was no longer living under my mother's roof. I knew how hurt she would be. My grandfather Pappy did tell me that he tried to locate Dwight when Mom got pregnant, so he could pressure him to do the right thing and marry her, but every time he came up with a lead to where he might be, the trail eventually went cold. Then Mom met Tucker and married him and he ended up adopting me as his own daughter, so Grandpa figured I finally had a stable father figure willing to take care of me and stopped trying to find Dwight."

"Betsy, all these years, every single time you checked me out with my groceries at the Shop 'n Save, you knew. You knew we were half sisters."

Betsy's face blanched, embarrassed. "I wanted to

say something, honestly, Hayley, but I was afraid how you would react. And like I said, I don't know you that well, mostly as one of my customers, so what right do I have to intrude on your life just because we share some of the same DNA?" She bowed her head slightly. "I'm sorry. Maybe I should have said something. It's okay if you want to just go our separate ways and pretend this conversation never happened. I won't blame you."

"There is something you need to know, Betsy."

She braced herself, fearing the worst. "What's that?"

"I have *always* wanted a sister."

The two women stared at each other and then shared a laugh. Not the exact laugh, like Randy's, but pretty darn close.

Chapter 27

"Excuse me, Betsy, I don't mean to interrupt," Liddy breathlessly gasped, hurrying up to them. "But I really need to speak with Hayley. It's an emergency."

"Of course. Hank's waiting for me anyway. It was nice talking to you, Hayley," Betsy said with a bright smile.

Hayley touched her hand, excited for the relationship they would be carving out in the future. "I look forward to doing it again."

Betsy trotted off as Liddy yanked on Hayley's coat sleeve, desperate to get her attention.

"Liddy, what's gotten you so wound up?"

Liddy tried to collect herself, but was having trouble breathing she was so upset. "The worst possible thing has happened!"

Hayley's stomach dropped. "Oh no, not another body! Has someone else died?"

Liddy wrinkled her nose. "What? No! Of course

not! Don't be so ghoulish. No, this is worse. Much, much worse than that."

Much worse than a dead body?

Hayley steeled herself, dreading what she was about to be told. "What?"

Liddy grabbed her by the arm and dragged her back over to the tented picnic area where people were enjoying their lobsters and assorted cookies and cakes from the local bakery.

Hayley glanced around.

Everything appeared perfectly normal to her.

"Last table on the right," Liddy moaned, pointing.

Hayley's eyes fell upon Dwight sitting on the same side of the table as Liddy's mother, Celeste. They were canoodling over lobster rolls. She finally understood why Liddy was so discombobulated. The idea of ne'er-do-well Dwight and rarified snob Celeste making a love connection made her sick to her stomach.

Hayley, in a lame attempt to deny what was happening, croaked, "Maybe they're just talking. They have known each other since high school. It could mean nothing."

Then they watched in horror as Dwight cracked one of his corny jokes and Celeste erupted in coquettish laughter, clutching his arm as if hanging on for dear life and resting her head on his shoulder. There was no mistaking it. Liddy's mother was shamelessly flirting with Hayley's father.

Liddy spun around and growled at Hayley. "There is absolutely no way I will stand having that good-for-nothing con artist nomad as my stepfather!" She then quickly added, "No offense."

"None taken," Hayley assured her.

Liddy gave her a gentle shove. "You need to put a halt to this right now before it progresses any further."

Hayley did not disagree. They raced over to the table, nearly knocking Hayley's old boss Sal to the ground as he tried passing them with a plate of lobster and a heaping pile of potato salad. When they reached the blossoming couple, Dwight stood up out of respect.

Celeste emitted a girlish giggle. "Oh, Dwight, when did you turn into such a gentleman?"

Liddy's eyes narrowed. "Mom, don't you have to be heading home soon?"

Celeste checked the diamond watch on her wrist. "No, dear. It's not even three o'clock. Besides, I'm having a marvelous time catching up with Dwight."

Hayley stared at the glittery diamond watch.

Another reason to disrupt this budding romance.

Celeste was loaded.

And Hayley wouldn't put it past Dwight to want to snag someone of means, given his typical precarious financial situation.

She stole a quick glance at her father.

He was staring at the diamond watch too.

And he was smiling.

"Dwight, can I have a word?" Hayley asked, trying to act breezy and upbeat, the polar opposite of how she was feeling on the inside.

"Sure thing."

Hayley led him away from the tent, out of Celeste's earshot. She stopped and turned to face him.

He lit up. "What's up, kiddo?"

"What are you doing?"

"Having a lobster roll with Celeste."

"It looks to me like it's a bit more than that."

"Celeste is an old friend."

"Look, that woman has been through a few bad marriages and she still hasn't fully recovered. The last thing she needs right now is to get involved with someone who is just going to take off again."

"We're reliving some old memories, that's all," Dwight promised.

"I'm just voicing my concerns."

"There's no need to do that. I'm not going to propose to Celeste. We're just having a nice time together. Don't worry, it's nothing serious."

Although he was convincing on the surface, somehow she found it hard to believe him.

Picking up on her skepticism, he popped the remainder of his lobster roll into his mouth and chewed, talking with his mouth full. "I swear on the Bible, Hayley."

"You've never picked up a Bible in your life," Hayley scoffed. She looked over to see Liddy trying to desperately reason with her mother, who appeared to be brushing her off.

Dwight scooped the napkin out of the paper holder to wipe his mouth, but stopped. He studied the napkin, a confused look on his face.

"What's the matter?"

"Someone wrote a note on this napkin."

Hayley snatched the napkin out of her father's hand and read it.

I know it was you who killed Carroll Flood. If you

don't want me going to the cops, meet me at the boat-house at the north end of the pond. Come alone.

Dwight guffawed. "What is this, an episode of *The Sopranos*? It's gotta be some kind of joke."

Hayley read the napkin again. "This sounds deadly serious."

Dwight shrugged. "Come on, Hayley, the idiot who wrote that note doesn't know squat because I wasn't the one who killed Carroll. This person, whoever they are, hasn't got one whiff of proof that I did anything wrong."

"We should call Sergio," Hayley said, reaching for her phone.

Dwight extended his hand to prevent her from making the call. "What for? This is nothing. Listen, tell Celeste I'll be back in a jiffy."

"Where are you going?"

"I want to meet the person who is trying to blackmail me," Dwight said before turning to leave.

It was Hayley's turn to stop him. "No, it could be dangerous."

"Oh, hon, don't. It's sweet that you're worried about me, but there's no need. Don't jump to the worst case scenario like your mother." Dwight chuckled before shaking free and marching away.

Liddy suddenly appeared by Hayley's side. "Hayley, please, you have to talk to my mother. Although she's denying it, it's crystal clear she has a huge crush on Dwight. You have to explain why it would be a monumental mistake to get involved with that worthless, no-good grifter. No offense."

"I will, Liddy, but I can't right now!" Hayley cried as she took off to chase after her father.

"Hayley, come back!" Liddy yelled.

But she did not have time to school Celeste on the pitfalls of dating Dwight because she feared his life might be hanging by a thread at this very moment. Because Dwight had been correct in pointing out that she always focused on the worst case scenario.

The trouble was, in the end she was usually proven right.

Chapter 28

The brisk winter air bit at Hayley's cheeks as she trudged through the snowy path, struggling to keep pace with Dwight's determined jog. The remote section of Long Pond loomed ahead, concealed from the vibrant chaos of the winter carnival.

Dwight's dark figure was now a mere speck in the distance, his strides purposeful as he continued his solitary race toward the arranged meeting point. Hayley's breath puffed out in quick, shallow bursts, the exertion causing white clouds to form around her lips. She pressed on, determination mingling with the growing unease that gnawed at her heart.

She instinctively knew Dwight's life was in serious jeopardy despite his lack of concern.

With each step, the ice beneath her feet seemed to grow slicker, more treacherous. She fought to keep her balance, arms flailing in the frigid air as if trying to capture stability. Her heart raced as the ground betrayed her, and in a sudden, jarring moment, her world toppled.

Hayley's body hit the ice with a resonant thud, a shock wave of pain reverberating through her as her backside met the hard, frozen surface. She winced, her fingers gripping the ice as if it were her lifeline. Her breath hitched in her chest, a mix of frustration and humiliation bubbling within her.

She rolled over, her nose touching the cold, frozen ice, and she tried lifting herself up, first to her knees and then slowly, carefully, to her feet, wobbling on unsteady legs. She didn't dare to move too fast or risk suffering another nasty fall.

Her eyes darted around, seeking her father amidst the stark landscape. But there was no sign of him.

"Dwight?" she called out, her voice tinged with both concern and urgency. The echo of her own voice was her only reply.

She took a few tentative steps forward, the slippery ice beneath her feet a constant reminder of her precarious situation.

The world around her seemed to hold its breath, the carnival's distant melodies fading into the background.

"Dwight! Where are you?"

Only the wind answered, its mournful howl carrying her plea away into the emptiness. It was as if Long Pond had swallowed him whole.

Hayley took tiny steps forward, arms outstretched to maintain her balance, across the sheet of ice toward solid ground. Once she was safely off the ice, she paused to assess the situation.

Still no sign of Dwight.

She suddenly caught something out of the corner of her eye.

A wooden sign. The bottom of the post had been sawed off and it had been discarded in some bushes. Hayley hurried over and yanked the bright yellow sign from the embrace of the branches, turning it over to read what was on it.

DANGER THIN ICE. Underneath the stark warning was the silhouette of a person falling through the ice into deep water that was crossed out with a red line.

Hayley's heart leapt into her throat.

Someone had deliberately moved the sign so people, most likely Dwight, wouldn't see it.

"Dwight!" Hayley yelled again, panic rising.

She rushed ahead blindly, not knowing where she was going, just hoping and praying she would find him soon, when suddenly she heard his voice calling faintly in the distance. "Hayley?"

"Dwight, where are you?"

"Over here!"

Her pulse quickened and she followed the sound, her steps now urgent as she navigated the labyrinth of trees and snow.

As she burst through a thicket of trees, reaching the north end of the pond near the boathouse where the note on the napkin had instructed Dwight to go, she finally spotted him. His features were etched with cold, his eyes filled with both recognition and a quiet plea. As their gazes locked, time seemed to suspend itself, and in the deafening silence, the cracks began.

Dwight didn't dare move.

Hayley could plainly see the terror written all over his face.

The ice beneath her father's feet trembled.

Hayley lunged forward, not sure what she could do, but willing to try anything to save him.

But it was too late.

With an explosive crescendo, the ice shattered, as though the world itself had split open. Dwight's figure plummeted through the splintering surface, disappearing into the icy abyss below.

Hayley stopped in her tracks and let out a blood-curdling scream. "No!"

Island Food & Spirits
By
Hayley Powell

If there is one thing my husband loves to do no matter if it's spring, summer, fall, or winter, it is grilling outside. Bruce's lifelong passion for grilling is now legendary among our close family and friends, and not because of his mouthwatering, delicious ribs, chicken, and steaks, which are admittedly to die for, but for an entirely different reason.

When Bruce and I first got married, it was the dog days of summer, and we were both so busy with work, that it was a few months before we could even entertain at our home because everyone was so busy during the frenetic summer tourist season.

Eventually the town finally quiets down when the last of the autumn "leaf peepers," as we locals like to call them, depart. I'm talking about the flood of people who travel north to New England to take in the incredible vibrant colors of the changing leaves in Acadia National Park and on the island itself before the leaves all fall to the ground, leaving the trees bare for winter.

Despite our intention to entertain as a married

couple, Thanksgiving had already passed and we still had not invited anyone over, with the exception of a handful of our closest family and friends to celebrate our new marriage.

Well, the week following Thanksgiving, we decided that now was the time to throw a casual gathering with friends, both old and new, before all of the Christmas festivities began ramping up in the next couple of weeks.

We emailed twenty-five people, friends, relatives, and work colleagues, to come on over to the house on Sunday afternoon to celebrate our new beginning with us.

Even though it was the first of December and there was a definite chill in the air, Bruce, for some inexplicable reason, insisted that he was going to grill his special ginger garlic wings, a recipe handed down to him by his grandfather, another self-proclaimed grill master, on his trusty charcoal grill that had indeed seen better days. I was constantly telling him he needed to replace that rusted, old dilapidated cooker with a new one, but he just wouldn't listen. I wouldn't say I nagged him (Bruce begs to differ). In any event, he told me in no uncertain terms, "Hayley, you just don't mess with perfection!" So I left it alone.

Bruce prided himself on using only charcoal and not propane, so my expensive propane grill I bought after seeing it on some barbecue competition show had been covered and stored in the back of the garage for months now. Not that I

minded, because Bruce really could work won-
ders with his rickety old charcoal grill.

The party was in full swing with cocktails and
appetizers flowing and the dining room table,
which had been set up with our makeshift buffet,
was loaded with pasta salad, potato salad, baked
beans, rolls, and even lobster and crab salad,
thanks to Mona.

Bruce had just brought in a baking tin filled
with the first batch of his delicious wings and
quickly headed out to grill more as our hungry
guests began to ravenously dive into them, chowing them down as fast as he could make them.

I noticed we were getting dangerously low on
wings and were about to run out, and Bruce still
had not been back to replenish yet, so I decided I
better nudge things along and go outside and
check on him and his grill master helpers Sal,
Randy, and Sergio.

When I walked out the door to the deck, I discovered that Bruce's helpers, Sal, Randy, and Sergio were not exactly assisting with the grilling,
but more like standing around, doling out lots of
unsolicited manly grilling advice. Bruce was asking Sal to hold a new tin so he could put the
cooked wings in it, when all of a sudden the entire bottom of the grill just fell out in a big pile of
burning hot charcoal, flames, and chicken wings
right onto the wooden deck floor!

We all just stood there, frozen, in shock, as the
burning flames and hot coals ignited the deck.
The same deck that was so old that I had been

begging Bruce to build a new one, but we had decided to wait until spring, unfortunately.

I let out a guttural cry, which luckily seemed to break the spell that the guys were in, and everyone started moving all at once.

Randy dashed off the deck to where we kept our water hose, only to discover the hose was now gone and the water to the hose had been turned off for winter. Sal started kicking at the burning pile of flames and charcoal with his boot, trying to contain it in one place. Sergio, being the police chief, was already on his phone calling the fire department to stand by for a possible assist of a small deck fire. Poor Bruce was more concerned with trying to save his wings, which by now were burnt to a crisp. Meanwhile, I was still yelling at anyone who would listen to put out the fire, but no one seemed to be listening to me! So I did the only thing I could think of as I spotted the snow shovel leaning up against the side of the house on the other end of the deck. I raced over, grabbed the shovel, and ran back to the burning pile of coals and flames, which now had spread out even more. Without thinking, in a panic, I frantically started shoveling them up and tossing them as hard as I could over the deck rail and onto the driveway over and over again until the deck was finally cleared of the hot, fiery coals.

Although I was breathing heavy and thinking that I really needed to get into shape, I turned to the guys with a huge smile on my face, awaiting the inevitable praise I was about to receive for saving the entire house from burning to the ground.

Instead, all eyes were staring at something in the driveway and I followed their gaze to what had transfixed them and let out a monumental groan. I had shoveled so hard and fast in my panic that the coals and flames had indeed made it to the driveway, but unfortunately they had all landed on top of the hood of Sal's brand-new Range Rover Sport that was parked there. We all watched in horror as the coals burned and bubbled the paint off the hood.

At that point, I could hear the siren of the fire truck blasting, growing louder, as it raced down the street (unfortunately, this wasn't the first time a fire truck had been to my house) and the party-goers inside all began to converge outside to see what had happened.

When all was said and done, thankfully Sal's car damage was mostly melted paint and dents, which Bruce and I gladly paid to have fixed, and being the good sport he was, Sal eventually got over the shock of it all and can finally laugh about it now (although it did take a few months).

Our deck was scorched pretty bad, but all in all, we were lucky we had homeowner's insurance, and we now have a brand-new deck and a great story to tell at future parties!

Oh, and best of all, Bruce finally got a new charcoal grill that Christmas from me, but I made him promise that when it gets old, he will, in fact, get a new one with no excuses, because we were not going to be replacing another deck. Once is enough.

I'm giving you an oven version of Bruce's chicken wings this week just in case our experience may have scared you off from grilling. But first, a delicious cocktail for you to enjoy while you wait for those delectable wings to bake.

GINGER ORANGE SPRITZER

GINGER SIMPLE SYRUP INGREDIENTS:
¼ cup sugar
1 cup water
8-inch piece of ginger root cut in thick slices

Heat the sugar and water in a small saucepan over medium high heat, stirring constantly to dissolve sugar. Add the ginger to the pan and reduce the heat to low. Let ginger simmer for 30 minutes, remove from heat and let ginger syrup cool.

SPRITZER INGREDIENTS:
1 cup ginger simple syrup
1 cup fresh squeezed orange juice
¼ cup fresh lemon juice
16 ounces club soda
ice

Fill four glasses with ice and pour equal parts orange juice, lemon juice, and ginger simple syrup and mix. Top each drink with club soda before serving.

Bruce's Ginger Garlic Chicken Wings

INGREDIENTS:
½ cup honey
⅓ cup soy sauce
4 cloves garlic, minced
1 tablespoon ginger, grated
¼ cup water
2 pounds fresh chicken wings cut into wings and
    drumettes
1 tablespoon olive oil
salt and pepper to taste

Preheat oven to 425 degrees.

With paper towels, dry your chicken wings so they are not wet.

In a bowl, toss your wings with the olive oil, salt, and pepper.

Place a piece of parchment paper on a baking sheet and put a wire rack on top of the parchment paper. Spread out your wings in a single layer onto the wire rack.

Bake for 45 minutes or until chicken is crispy and done.

SAUCE:
Add honey, soy sauce, garlic, ginger, and water to a small saucepan and bring to a boil.

Reduce the heat to low and simmer for 10 minutes until a little reduced and thickened.

Remove your sauce from the heat and it will thicken as it cools.

When your chicken is done, remove from the oven and toss in the sauce. When the wings are all coated, put back on the rack and return to the oven for 15 more minutes. Remove and enjoy!

Note: I like to double the sauce, so we always have some for dipping our chicken into it. I promise you will love it, but it is not necessary.

Chapter 29

Hayley's heart skipped a beat as she watched Dwight struggling in the icy waters of the pond. With panic seizing in her chest, she at first ran toward him, but stopped, realizing if she tried reaching him, chances were she would just end up in the water with him. Spinning around, she sprinted back toward the carnival grounds, her voice piercing the air as she frantically screamed for help. A crowd gathered around as she tried not to get hysterical, her eyes pleading for help.

"Dwight, my dad, he's fallen through the ice! He's going to die of hypothermia if somebody doesn't help him!"

Lots of gasps.

Buster Healey, a local fisherman, rushed forward. "Come on, we can take my truck."

Hayley shook her head. "No! It's too big! The ice will collapse under its weight! It'll just make things worse!"

Just then, Bruce rode up on his Thundercat, a happy boy behind him, his cheeks red and his little arms clutching the sides of Bruce's snow vest.

"Bruce!" Hayley cried.

Bruce's face instantly registered concern. "What's wrong?"

"It's Dwight! He walked out on some thin ice and fell through!"

Bruce's eyes widened with concern. "Anybody got some rope?"

Buster reached into the flatbed of his truck and grabbed some thick rope and then hustled over and handed it to Bruce. He turned to Hayley. "Show me where!"

Hayley hurried over and grabbed the boy crouched on the snowmobile behind Bruce by his mitten. "Okay, Aaron, it's my turn for a ride." She helped him off and handed him to his mother before hopping on the Thundercat and wrapping her arms around Bruce. "Go!"

He cranked the throttle, revving the engine, and then the snowmobile jetted off across the pond. Hayley clung to Bruce as the cold air whipped against their faces as she directed him on where to go. Once they got closer, Bruce skidded to a stop about twenty feet from where they spotted Dwight splashing and flailing in the freezing water, his face a mask of fear and desperation. Bruce and Hayley scrambled off. Hayley's heart pounded as Bruce quickly made a lasso out of the rope and tentatively made his way closer to Dwight, careful with each step, making sure the ice was thick enough to support him. Then, like a rodeo cowboy, he swung the loop of the rope in a circular motion above his head, hurling it toward Dwight's trembling fingers. It landed about a foot and a half from him. He tried reaching for it, clawing at the chunks of ice, almost succumbing and sinking below the surface.

"Come on, Dwight! You can do it!" Hayley cried.

After a few tries, Dwight managed to wrap his middle finger around a piece of the rope and pull it toward him, inch by inch.

Hayley realized she was holding her breath.

With a final tug, Dwight was able to get a good grip on the lasso and secure it around his waist. Bruce, meanwhile, grasping the other end of the rope, tied it to the Thundercat's sturdy frame. Without any hesitation, Bruce jumped on his snowmobile and cranked the handle, the machine's engine roaring once again, and started moving in the opposite direction.

Slowly but steadily, the rope began to tighten, pulling Dwight out of the frigid water. He clung to the edge of the ice, his strength waning. But Bruce was not about to lose him at this point. With grim determination, he continued driving as Hayley shouted words of encouragement to Dwight to hang on, he was almost there. Inch by inch, his muscles straining against the effort, Dwight emerged from the icy depths, finally collapsing on the solid ice. Hayley rushed to her father, helping him to his feet and wrapping her coat around him to keep him warm as Bruce joined them. Dwight's shivering body pressed close to Hayley's and she rubbed his arms vigorously, trying to infuse warmth back into his chilled frame.

Bruce stared into Dwight's shell-shocked eyes. "You okay, buddy?"

Unable to speak, his lips quivering, he managed a slight nod as Hayley continued holding him.

Hearing people yelling, they turned to see some men running toward them to offer help.

Bruce waved at them, signaling everything was going to be all right. Hayley could tell Bruce was proud his Thundercat had saved the day.

But then, they heard cracking noises reverberating through the air, and the ice beneath Bruce's snowmobile began to groan and slowly give way.

"Oh no . . . No . . ." Bruce muttered.

They watched in horror as the ground beneath the Thundercat crumbled and the snowmobile plunged through the fragile surface, disappearing into the icy, murky water below.

Bruce's face turned ashen.

All of them, Hayley, Bruce, Dwight, the men who had run there to offer their aid, stood motionless and silent, the crackling ice and gentle winter breeze the only sounds breaking the silence.

Finally, Buster Healey, who was among the men who had come to help, spoke up. "Damn, Bruce, I sure hope you have insurance on that thing!"

Bruce didn't respond.

He just stared hopelessly at the spot where he had lost his beloved Christmas gift. There was no way to recover it, not until the spring thaw at least.

Dwight placed a comforting hand on Bruce's shoulder. "I don't know how to thank you, Bruce. You saved my life."

Bruce offered him a rueful smile.

But Hayley knew he was inconsolable.

He had been the proud owner of that awesome Arctic Cat ZR 9000 Thundercat he had coveted for a whopping three whole days.

Chapter 30

Dolly's Craft Castle had only been open for a year. Nestled in between the pet shop Bark Harbor and a takeout deli, Dolly Halperin had struggled to keep her shop open year-round, but during the holidays, she enjoyed enough business to keep her going until the summer months when the tourist season flooded the town with potential customers, not to mention the cruise ships that docked in the harbor and unleashed their passengers for the day.

Hayley and Sheila entered the store and were not surprised to see Marlene Shaw, Betsy's mother, behind the counter with a cup of coffee, and reading a Nora Roberts novel. Hayley was aware that Marlene, also a crafts lover, recently began working part-time for Dolly, covering for her whenever Dolly had choir practice at the Congregational church. Hayley had pre-planned this drop-in ahead of time, using the excuse that they would check out the post-Christmas sales.

She had hoped to speak to Marlene alone and suss

out some information about her past relationship with Dwight, but once Sheila got wind of Hayley's plan, having overheard her talking to Bruce in the kitchen over breakfast, Sheila had insisted on accompanying her.

Hayley was already annoyed with her mother. Not only had she insisted they leave the car behind and walk downtown in order to get some brisk exercise that might help melt the pounds gained over Christmas, but also as they trudged along the slippery sidewalk trying not to fall. When the subject of Dwight's near-death experience came up, Sheila dismissed it out of hand, not the least bit moved or concerned that someone might be targeting him.

"Mom, this is serious. It appears he has a bull's-eye on his back and could be in real danger."

Sheila just sniffed. "We reap what we sow, Hayley. That's what the Bible says, if you ever bothered coming with me to church."

Frustrated by her mother's lack of worry or alarm, Hayley decided to simply drop the subject. There was no getting through to Sheila. Her mother's wounds were still just too deep despite the decades that had passed.

"Oh, Hayley, look! Don't these gingerbread-scented candles smell divine?" Sheila cooed, holding up a wax candle decorated with pinecones and holly leaves and then shoving it underneath Hayley's nose.

Hayley nodded, brushing the candle away from her face, and focused on Marlene, who glanced up from her paperback novel. "Good morning, Marlene! I didn't see you at the winter carnival yesterday."

"I was covering for Dolly here so she could sell her wares to everybody at Long Pond," Marlene explained. "How are you, Sheila?"

"Fine," Sheila snipped, stone-faced.

Hayley sighed. She had warned her mother not to act this way if she was so determined to come with her to Dolly's craft store knowing they would run into Marlene. Sheila for years had taken great pains to explain why she despised Marlene. Apparently, they were bitter rivals in high school, much like Hayley and her former nemesis Sabrina Merryweather. Although the details were sketchy, Hayley was able to deduce that their decades-long feud had something to do with Marlene spreading a false rumor about Sheila canoodling with the football coach, a much older married man, costing her a coveted spot on the cheerleading squad, which Marlene was only too happy to fill, and eventually was named captain.

"I'm not saying I would have become captain of the cheerleading squad like Marlene," Sheila would explain. "But she robbed me of the chance. She took that opportunity away from me when she spread those vicious lies about me!"

Sheila had never forgiven Marlene, which made the revelation about Dwight's affair with her sworn enemy all the more hurtful. It was a betrayal she would never get over.

"How long are you in town for?" Marlene asked.

"Just until after New Year's. My boyfriend Carl needs to get back to Florida for a golf tournament at our club. You remember Carl, don't you, Marlene? Tall, devastatingly handsome. Used to be a local."

"Of course I remember Carl. I heard he had moved down to Florida."

"Yes. To be with *me*," Sheila said pointedly.

Marlene nodded and went back to reading her book.

But Sheila could not help herself despite Hayley's eyes begging her to stop. "We're very happy together, so don't you get any ideas in your head!" She said it with a friendly lilt in her voice as if she was just complimenting the wallpaper.

"Mom!" Hayley growled.

Marlene was not anxious to rehash any old grudges and past transgressions, but she simply could not ignore Sheila's last comment. She closed her book and set it down on the counter, looking up at Sheila, whose face was flushed. "I'm a happily married woman, Sheila."

"So was I," Sheila hissed.

Hayley snatched the candle out of Sheila's hand. "You know what, I think I'm going to buy this gingerbread candle. It smells so good!"

Marlene stood up and came around from behind the counter. Hayley feared she might pop her mother right in the eye. But she didn't. She crossed to her, arms at her side. "I understand how you must feel, Sheila. It was a lousy thing for us to do. Dwight and I both acted horribly. For years I felt guilty about that affair, knowing how you and Hayley and Randy might feel if you ever found out."

"And lo and behold, we did. All these years later," Sheila snapped.

"Yes, Betsy told me everything. It's a lot to process, for all of us. Not to make excuses, but I want you to know that when Dwight and I got together, you two were already separated—at least that's what he told me."

"We weren't. I didn't even know the marriage was in trouble until he up and vanished from our lives one day, leaving me all alone to raise two children."

"I'm sorry," Marlene whispered. "That must have been a very difficult time."

"You have no idea."

Sheila steeled herself before speaking again. "Tell me something, Marlene. Did you frame Dwight for Carroll Flood's murder in order to get revenge on him for skipping town after he got you pregnant way back when?"

Hayley emitted a low gasp.

She could not believe her mother went there so quickly.

There was a prolonged silence.

Marlene fixed an unwavering gaze upon Sheila, who stood her ground, her fists clenched. Then Marlene erupted in laughter, as if the accusation was a hysterical joke. "No, Sheila, I didn't! Seriously, I could ask you the same question!"

"What? I-I would n-never," Sheila sputtered. "How could you ask me that?"

"Because despite what you might think of me, we're not so different. I don't believe either of us is capable of something so heinous. I was fond of Carroll and Althea. They were friends of mine. I was heartbroken when he died."

Hayley noticed her mother's cold veneer starting to slowly melt, although she struggled mightily to maintain her distant and unsympathetic posture.

"I will admit, running into Dwight at the Criterion Theatre, that was a shock. I never expected to ever again see that man's face in Bar Harbor," Marlene said. "I had no idea how to act, what to say. But honestly, I have no ill will toward the man. Not after all this time. What he did to me was ages ago. Yes, he left me a cowardly note and then just ran away, leaving me with a baby on the way. At the time, I couldn't imagine my life getting any worse. But I persevered, gave birth to Betsy, and eventually I met Tucker. I never knew what real love was until I met that man. Dwight was just an infatuation. Tucker was the man I was meant to be with. And he adopted Betsy as his own. Our daughter is our pride and joy, our reason for living. I have Dwight to thank for helping bring her into this world."

Sheila was now on the verge of tears. She took a step toward Marlene. Hayley feared she might strike her. But instead, Sheila wrapped her arms around Marlene and gave her a hug. Marlene stiffened, not sure what to do at first, but then she patted Sheila softly on the back.

Hayley watched the scene, confident about Marlene's sincerity, and she knew in her gut that Marlene Shaw had not been the culprit who poisoned Carroll at the gingerbread house contest in some misguided attempt to frame Dwight.

Which only raised the question.

Then who did?

Chapter 31

Nestled away on the west side of Mount Desert Island, about four miles from Southwest Harbor, was a serene little hideaway spot known to the locals as the Seawall Dining Room that boasted a minimalist menu of fresh seafood, offered either fried or sautéed, accompanied by crispy French fries or a side of cole-slaw. That was about the extent of their menu besides a selection of beers and soft drinks. Bruce's favorite item to order was the fried shrimp that he loved dipping in the owner Harry's homemade tartar sauce. Harry had inherited the small establishment that had room for only twelve tables from his grandparents, who started the business in the 1950s.

Bruce had been despondent all day after losing his beloved Thundercat to the depths of Long Pond, so in an effort to cheer him up, Hayley had offered to treat him to dinner at Seawall, inviting Sheila and Carl to tag along as well. They jumped at the chance, since both of them had been coming to Seawall with their own parents since they were little kids. When they pulled into the gravel parking lot they counted twelve cars, which suggested they might have to wait a while for a table.

Hayley was ravenous as she led the way inside and stepped up to the host station, manned by Harry's daughter, Cammie, a sweet, button-nosed, soft-spoken girl in her mid-twenties.

"Hi, Cammie, how long is the wait?" Hayley asked.

She glanced around. "Not too long. There is a check down at a window table for four. We're just waiting on a credit card."

"Great. You're always so busy here. I'm surprised you haven't expanded."

"Dad thinks it would take away from the charm of the place and the service would suffer. Plus, the locals might put up a fuss if we have to raise the prices to cover renovations."

"That makes perfect sense," Sheila said.

Once the tourists discovered the place after a few stellar Yelp and Tripadvisor raves, business boomed and now there was usually a long line out the door, especially during the busy summer months.

Hayley scanned the small dining room. "The out-of-towners are definitely crowding out the locals. I don't see one familiar face."

Cammie nodded in agreement. "Other than Mrs. Crawford, I haven't sat one person who lives on the island all night."

Hayley perked up, surprised. "Celeste Crawford is here?"

Cammie pointed to a private table for two on the far

side of the restaurant near the kitchen. "Yes, they just sat down. I think she's on a date," Cammie whispered, winking.

Sure enough, Hayley spotted Celeste seated across from Dwight. They were holding hands, mooning over one another.

"Oh no!" Hayley cried.

Sheila, who was chatting up Bruce and Carl, spun around, smelling a crisis. "What is it?"

"Nothing! Let's go somewhere else to eat. It's going to be too long of a wait!" Hayley fibbed, pushing them all toward the door.

But it was too late. Cammie had grabbed four menus and had already come out from behind the host station. "Your table's ready, Hayley. Right this way."

Luckily, their table was clear across the room from where Dwight and Celeste were sitting, but it was such a small dining room, someone in their party was sure to spot them at some point. And it did not take long.

"Look, Dwight's here!" Carl bellowed, loud enough for everyone in the restaurant to hear.

Startled, Sheila clutched Carl's flannel shirtsleeve. "What? Where?"

Dwight pointed in their direction. "Over there." He then began waving. "Hey, Dwight!"

Dwight sheepishly waved back, knowing the scandal he and Celeste were causing. Celeste sat up proudly. She was not going to be shamed for having a romantic dinner with Dwight.

As Bruce and Sheila sat down, Carl bounded off across the room.

"Carl, where are you going?" Sheila gasped.

Carl stopped and turned back. "I'm just going to pop over there and say hello."

"Why?" Sheila cried.

He stared at her incredulously. "Because Dwight is my friend and it's the polite thing to do. Do you have a problem with that?"

Sheila threw her hands up in the air, frustrated. "No, knock yourself out."

Cammie, confused by the whole situation, set the menus down on the table. "Enjoy your meal."

Hayley stopped her. "Cammie, do me a favor, don't tell Liddy that we saw her mother here on a date with Dwight. It's just easier for everyone."

"She already knows," Cammie replied flatly.

"What do you mean, she already knows?"

"My dad is a huge fan of Liddy. She sold his cottage on Hodgdon Pond Farm last year for three times what his parents bought it for in the 1970s. He's a loyalist and he knows she would want to know who her mother showed up here with and he texted her even before I had a chance to show them to their table."

"How did she react?"

"He didn't say, but I got a glance at his phone and all I saw was that exploding head emoji."

"That's not good," Hayley moaned.

"Probably not," Cammie agreed.

Cammie wandered off to greet a couple who had just walked through the front door.

"Hold on. I'll be right back!" Hayley said to Bruce and Sheila before dashing across the restaurant to Dwight and Celeste's table, where Dwight was in the middle of recounting his harrowing brush with death to Carl as Celeste, who had probably already heard the dramatic story multiple times by now, listened with rapt attention.

"That sounds pretty scary," Carl said, shaking his head.

"If it hadn't been for Bruce and Hayley, I would've been a goner!" Dwight declared.

Celeste reached across the table and squeezed his hand. "Well, thank God we didn't lose you!" Then her eyes settled upon Hayley. "What a coincidence. There are over sixty-five restaurants on the island and we wind up at the same one for dinner! I didn't expect to run into any familiar faces all the way over here."

"I'm sure you didn't," Hayley said, folding her arms. "But it's December. Only a handful of those restaurants stay open during the winter months, as you know."

"I would appreciate it if you showed a little discretion and not mention you saw us here tonight," Celeste whispered.

"Of course, Celeste," Hayley reassured her. She paused before adding, "But Liddy already knows you're here."

"You told her already?"

"No, but you know your daughter. She has spies all over this island."

A cloud passed over Celeste's face.

Hayley and Carl returned to their table to join Bruce and Celeste to enjoy a delicious meal of fried shrimp and clams and sautéed scallops as they watched the beautiful sunset, knowing a major storm was brewing for tomorrow.

Hurricane Liddy.

Hayley's phone started buzzing with texts just after six in the morning. She tried ignoring them, but Liddy was adamant. She needed Hayley to come to her house and help her talk some sense into her wayward mother.

Bruce wanted no part of it, but Sheila offered to go with Hayley for this emergency intervention.

When they arrived at Liddy's sprawling mansion off Eagle Lake Road just outside of town and were hurriedly ushered inside by a fluttery and discombobulated Liddy, they found Celeste calmly sitting at the table, sipping coffee and enjoying a healthy breakfast of granola and yogurt and some dry whole grain toast.

"Good morning, girls," Celeste chirped.

"Morning, Celeste," both Hayley and Sheila muttered, both curious as to how this was going to go.

Liddy decided to start. "Mother, I asked Hayley and Sheila to come over this morning because—"

"Wasn't the food scrumptious last night at Seawall?" Celeste interrupted. "Nobody can fry a piece of haddock like that Harry Carter. How were your meals?"

"Mother, stop trying to change the subject!"

Celeste took a bite of her toast. "Fine. I won't say another word. Go on. Continue with your meddling into my private life."

Liddy heaved a sigh. "I'm just looking out for you! You would do the same if you caught me dating a man who has more red flags than a bullfighting arena during a championship match!"

Celeste sipped her coffee. "I believe you're overreacting, dear. We're just having fun. It's not like I'm going to marry the man . . . any time soon."

Liddy gasped. "So you've already thought about it!" She whipped around to Hayley and Sheila. "This is nuts! Please! You have to help me! Say something! She won't listen to reason!"

"How many men have you dated who were completely wrong for you, and when I tried to warn you, you refused to listen?" Celeste wondered out loud.

She was absolutely correct.

But Hayley had no intention of pointing out to Liddy that she took after her mother. Not if she wanted to leave this house with their friendship still intact.

"Dwight has changed," Celeste said matter-of-factly. "He's become a better man over the years."

Sheila could not help but loudly scoff.

Celeste raised an eyebrow. "You don't agree, Sheila?"

"No, I don't, Celeste. I've known that man for a very long time. I don't think he's capable of changing."

"I respect your opinion, but you haven't seen him in decades, so I don't believe you are in a position to truly know that to be true," Celeste surmised. "Everyone deserves a second chance."

"Not him! He not only deserted Sheila, he also left behind Marlene, two young mothers who were forced to raise their children all on their own with no help!

How do you come back from something like that? It's unforgivable!" Liddy cried.

As much as she tried reasoning with her, Liddy knew it was hopeless because Celeste was just as stubborn as she was, and when pushed hard, she just became all the more intractable.

Celeste stood up and said in a singsongy voice, "Would anyone like some coffee? I just brewed a fresh pot."

Liddy rushed up to Hayley. "You have to talk to her, get her to see Dwight as he truly is, a player who will only break her heart in the end with all of us left behind to pick up the pieces!"

"I don't know what else I can do—" Hayley began before her phone buzzed and she looked at the screen. There was a text from Sergio. The blood suddenly drained from Hayley's face.

"Hayley, what is it?" Sheila asked tentatively.

Hayley slowly looked up from the phone, her voice shaky. "It's Dwight. He's been shot."

Chapter 32

Hayley thought she might be pulled over for speeding as she and Sheila raced to the Bar Harbor Hospital. Squealing to a stop in the guest parking lot, they both shot out of her car and dashed through the automatic doors to the emergency check-in where they were told by the receptionist, who had been in Gemma's class and recognized her immediately, that her brother Randy and some others were up on the second floor in the waiting room. Hayley thanked the girl and she and her mother hurried into the elevator, Hayley's hand trembling as she pressed the button to take them up one floor. Neither spoke as the elevator ascended. When the doors opened, Hayley's eyes fell upon Randy, sitting between Mona's father, Bubba, and Liddy's father, Elmer. They rushed toward them.

Randy raised his eyes and then stood up to greet them. "It's just a flesh wound. He's still in with the doctor, but I'm sure he's going to be fine!" Randy assured both of them.

Hayley emitted a huge sigh of relief and threw her arms around Randy in a tight hug. "Thank God!" Then she let go and shook her head. "I don't understand. What happened?"

Bubba gripped both armrests of his chair and hauled himself to his feet, speaking gently to Hayley. "We, um, were out in the park on a hike—"

Sheila interrupted him, suddenly suspicious. "A *hike*? When have you three ever gone on a hike?"

Hayley whipped around toward her mother. "Mom, please. Let him speak."

Sheila threw up her hands and then folded her arms, anxious to hear what was going to come out of his mouth next.

Bubba and Elmer exchanged troubled glances, which was not lost on Hayley.

"Anyway, we were out in the park . . ." His eyes met Sheila before he emphatically continued. "On a *hike* . . . when somebody started, um, taking potshots at us with a rifle."

"What?" Hayley cried. "There was a sniper on the loose in Acadia National Park?"

Elmer still sat hunched over in his chair, hands on his face. He slowly lowered them. "We think someone followed us out there and—"

Sheila could not contain herself. She interrupted again. "And just started firing random bullets at you? Why, that's the craziest thing I have ever heard! And frankly, I'm still having trouble with the whole hiking story. I couldn't even get Dwight to walk to the refrigerator to get his own beer! What were you three really doing?"

"Mom, please!" Hayley scolded before turning back to Bubba. "Are you sure it wasn't a hunter who mistook you for some deer?"

"Probably not," Bubba said quietly. "Deer season ended in November. It's illegal to be out there hunting now."

Once again, Hayley noticed Bubba and Elmer trading apprehensive looks.

Sheila picked up on the furtive glances as well. "What are you two not telling us?"

"Nothing!" Bubba yelped defensively.

"I know something's up. I can feel it in my bones. Whenever you get together with Dwight, trouble *always* follows. You three never learn. When are you going to finally grow up and start acting like responsible adults, like my Carl?"

Suddenly, as if on cue, Carl appeared carrying a cardboard tray of hot coffees for the group.

Sheila's eyes widened in surprise. "Carl, what are you doing here? I thought you were at home watching a Patriots game on TV."

"Uh, no, I mean I was, but after you left, Dwight called and asked if I wanted to go—"

Elmer quickly cut him off. "Hiking!"

Carl looked at him quizzically.

"That's right. After everything we ate over Christmas, we thought we could all use a little exercise!" Bubba explained, patting his round belly. He stared at Carl, his voice tightening. "Right, Carl?"

Carl nodded and smiled. "Yup. So I had them swing by the house and pick me up. I thought we'd commune with nature, maybe see a deer, or even a bear. Last thing I expected to find deep in the woods was an active shooter."

Sheila's knees buckled. "My God, Carl, you could have been killed! Who on earth would want to harm you? You're so nice! You just won a congeniality award from the Florida Federation of Square Dancers!"

"Carl wasn't the target. None of us were. It was clearly Dwight," Elmer said solemnly. "All the bullets that were fired were aimed at him—most of them missed, one hit a tree—but that last one got him right in the left shoulder and he went down. Luckily, Bubba's phone had service and we were able to call for an ambulance to meet us on the roadside."

The elevator dinged and the doors opened and Bruce, distressed, charged off and hastily joined them. "How is he?"

"We're still waiting to hear, but they think he's going to be okay," Hayley answered, falling into her husband's arms. He gently patted her back as he spoke to the group. "How on earth did he get shot?"

"Apparently Lee Harvey Oswald is in Maine and stalking my ex-husband!" Sheila wailed.

Bruce, still holding Hayley, gaped at Sheila incredulously. "You mean this wasn't an accident?"

Hayley pulled out from the hug and took a step back, worry lines on her forehead. "Think about it, Bruce. First, the warning sign for thin ice on Long Pond was mysteriously moved so Dwight couldn't see it, and now this!"

Bruce rubbed his chin, mind racing. "But who would want him dead?"

"It could be anyone!" Sheila yelled. "At least anyone old enough to remember him when he lived here. Not to mention the scores of others he left in his wake all over the world that we don't even know about! We could be talking thousands, maybe more than the head count on a Princess cruise ship!"

Hayley opened her mouth to admonish her mother again, but stopped herself. Because this time Sheila's assessment of the situation was dead-on.

The shooter could be anyone who passed through Dwight Jordan's orbit, someone he had wronged along the way. And given Dwight's checkered history, that number could very well be in the thousands.

Chapter 33

Hayley's heart leapt into her throat when she saw a grim-faced Dr. Cormack approaching. She gripped her brother's hand. "Randy . . ."

Randy spun around and his face fell at the sight of Dr. Cormack. By his somber expression, the news did not look good.

They scurried up to meet him halfway. "Dr. Cormack, what is it? What's wrong?"

He looked at them curiously. "Huh? Oh, nothing. Dwight's going to be just fine. The bullet's out, we bandaged him up, and after he signs some paperwork, he'll be good to go."

"You just looked upset when you came out to talk to us," Hayley said.

"That's because I just got off the phone with my wife," he sighed. "She ripped me a new one for forgetting our wedding anniversary today. Honestly, after thirty-four long, arduous years, is it really still worth celebrating?"

Dr. Cormack's marriage had been on the rocks ever since his extramarital affair with a coworker, Nurse Tilly, became public not too long ago. Although the relationship ended and Tilly quickly moved on by dating one of Sergio's officers, Lieutenant Donnie, Dr. Cormack stayed with his wife and was still paying for his sins. Word around town was Mrs. Cormack was not the forgiving type and took great pleasure in reminding him of his shortcomings on a daily basis.

Hayley turned to everyone in the waiting area, calling out, "He's going to be okay!"

Everyone cheered except for Sheila, who shook her head and muttered, "I swear that fool is like a cat with nine lives. He always manages to survive."

"Can we see go see him?" Randy asked.

"We can't have a big crowd back there, so only family at this time. He's in exam room three. The rest of you can wait here. He'll be out in a few minutes," Dr. Cormack said with a bright smile, trying to make up for scaring them so badly moments earlier with his gloom-ridden expression.

Hayley and Randy started off toward the exam rooms.

"I'm coming with you!" Sheila cried, following them.

Hayley turned to her mother and held a hand up. "Mom, perhaps you should stay here with the others."

"Why? I'm family too," Sheila snorted.

"Yes, but Dwight's recovering from a gunshot wound. That's very traumatizing. So he probably doesn't need you berating him right now. There will be plenty of time for that later."

"Somebody has to keep his feet on the ground!" Sheila protested.

Carl came up behind Sheila and firmly planted his hands on her shoulders. "You two go ahead. We'll wait here."

Carl's soothing voice seemed to placate Sheila. She made no further move to join them.

Hayley and Randy bustled through the swinging metal doors and down the hall to the last room on the left, number 3, where they found Dwight sitting up on an exam table. His shirt was off and there was a large white bandage on his right shoulder. Nurse Tilly gripped a clipboard of papers and Dwight was signing the last page. He went to hand the pen back to her, but before she could take it, he slipped it out of her reach. "How about I give you your pen back if you agree to have a drink with me?"

"I have a very jealous boyfriend, Mr. Jordan," Tilly warned. "He's a lieutenant with the Bar Harbor police department." She made a move to grab the pen from him, but he hid it behind his back with his good arm.

"I won't tell if you won't," he whispered with a wink.

"Dwight, please, you're embarrassing yourself!" Hayley wailed and then turned to the nurse with an apologetic smile. "Sorry about that, Tilly."

"I'm used to it! If he gets too out of line, there's a bedpan within reach that I can use to conk him on the head. You look after that arm, Dwight. Happy New Year, everyone!"

As she scuttled out, Dwight called after her, "I'm available to ring in the new year if your cop boyfriend has to work that night! People say I'm an excellent kisser!"

"You're impossible, Dwight!" Hayley howled. "Have you never heard of the Me Too movement? You can't do things like that anymore."

"You can't teach an old dog new tricks, and thank the good lord for that!" Dwight exclaimed.

Randy laughed. "So much for a long recovery."

"I've never felt better!" Dwight crowed.

"Why are you in such high spirits? Someone tried to kill you today!" Hayley gasped.

"And they failed! I cheated death! I feel invincible!" Dwight raised his arms and flexed his muscles, but the pain from his freshly bandaged shoulder caused him to wince and moan and he slowly lowered his arms.

"Eventually your luck is going to run out if we don't catch whoever it is who wants you dead," Hayley said.

Dwight reached out and took hold of Hayley's hand. "I have all the faith in the world in you, Hayley. There is no doubt in my mind that you'll track down this mystery shooter in the woods, along with the culprit who poisoned poor Carroll Flood."

That was a pretty tall order.

And Hayley didn't have half the confidence in herself that her father apparently did.

Sergio appeared in the doorway with a wheelchair.

Dwight arched an eyebrow. "What's that for?"

"Dr. Cormack says it's hospital policy after you're discharged to be wheeled out."

Dwight hopped down off the exam table. "I don't need that thing. I can walk just fine."

"Everyone here worked very hard to make sure you leave this hospital in better shape than when you came in, Dwight, so why not return the favor and just follow the rules?" Hayley begged.

"Okay, okay," Dwight groaned as he shuffled over and plopped down in the wheelchair. Before he could react, Sergio unhooked a pair of handcuffs and snapped one on Dwight's wrist and the other on the arm of the wheelchair.

Dwight struggled to free himself. "What is this? What are you doing?"

"I'm placing you under arrest," Sergio replied matter-of-factly.

"*What*?" Randy cried, his breath catching.

As Sergio wheeled a shell-shocked Dwight down the hall toward the waiting room, Hayley and Randy followed behind them, manic.

"Have you uncovered more evidence that we don't know about besides the vial of poison someone obviously planted in Dwight's pocket?" Hayley asked.

Sergio shook his head. "This has nothing to do with the Carroll Flood murder."

Sergio pushed the wheelchair through the metal doors and out to the waiting area, where Lieutenant Donnie and Sergeant Earl were in the process of arresting Bubba, Elmer, and Carl and reading them their rights.

Sheila had a hand over her mouth, shaking, as Bruce watched with amazement.

"I'm arresting them all for deer hunting out of season. That's against the law and subject to a very steep fine," Sergio calmly explained.

"I knew the whole scenic winter hike explanation sounded fishy!" Sheila bellowed.

"You got no proof, Sergio!" Bubba said. "Who's to say we weren't just out in the park taking an innocent nature walk?"

Sergio chuckled. "Because I have a series of photos of you four in the park, all carrying rifles. I'm sure if I send Donnie and Earl out there, they'll no doubt find your guns buried in the snow, exactly where you left them when you attempted to cover up your crime before the ambulance arrived to take Dwight to the hospital."

"How in hell did you get your hands on photos? Who took them? Are you saying the shooter who tried taking out Dwight took the time to snap some pictures?"

"No, it wasn't the shooter. I happen to follow Carl's Instagram account. They're everywhere."

Bubba whipped around and glared at Carl. "You posted photos of us on social media?"

Carl's face flushed with embarrassment. "We were having so much fun. You guys made me feel like one of the boys. I wanted to show my followers back home in Florida the awesome new friends I made up here in Maine."

Elmer slapped the palm of his hand on his forehead. "Carl!"

"In my defense, nobody told me we were breaking the law!"

"You grew up here!" Dwight yelled, reaching out in

frustration with his hand, but the handcuff snapping it back.

"My dad didn't hunt. He usually took me ice fishing instead," Carl said sheepishly.

"Let's move 'em out," Sergio said as he and his officers herded the men out of the waiting room like cattle, leaving a stunned Hayley, a horrified Sheila, and an amused Bruce behind.

Chapter 34

Edie Shilling did not look like your typical bail bondsman in Ellsworth, Maine, at four feet nine inches tall, eighty-three years old, with gray hair tied up in a bun, and wearing a sweater with *Badass Nana* stitched across the front that was a gift from one of her twelve grandchildren. But Edie wasted no time in providing the Ellsworth District Court with a surety bond in order to secure the release of all four defendants after their arraignment. Dwight wanted to stick around and tell her how grateful they all were that she acted so quickly and they didn't have to spend any time behind bars in the county jail, but she was late to a baked bean supper at the Masonic Hall and didn't have any time to waste with any small talk.

Jane and Rocco arrived to whisk their spouses, Bubba and Elmer respectively, back to the island. Randy pulled up shortly thereafter to spirit Dwight away before he suffered too much hassle from an apoplectic Sheila, leaving poor Carl behind to face her wrath.

"Carl, what were you thinking getting mixed up with the Three Stooges?" Sheila huffed as they walked with Hayley to her car parked in the lot outside the courthouse. "How many times do I have to warn you that no matter how charming he can be, Dwight Jordan will eventually cause you nothing but chaos and pain!"

Carl did not appear to be too upset about the series of unfortunate events and just shrugged. "I guess he didn't think we'd ever get caught. And we wouldn't have if I hadn't posted those pictures on Instagram."

"Is that how you're rationalizing their criminal behavior? It was all your fault? Really, Carl! You're too nice! It's irritating sometimes!"

"Mom, what's done is done," Hayley interjected. "There's no point in belaboring the point. You heard the public defender. Carl will probably just have to show up for his court date in February, pay a fine, and be done with the whole matter. No one is expecting any jail time. So let's try and just put it behind us."

"There's nothing more I would like to do, but I have my reputation to consider!" Sheila sniffed.

"*Your* reputation? Carl was the one who got arrested, not you."

"Well, I don't want it getting around town that I'm dating a criminal."

"Oh come on, Mom. A criminal? It's a misdemeanor. Carl isn't exactly Al Capone. And I think it's safe to assume that Dwight, Elmer, Bubba, and Carl are not going to be singing from the rooftops about how they got arrested. So you have nothing to worry about."

Sheila stopped at the car and put her hands on her hips. "Have you forgotten about the newspaper you work for?"

Hayley's jaw dropped.

She had indeed forgotten.

Hayley had once been the trusted office manager for the *Island Times*, as well as the food columnist. She resigned her post after opening her restaurant, but continued writing her food and cocktail column, once a week for the print edition and several more a week for the digital version. As popular with the locals as her column was, it did not rise to the level of crowd-pleasing appeal as the police beat column, which listed all the names in black and white of every local who broke the law during the past week. It was a time-honored tradition dating back to the early 1900s, and Hayley knew her boss, editor in chief Sal Moretti, was probably already aware of the unlawful shenanigans of her father and his buddies in the park. Bruce wrote a much more detailed thrice-weekly crime column and Hayley was reasonably sure illicit deer hunting would not be a scintillating topic to write about, but the police beat column—that would be far more challenging to avoid. It was only a matter of days before the whole town would be buzzing about the arrest.

"You have to talk to Sal," Sheila insisted. "You have to convince him to leave Carl's name out of it. I don't care about the others, they're used to scandal, but you heard Carl: He didn't even know what they were doing was illegal, so the paper should cut him a little slack."

"This smacks of favoritism," Carl piped in. "It doesn't seem right."

"Stay out of it, Carl!" Sheila snapped.

"But you're talking about *me*!" Carl shot back a little more forcefully. "Look, I appreciate you trying to protect me, Sheila, but I deserve to be listed right alongside the others. It's only fair."

Sheila threw her head back with a heavy sigh. "All right! All right! Good lord, you and your unshakable moral compass!" She turned to Hayley. "Well, I wanted to wind up with somebody who was the exact opposite of your father and look what happened, I did! Get in the car, Carl!"

Sheila waited for Carl to slide in the passenger seat and close the door before whispering to Hayley, "See what you can do to get Sal to scrub this, will you, dear? It will be our little secret." She gave her a conspiratorial wink and then got into the back seat of Hayley's car.

After driving Sheila and Carl back to the house where Bruce was waiting, Hayley sped off to the local bakery to buy a box of gingerbread cookies, Sal's favorite kind to eat during the holiday season. Then she drove straight to the *Island Times* office. It was almost five o'clock, the end of the workday, and when she breezed into the reception area and saw that the office manager, her replacement, had already clocked out for the day, she worried Sal might have gone home too. But then she heard Mötley Crüe, Sal's favorite band from when he was younger, blasting in the bullpen out back, and she knew he was still toiling away on the next issue of the paper.

She found him staring at his desktop computer, the

glow from the screen reflecting in his reading glasses. He did not hear her come in because of the loud music.

"Sal?"

He kept typing away, no doubt editing someone's article.

"Sal!"

This time he heard her and raised his eyes toward her. He tapped his phone to stop the music that was playing through the Bluetooth speaker on the credenza behind him, took one look at the box from the bakery Hayley held in her hand, and chuckled. "Nice try, but I'm not deleting your dad and his cronies from next week's police beat column."

"I would never ask you to do something like that. If Dwight, Bubba, and Elmer broke the law, then the public has a right to know. But Carl, he's not a local, he just got swept up in a scheme he didn't even know was illegal. I'll be surprised if the DA doesn't drop the charges against him before you go to press."

Sal, unmoved, continued typing.

Hayley stepped closer to the desk, opening the box. "Look, they're gingerbread."

He studied the cookies, then grabbed the biggest one and took a big bite, talking with his mouth full. "No."

Hayley plopped down in the chair opposite his desk, resigned. "I know, I just had to take a shot." She set the box of cookies on the desk next to Sal.

He had already finished his cookie and plucked another from the box. "Your mother put you up to this, didn't she?"

"My mother's thoughts have always been consumed by what others might think."

"I know, and I'd like to help her out. I've always had a soft spot for your mom, but I can't compromise my journalistic integrity and make special concessions for one of my employees."

Hayley was not going to press the point any further. She knew this had been a fool's errand. But now she could tell Sheila she had at least tried. That had to count for something.

"On the bright side, there's been a lot of police activity this week. Four DUIs, property theft, a bunch of speeding tickets, not to mention the unapprehended shooter who tried to use your father for target practice. Here, take a look," Sal said, shoving a piece of paper in front of her, a list of this week's lawbreakers.

Hayley scanned the list, taking solace in the fact that Carl's name was near the end. Maybe a few readers might miss it. But then, at the bottom, was a name that popped out at her.

"Dolly Halperin got a speeding ticket?"

Sal nodded. "I know. Surprised me too. That woman usually drives so slow a turtle could outrun her and not break a sweat. I got stuck behind her once and missed a dentist appointment."

Hayley continued reading. "In the park?"

"Yeah, the rangers pulled her over."

"What was she doing out there in the dead of winter? Most of the roads are closed."

"She told them she was just taking a ride to clear her head and wasn't paying attention to the speedometer."

Hayley noted the location. "Sal, it says here she was pulled over very near the exact location where the shooting took place."

Curious, Sal snatched the paper out of Hayley's hand and read it for himself. "I'll be damned. I didn't notice that before." He looked at her in disbelief. "The woman spends her whole day selling her handcrafted knickknacks. You don't honestly think . . . ?" He paused, running the possibility through his own mind before returning his gaze to Hayley. "Do you?"

Hayley didn't know what to think.

Dolly despised Carroll and was still bitter about him dumping her for Althea. So she really had no motive to target Dwight in some revenge plot if she believed he was the one who had poisoned her ex-husband. It didn't make sense.

But the fact that she was near the scene, a desolate area, at the exact time of the shooting, was just too big of a coincidence to ignore.

Island Food & Spirits
BY
HAYLEY POWELL

Recently I have been experimenting with a new pizza recipe—Thai chicken pizza! Bruce and I both think it is absolutely delicious, but I wanted a few more trusted opinions before I served it up at one of my get-togethers or offer it as a nightly special at my restaurant.

I decided to invite my brother Randy and his husband Sergio over to the house for a pizza night so I could gauge their honest reactions, since both of them love their pizza just as much as Bruce and I do. I also wanted to have them try my whiskey ginger cocktail that we have become obsessed with lately.

The four of us were having a grand time sitting at my kitchen table, downing our cocktails and my new pizza recipe, which, I must admit, was pretty darn tasty, when Sergio, out of the blue, casually asked me if Mona was enjoying dating Sergeant Earl as much as Earl seemed to be enjoying his time with Mona.

I had just taken a big bite of my pizza, and the shock of hearing this news caused me to swallow too fast. I began coughing and choking as I looked at Sergio like he was sporting two heads.

While still hacking and sputtering, Bruce started pounding me on the back a few times with the palm of his hand, and I was finally able to get the pizza down. Waving Bruce off, I focused my attention on Sergio. "That's not funny, Sergio! I almost choked to death, and it would've been all your fault!"

"I'm dead serious," Sergio said with a straight face.

"Oh, please!" I scoffed. "Mona and Earl don't even get along. Any time he and Lieutenant Donnie even see Mona in town, I've actually seen them cross the street so they don't have to take any guff from her!"

"It's true," Sergio insisted.

"Honestly, Sergio, where did you hear this ridiculous gossip? And you should warn whoever told you that they better stop spreading lies, because if Mona hears about this, I shudder to think what she would even do to this poor person!"

Sergio just smiled and shook his head. "All I will say is, I have it on good authority from a very trusted source."

I laughed out loud and told Sergio that if Mona was dating Earl, then I was the queen of England!

Sergio just shrugged. "Well, Your Majesty, if it pleases the crown, I would love another piece of pizza, please."

Handing Sergio another slice of pizza, I turned

to Randy and asked, "What about you? Have you heard anything about this crazy rumor?"

"No, not a word!" Randy declared.

I spun back around toward Sergio. "Come on, spill it. Where did you hear this cockamamie rumor, because if Mona was dating anyone, as her best friend, I would be the first to know about it, and she hasn't said one word to me, so it can't be true!"

At this point, Bruce and Randy jumped in, wholeheartedly agreeing with me, further bolstering my confidence that it must be a bald-faced lie.

Finally, I couldn't take it anymore, snatched the slice of pizza out of Sergio's hand just as he lifted it to his mouth, and cried, "Who? Who, Sergio? Tell me now or no more pizza!"

Sergio grinned. "Earl."

As Sergio grabbed his pizza back from me and stuffed it in his mouth, grinning from ear to ear like a Cheshire cat, the rest of us just sat there, slack-jawed and in total shock.

"I don't believe it," I muttered.

Unlike me, Sergio made sure to chew properly before swallowing. "Earl asked for a night off a couple of weeks ago because he said he had a date with a special lady. When I pressed him, curious to know who, he said it was with Mona Barnes, but it was all fairly new and he wasn't ready to talk about it yet, so I adhered to his wishes and never mentioned it to him again."

Well, you could have knocked me over with a feather.

Mona and Earl? I could not believe it. One thing was for sure: I was going to get to the bottom of this. But there was no way I could just come out and ask Mona, because I was not about to play into the whole "kill the messenger" scenario if she somehow blamed me for word getting out!

When Randy and Sergio finally left that night, I immediately called Liddy to tell her what I had learned, and asked her if she had heard this news anywhere around town. Liddy, of course, began laughing uncontrollably before finally sputtering, "Oh, come on! Where did you hear this nonsense?"

I told her what Sergio had revealed to us at dinner. Liddy, like me, refused to believe such a wild tale. We decided it would be best to get Mona to go out with us to Drinks Like a Fish, and after she had a few beers and was relaxed, we could delicately pepper her with a few innocent questions about her dating life, feel her out, and see if she would corroborate anything about what we heard (a sucker's bet) or flatly deny it (I would put my money down on this outcome).

Unfortunately, scheduling a girls' happy hour with Mona proved nearly impossible. She was always ready with an excuse: too much work to get done, bone-tired from a long day, plans with her grandkids. We were starting to take it personally.

After Mona turned us down for a fourth time in less than two weeks, Liddy and I were now more determined than ever to get to the bottom of this situation.

Bruce suggested we give Mona the benefit of the doubt, that we should stop pressing the issue and allow Mona to tell us in her own time if there was anything to tell. We both just laughed in his face. If we waited for Mona, we would go to our graves never knowing the truth!

We decided to call Mona the next day and try again to make a date to meet at Drinks Like a Fish after work. She politely declined, claiming she had to take her dad to Ellsworth to pick up one of his prescriptions at Walmart.

When I told Liddy her latest excuse, she had an "ah-ha!" moment. Liddy had seen Mona's mother, Jane, at the Shop 'n Save that very day, and Jane had told her that she and Bubba were going to the Criterion Theater that evening to watch one of Albie's classic old movies. Mona was lying!

As Mona's best friends, we decided that it was in her best interest for us to make sure that she was okay and not in any kind of trouble. At least that's how we convinced ourselves to conduct a stakeout down the road from Mona's house. When her truck pulled out of her driveway at 5:30 that afternoon, Liddy and I followed her at a safe distance, hoping she wouldn't spot us.

Twenty-five minutes later, Mona pulled into the China Hill Buffet restaurant in Ellsworth. We parked on the opposite side of the restaurant and followed her inside.

We could see the host escorting Mona to a table, so we inched our way closer, hiding behind a large dragon statue, straining to get a good look at who she was meeting. That's when I felt a tap on my back.

It was the host, asking us if we would like to be seated and I panicked because I didn't want Mona to spot us, but quick-thinking Liddy told him we would be eating at the bar on the other side of the restaurant. The host shrugged and led us over to the bar. We each ordered a mai tai and decided to work up some liquid courage to search the restaurant and finally get a glimpse of Mona and her mystery date. I may have needed more than one mai tai to psych myself up, and before I knew it, I was volunteering to conduct a reconnaissance mission. I hopped off the barstool with Liddy's encouragement and stealthily made my way around the restaurant. I guess I was so busy searching the dining room for any sign of Mona, and was not looking where I was going, because the next thing I knew I slammed into a waiter carrying a tray with seven plates of food and drinks, and everything went flying into the air and came crashing down all around us. All eyes in the restaurant were suddenly upon me, including those of Mona and Earl, who were tucked away in a romantic corner booth!

I could see Mona standing up, eyes wide with horror, as she watched me bend over and help the waiter pick up all the broken plates and shards of glass. The waiter very firmly informed me that he did not need my help, I had caused enough damage; and so, tail between my legs, I scurried back to the bar where Liddy was waiting.

"Do you think she saw me?"

Liddy's face fell as she glanced over my shoulder. "Um, yeah, I think so."

"How do you know?"

"Because she is right behind you."

I slowly turned around to confront a red-faced Mona, hands on her hips. She spoke slow and evenly. "All I want to know is, Who knows about this?"

We both began babbling at the same time.

"Just Bruce and Sergio and Randy—" I wailed.

Liddy backed me up. "Yes, that's it! Oh, and my secretary, my mother . . ."

"Is that it?" Mona snapped.

Liddy guiltily shook her head. "And possibly Mary at FedEx—oh, and Dr. Klein, my gynecologist."

Mona took a deep breath.

We waited on pins and needles for Mona to erupt like Mount St. Helens. But instead, she just nodded and said quietly, "I have no idea where this thing with Earl is going; it's in the very early stages, which is why I want to keep things on the down-low and not announce anything. We all know what a small town can be like when it comes to people's private lives. So this is what you two are going to do. You're going to stick a sock in it from this moment forward, no more kaffeeklatsches with Mary at FedEx or Dr. Klein, who is also my gynecologist! Do you hear me?"

We both nodded.

"And when I'm ready to talk about this, if I'm ever ready to talk about this, I assure you, you two will be the first to know. Got it?"

We both nodded again.

"Okay, then. End of discussion. Now, if you'll excuse me, I'd like to get back to my date!"

She was right, of course.

I made a vow to just stay out of Mona's business.

But then I thought, What harm could it do to invite Mona and Earl over to taste test my new Thai chicken pizza recipe and enjoy some whiskey ginger cocktails, just to, you know, gently nudge things along.

As my husband Bruce routinely likes to tell me, "You never learn."

WHISKEY GINGER COCKTAIL

INGREDIENTS:
2 ounces rye whiskey
½ ounce simple syrup
½ ounce fresh squeezed lemon
1 ounce ginger liqueur
cherry for garnish

In a shaker, add ice and all ingredients above, except the cherry.

Shake until well mixed and pour into a chilled glass.

Add a cherry, sip and enjoy!

THAI CHICKEN PIZZA

INGREDIENTS:
dough for one large thin crust pizza (homemade
    or store-bought).

PIZZA SAUCE:
3 tablespoons peanut butter (chunky or smooth,
    your choice)
2 teaspoons rice vinegar
2 teaspoons soy sauce
1 teaspoon olive oil
½ teaspoon crushed red pepper (more if you like
    spice)
1 tablespoon freshly grated ginger
2 teaspoons honey
1 teaspoon sesame oil
3 tablespoons water

In a food processor or a blender add all of the ingredients and combine. Feel free to add a little more water
so the sauce is smooth and spreadable. Set aside.

TOPPINGS:
1 to 2 cups of shredded chicken
½ cup red or green onion
3 tablespoons shredded carrots
1½ cups freshly shredded mozzarella cheese
    (more if you like)
¼ cup cilantro (optional)

Preheat oven to 475 degrees.

To assemble, roll out your pizza dough for a thin crust pizza and place on a pizza pan or baking sheet.

For your pizza sauce, combine all of the above ingredients for the sauce in a food processor or blender and add enough water to make a thin, smooth spreadable sauce.

Spread the sauce over the pizza crust.

Add the toppings of your choice on top of the sauce.

Chicken, onions, cheese, and whatever else you like.

Bake for 10 to 12 minutes or until crust is browned and cheese is melted.

Remove from the oven, slice, and just let it melt in your mouth!

Chapter 35

Hayley spent most of the day with Dwight, sitting at her kitchen table with a pad of paper and a pen, writing down the names of everyone her father could think of who might have had a serious grudge against him over the many years he had been alive.

There was no getting past it.

The list was long.

Super-long.

By four in the afternoon, they had hundreds of names written on over a dozen pages.

Bruce joined them for a little while but got bored quickly and took his leave to the dining room, where he sat down at the table, popped open his laptop, and began the process of filing the insurance claim for his beloved snowmobile now resting at the bottom of Long Pond. He was within earshot of their conversation, however, and every now and then shouted a name that came to mind who might be anti-Dwight.

Acutely aware that Dwight was coming over to Hayley's house to compile a list of suspects who might be the shooter, Sheila chose to drive to Bangor with Carl to do some shopping and to go to a movie. They had left at eight in the morning, purposely to miss seeing Dwight altogether, but when they returned in the late afternoon, Sheila grimaced as she sailed through the front door, hardly pleased to see Dwight still there. Carl, on the other hand, was happy to see his new buddy, and even offered to make everyone his famous Grinch cocktail, a sickly-sweet concoction made with melon liqueur, clear rum, and fizzy lemon-lime soda. Hayley and Sheila both politely declined, but Dwight and Bruce were more than happy to give it a try.

Hayley noticed her mother's obvious discomfort with how chummy Carl was becoming with Dwight, plopping down next to him at the kitchen table after serving them drinks and perusing the long list of suspects.

"Wow, Dwight, I think there were less people at King Charles's coronation," Carl cracked.

Dwight shook his head. "I know. Half the town must be on this list."

"Well, you've alienated a lot of people during your lifetime," Sheila said, sniffing.

Carl picked up a pen and started crossing off a few names. "This one's dead. So is this one. Not sure about him, but I heard he divorced his wife and is living in a Buddhist monastery studying Tibetan literature, so I would assume he's really not the violent type." He crossed off the name and continued pouring over the others.

Sheila, unable to stop herself, scuttled over to the table and hovered over Carl's shoulder, reading all the names. She pointed out one. "I follow her on Facebook. She's in Solvang, California selling German knick-knacks. She just posted this morning, so it couldn't be her."

Carl crossed her name off the list.

Sheila pointed out another name. "I just heard from Kathy Leighton. She and her husband Ronnie are spending the holidays in Australia's Gold Coast, where it's the summer season right now. You know how much Kathy hates the cold weather, so why she still lives in Maine I'll never know!"

Getting more curious, Sheila snatched up the pad of paper and began rifling through all the names. "I can pick out at least ten names here that are immobile and incapable of taking a potshot at Dwight or who are no longer around." She grabbed the pen from Carl and started crossing out more names, then continued reading.

Hayley piped in. "I'm sure a lot of these people have either forgotten about what you did to them or have forgiven you. You know the saying, Time heals all wounds. We just need to make sure they've let bygones be bygones."

"With the exception of Carroll Flood. He hadn't forgotten anything!" Bruce called out from the dining room.

"Yes, but Carroll Flood has an airtight alibi for the time of the shooting. He was safely tucked away in a casket at McFarland's Funeral Home!" Hayley replied.

Sheila sighed. "It's going to take years to sort

through all these names. And I can come up with a bunch more names who aren't even on this list! People who complained about you to me but didn't have the guts to do it to your face!"

Frustrated, Dwight guzzled the rest of his Grinch cocktail and slammed the glass down on the table. "Well, I'm not going to worry about it anymore. People have been wanting to kill me ever since I can remember."

As Bruce tapped a few keys on his computer, filling out his insurance form, he added, "Maybe seeing all those names of people out to get you might be the motivation you need to course correct your behavior."

"Bruce!" Hayley scolded.

"No, he's right, Hayley," Dwight muttered. "It's taken me fifty years to come to grips with the consequences of my actions. But I am trying. Every morning I wake up and say to myself, 'Dwight, today is the day you make amends for all the hurt you caused. Today is the first day you can be a better person, a positive force in the world.'"

"And then you get out of bed and go straight back to your old habits," Sheila sneered.

Carl gave Sheila an admonishing look. "Sheila, that's enough. Give the poor guy a break. Now, if you can't say anything helpful, don't say anything at all."

This was the first time Hayley had ever seen Carl forcefully stand up to her mother and she feared there might be some kind of volcanic eruption, but much to her surprise, and Bruce's shock, Sheila buttoned her lips and remained silent.

Hayley smirked at Bruce, whose jaw dropped open, marveling at how Sheila actually listened to Carl.

Sheila finally finished going through all the names on the suspect list and shot her hand in the air.

"Mom, why are you raising your hand?" Hayley asked.

She gave Carl a little side-eye. "Permission to speak?"

Carl dropped his head. "Of course, dear."

"There is one very prominent name missing from your list," she said. "Dudley Vickers."

Dwight lit up and slapped his forehead with his hand. "Of course! Dudley Vickers! He despised me back in the day! How could I have forgotten about him?"

"I certainly couldn't!" Sheila shivered. "I'll never forget him showing up at our front door, waving a firearm, threatening to drop you where you stood. I thought he might barge in and take us all out." She turned to Hayley. "You were in your bassinet upstairs, maybe six months old, so I called the police, but Dudley left before they even got there."

Bruce sauntered into the kitchen for another Grinch cocktail. "Wow, Dwight, what did you do to the guy?"

Dwight bowed his head, embarrassed, not anxious to relive it.

"Go on, Dwight, tell him," Sheila nudged.

"I—uh—I wanted to open my own restaurant here in town—"

Sheila interrupted. "After a string of other small business failures!"

"Mom, let him finish!"

"Dudley was the bank president at the time—this was way back in the mid-1970s—and he, well, he didn't think I was responsible enough, and so he rejected me for the loan I needed to open my doors."

"He didn't even bother letting Dwight fill out the proper paperwork, let alone consider his application. He just laughed him right out of his office!" Sheila declared.

"That must have been very disappointing," Carl sympathized, much to Sheila's consternation.

"Yes, it was," Dwight murmured, recalling the painful memory. "That loan would've changed my life."

"He didn't stay disappointed for long, because then he got mad. He decided to get revenge," Sheila said.

Bruce chuckled. "I'm almost afraid to ask."

Dwight hesitated elaborating any further.

"Go on, tell him!" Sheila snapped.

"I, uh, knew Dudley loved going to this one seafood restaurant down on lower Main Street at the time, the Codfather's Corner, where he always ordered the same dish, the fish and chips, and so, uh, I got a part-time job there as a dishwasher in the kitchen . . . and . . ."

Sheila impatiently took over. "Dudley loved dousing his fish and chips with this rich ketchup sauce, so when the waiter wasn't looking, your father swapped out the ketchup with ghost pepper sauce!"

"Oh no!" Hayley cried.

"Oh, yes, and it was bad. Dudley never forgave him because he had stomach issues for years after that prank."

"He had an ulcer! It had nothing to with the ghost pepper sauce!" Dwight said, lamely trying to defend himself, then, realizing he had no leg to stand on, sighed. "Like I said, I'm trying to change."

Sheila scribbled Dudley's name at the top of the list. But then, Bruce plucked the pen out of her hand and crossed it out. "Sorry to break it to you, but Dudley died. About three months ago. Went in his sleep. I read the obit in the *Island Times*. He was something like ninety-six years old."

"I must have missed that," Hayley said.

"Well, his wife is still alive and she was even madder than Dudley over the whole sordid incident," Sheila interjected.

"That's right! Zelda!" Dwight shouted, slamming his fist down on the kitchen table. "Man, oh man, I remember her. She was in her forties at the time, I was in my twenties, but I remember what a body she had! All the young bucks in town were gaga over her. What are women like that called now, cougars?"

"Dwight, now might be a good time to keep your thoughts to yourself. They're not helping your whole 'trying to be a better man' resolution," Hayley advised.

"Then it's very possible that Zelda might still hold a grudge against Dwight on her late husband's behalf," Carl surmised.

"But she's in her nineties now too," Hayley said skeptically. "I can hardly picture Zelda Vickers carrying out an assassination attempt in Acadia National Park in the dead of winter." They all nodded in agreement before Hayley continued her thought. "Unless she had help."

Chapter 36

The Sonora Estates, an assisted-living facility just outside of town, had been in operation since the 1940s, privately owned by a family with ties to the island, along with state and federal financial assistance. Many of Bar Harbor's elderly were on waiting lists for admission, given its staff's sterling reputation for caring for their loved ones. There were also many weekly activities to keep the residents busy, including a classic TCM movie night, showing films from Hollywood's golden age alongside more contemporary offerings, all PG-rated. Game night was particularly popular to keep minds sharp, and dinnertime often featured a theme night like taco Tuesday or spaghetti Western Wednesday (a pasta entrée followed by a screening of an old Clint Eastwood Italian Western flick). But the residents, especially the ones with no family around to visit them, most of all looked forward to the guest speakers who would come by once a month and deliver a lecture or teach a class. The activities director,

Linda Scully, worked tirelessly to come up with an interesting lineup to entertain or inspire the residents. When she invited the author of a self-help book on the senior sex drive, who summered on the island, the event was standing room only (except those in wheelchairs).

Linda had been chasing after Hayley for years to teach a cooking class to the residents, which Hayley had every intention of doing—that is, until she opened the doors of her restaurant and was hit with just how much work was involved. Since then, she had been promising Linda she would find some room in her busy schedule, but unfortunately she never did.

So when Hayley discovered that Dudley Vickers's widow, Zelda, was now residing at the Sonora Estates, and loved helping out in the kitchen at mealtime since she missed cooking for her late husband, Hayley fired off an email to Linda to let her know her schedule had miraculously freed up and she was now available to teach a holiday cooking class on Thursday afternoon. Normally, Linda would like to have more time to promote the event for a good turnout, but she was not about to risk losing out booking Hayley, and immediately wrote back with a one-word response: *YES!!!*

Hayley had spent the morning shopping for ingredients for her students so they could prepare a simple spicy gingerbread loaf. Linda had informed her that morning that she had six residents signed up, four women (including Zelda) and two men, so she stocked up accordingly.

The kitchen had three ovens in order to serve all the residents their meals at the same time, so Hayley paired up everyone in twos to work together. Zelda, who was sharp and fiery and very opinionated, refused to be partnered with Abe Foley, who had pinched her left butt cheek at last fall's Halloween costume party. Abe had claimed he was just staying in character, having dressed up as Don Juan, but Zelda was not buying that lame excuse. She had not spoken to him since. Instead, she coerced Glenda Richardson, a very meek, shy woman, to be her partner, so she could easily boss her around.

Abe instead teamed up with the other man in the class, Johnny Damiano, and boasted that he had been a cook in the army and could probably out-bake the women, setting up a battle of the sexes competition. The third team, two women both named Diane, were busy gossiping among themselves and barely listened as Hayley commenced with the class once Linda quickly slipped out after introducing her.

"Okay, now make sure you have all the ingredients you will need at your station before we begin. Flour, sugar, baking soda, eggs, buttermilk, vanilla extract, molasses. Then line up your spices like little soldiers on the battlefield. There should be five altogether, the most important being your ground ginger."

"I only have four!" Zelda huffed. "Ginger, cinnamon, cloves, and allspice."

Abe glanced over at her station. "You forgot the salt."

"Salt is salt! It's not a spice! Who on earth considers salt a spice?" Zelda cried.

"Um, just about everyone, sweetheart," Abe laughed.

"Don't call me sweetheart!" Zelda growled.

"Oh, come on, you love it!" Abe said, winking.

Hayley chose to ignore the testy exchange. "Okay, also make sure you have everything for your vanilla glaze drizzle. You'll need one cup of confectioners' sugar, one tablespoon milk, and two teaspoons of vanilla extract."

"Where's the milk, Glenda?" Zelda snapped at her partner. "I don't see the milk."

Glenda timidly pointed to a one-pint carton of milk directly in front of her. "It's right there, Zelda."

"Oh," Zelda sniffed. "Why is it with the other baking ingredients? It should be with the topping ingredients! My word, Glenda, you've got to start pulling your weight. I can't do it all by myself!"

"Sorry," Glenda murmured.

This was going to be a long afternoon.

Hayley was amazed with how fast her students worked and within fifteen minutes they were pouring their gingerbread batter into their greased loaf pans and sliding them into their ovens. Hayley now had fifty- to fifty-five minutes to fill before the next step. After a talk about her own checkered history with baking, how she had trouble with the exact science of the recipes, she polled the others on what they liked to make in the kitchen. Zelda rattled off a cookbook's list of her favorite recipes, hearty stews, seafood casseroles, meat pies her grandmother from England taught her to make; anything that popped into her mind, leaving poor Glenda left to shrug and say she could not think of anything off the top of her head and would like to pass. Abe and Johnny went next. Abe proudly listed his best dishes during his time in the military (most were large-scale recipes that would feed a hundred hungry soldiers) and Johnny talked about his Italian heritage and how his mother had schooled him on how to make the perfect homemade marinara sauce. The two Dianes could not have cared less about what was going on in class and were preoccupied with some scandal brewing between two of the staff members over some missing petty cash.

Hayley checked the time on her phone. "Okay, we still have twenty minutes left on the timer, so everybody just hang out and we will pick it up when our loaves are ready to come out of the oven." She made a beeline for Zelda, trying to come up with a natural way to bring up her late husband Dudley's dislike of Dwight, but ultimately she didn't have to say a word. As soon as she approached Zelda and Glenda's workstation, Zelda turned to her and spewed out, "I hear that deadbeat dad of yours has come crawling back to town!"

Bingo.

All the work was done for her.

"Yes, it's been rather stressful ever since he became a person of interest in Carroll Flood's death, not to mention the harrowing incident in the park."

"I heard about Carroll, but what harrowing incident?"

"You don't know?"

"Know what?" Zelda turned to Glenda. "Glenda, do you have any idea what she's talking about?"

Glenda, afraid to speak and suffer more berating from Zelda, simply nodded.

"Someone tried to kill him," Hayley said.

"Did they get him?" Zelda asked hopefully.

"Yes. In the shoulder. But he's going to be fine."

Zelda shrugged. "Huh, maybe next time someone might have better luck. Sorry, Hayley, I know he's your father, but if they catch the guy taking potshots at Dwight Jordan, I bet the town will hand him a medal!"

Glenda gave her an admonishing look. "Oh, Zelda . . ."

"What, Glenda? I'm just speaking the truth. I'm too old to sugarcoat anything anymore."

"You never did when you were young either," Abe chuckled.

"Mind your own business, Abe!" Zelda glowered.

"I know just the mention of Dwight's name leaves a bad taste in people's mouths. He made a lot of people very angry over the years, especially your husband Dudley," Hayley said.

"You have no idea! Making my poor husband sick like that! He never fully recovered! He wanted to sue Dwight, but we could never find him. Any time we got close to tracking him down, narrowing our search to a village outside Anchorage or a little hamlet near Lake Michigan, wily Dwight would just up and vanish again without a trace. Finally, I convinced Dudley to give up the search. All that built-up anger was having a bad effect on his health. It wasn't just his stomach. He was having heart issues, ulcers, you name it."

"Do you blame Dwight for Dudley's death?"

"Absolutely!"

"What about your two sons? How do they feel?"

"After we buried Dudley, I tried convincing them

that they should be as mad as I was about Dwight Jordan and what he did to their father, but they just couldn't muster up the same hatred as me because, after all, they never met the man. They were babies at the time."

"Where are your sons now?"

"Peter's in Boston. Walt is in Colorado. Both married with families. They have too much to lose trying to avenge their father, who lived another fifty years after the notorious ghost pepper sauce incident."

"What about you, Zelda? You still seem very angry," Hayley noted.

"She's no different than usual. She's always angry about something," Abe joked.

"I swear, Abe! One more word out of you—"

Abe snickered, not the least bit intimidated. "You've got something on your face, Zelda."

Zelda started brushing her face with her hands, although there was nothing there.

Abe reached out with his finger and touched her cheek. "Right there."

Where there had been nothing, now there was some confectioners' sugar he had intentionally put there.

Johnny erupted in laughter and so did the two Dianes, who had finally stopped chattering to each other. Glenda was frozen in place. Zelda scowled, grabbed a dishrag, and wiped her entire face, sensing she was the butt of some kind of joke.

Hayley gently pushed Abe aside. "Zelda, where were you this past Saturday?"

Zelda folded her arms confidently. "Here. Where else would I be? They took away my driver's license. I can't go anywhere. What would you expect me to do? Hot-wire the Sonora Estates shuttle van and drive out to the Park Loop Road with a loaded shotgun? You're in fantasy land. No, I was here playing cards with Pappy."

"Pappy? Marlene Shaw's father? He lives here?"

"Yes, he moved in about two years ago," Johnny answered. "His daughter Marlene and his granddaughter Betsy are here visiting him all the time, always bringing him sweets and puzzles."

Pappy had searched high and low for Dwight when he learned he had impregnated his daughter Marlene all those years ago, and like the Vickerses, he never managed to find him. Maybe he had heard Dwight was back in town and finally decided to do something about it.

"Where's his room?" Hayley asked Johnny breathlessly.

"Just down the hall. Unit four," he said. "But just so you know, his mind's been going for a while now. There's not much of the old Pappy left."

Hayley still had to try.

"Keep an eye on your ovens. Once the timer goes off, remove your loaves and leave them out to cool. I will be right back!" Hayley yelled as she bolted out of the room and down the hall to unit four. The door was open halfway, but she knocked anyway before poking her head inside. "Pappy?"

The room was dark because someone had closed the blinds. Pappy was fully clothed, but lying on top of his unmade bed, his eyes glued to an old episode of the classic 1960s Western TV show *The Big Valley*, starring Barbara Stanwyck, playing on some local broadcast channel.

"Pappy, do you remember me? I'm Hayley Powell. Dwight Jordan's daughter."

His eyes stayed fixed on the old-fashioned television set with rabbit ears.

She sat down on the edge of the bed. "Do you remember Dwight? He used to date your daughter Marlene way back when."

Pappy tensed and Hayley thought he might be responding, but then she glanced at the screen where Adam West, playing a decorated but mentally unstable Army major, had just thrown a nightgown-clad Linda Evans—Barbara Stanwyck's daughter, Audra—down a flight of stairs in a homicidal rage. No wonder Pappy had just tensed up. He either didn't recognize Hayley, or was so far gone, he had no idea she was even there. She reached out and touched his arm. "Pappy?"

The only life Hayley could see in his eyes was the flickering glow of the TV screen.

Whatever he might know, whatever lingering resentment he had toward Dwight, was locked up tight inside his brain and would probably never come out.

Hayley reached out and squeezed his hand. She could see the corners of his mouth turn up briefly, then sag again as he watched Barbara Stanwyck valiantly fighting Adam West to protect her daughter. Like Pappy had tried to do all those years ago.

She stood up and returned to the kitchen, where she found Zelda and Abe engaged in a full-on food fight.

Abe's shirt was covered in raw egg yolks and Zelda's gray hair was dusted white with flour and confectioners' sugar. Johnny and the two Dianes stood off to the side, watching with glee.

"What is going on here?" Hayley gasped.

"You saw what he did! He started it!"

It was as if she had walked into a kindergarten classroom she had left unattended for just a few minutes.

"You two are going to clean this mess up while I work with the others on their vanilla glaze drizzles!" Hayley declared.

Abe nodded, chastised.

Zelda was less intimidated by Hayley. "Is this how you run your restaurant, Hayley? My goodness, how quickly you lost control. I can't imagine what it must be like to work for you."

"Thank you for your concern, Zelda, but I get by just fine," Hayley said through clenched teeth.

"Maybe you should follow in your father's footsteps and consider taking on a partner to help run your business."

Hayley, seething, glared at Zelda. "If I want your advice—" She stopped suddenly. "Wait, what did you say?"

"I said, It looks like you're in way over your head."

"No, what did you mean when you said follow in my father's footsteps? Are you saying he had a partner when he applied for that loan with Dudley back in the seventies?"

"Yes, I thought you knew."

"No, I didn't. Who was it, do you recall?"

"Of course I recall. I'm not senile!"

"Pretty darn close," Abe chuckled, wiping the egg off his shirt with his dishrag.

"Zip it, Abe!" Hayley shouted, pointing a warning finger at him before returning her attention to Zelda. "Who?"

"It was Albie Schooner."

All the oven timers suddenly went off like alarm bells as if it was some universal sign.

Chapter 37

As Hayley dashed across the street toward the Criterion Theatre, she spotted Albie teetering on top of a ladder trying to put up the marquee letter lights to spell the next film showcased in his tribute to Alfred Hitchcock. So far, he had managed to complete the first word: *Shadow*. That could only mean his next featured title was *Shadow of a Doubt* from 1943, starring Teresa Wright and Joseph Cotten about a homicidal criminal on the run from the police after a series of murders of wealthy widows, who hides out at the family home of his older sister in northern California, where his young niece slowly begins to suspect he may not be the perfect uncle she has idolized all her life. Hayley remembered from watching it not too long ago with Bruce on TCM that Hitchcock ranked this picture as his own personal favorite.

Albie stretched to reach the far-right side of the marquee, clutching a lower-case letter *o* in order to add an *of* after *Shadow*. Hayley gasped as he nearly lost his balance and toppled to the pavement below, but he stopped himself by grabbing ahold of the top of the ladder as it rocked back and forth unsteadily.

Hayley hustled up to him and gripped one of the lower rungs on the ladder, keeping it firmly in place, and called up to Albie, "If you're not careful, you're going to fall and crack your head open!"

He looked down at Hayley and broke into a wide grin as he waved with his free hand, almost losing his balance again. "Hi, Hayley! I didn't see you down there!"

"Albie, you shouldn't be the one to put those letters up! Let one of the maintenance men do it."

"They never get the spacing right! Hey, are you suggesting I'm too old to be doing this?" Albie asked with a raised eyebrow.

"I'm saying if you fall, then that would be really bad. For everyone. If something happened to you, who would host the Criterion's classic movie night? No one can talk about the movies like you can."

His face lit up. "Are you and Bruce coming tonight? I've got a whole presentation planned before the film! Plus, there's a raffle and the grand prize is a complete DVD collection of Hitchcock's Hollywood films up until *Marnie*. After that, they're practically unwatchable! Seriously, *Topaz*? Somebody should have taken away his director's chair!"

Does anyone even own a DVD player anymore? Hayley asked herself before shouting up to Albie, "We're sure going to try. I'm a big fan of this one. Joseph Cotten gives a mesmerizing performance!"

That was what she had remembered most about the film.

"Yes, Cotten and Wright are fantastic, but there is so much more to admire about the film. This is truly Hitchcock at his finest. Did you know the movie includes subtle references to Hitchcock's own childhood experiences, further deepening the connection between the director and his work?"

"How interesting," Hayley noted as Albie went back to adding an *f* then an *a* before sifting through his bucket of letters for what he needed to finish with *Doubt*.

"Of course, with a script by Thornton Wilder, the writer of *Our Town*, the perfect homage to small-town Americana, how could you lose? I also want to talk about the humor, how it's spread throughout the film, but doesn't at all take away from the gripping suspense!"

As Albie leaned toward the marquee again with his capital *D* to start the second row of words, the rickety ladder began to shake again and Hayley gripped it tighter to keep it in place so it would not tip over and send Albie flying. "I've never met anyone with such a steel-trap mind for movie trivia."

"I've always had a razor-sharp good memory. My head is so full of interesting facts and information, sometimes it can be overwhelming! But by golly, you can be sure when I'm at the store, I'm going to forget half my grocery list and then I have to go back the next day!" Albie laughed, snapping on the last letter *t* to finish spelling *Doubt*. He called down to Hayley. "Does it look even to you?"

She stepped back to get a better view. "It looks perfect!" As Albie started to climb back down the ladder, Hayley casually said, "Hey, I heard an interesting fact recently that I'm sure you will remember."

"What's that?"

"That you were once business partners with my dad."

Albie suddenly missed a rung on the ladder with his foot and slid all the way down to the ground, stumbling on the pavement and waving his arms to steady himself before Hayley rushed over and caught him.

"Sorry, Albie, I didn't mean to startle you."

"You didn't startle me," Albie barked defensively. "I just slipped. It's no big deal. What was that you said about me and Dwight going into business together? I honestly don't recall that."

"Well, it was a long time ago. I'm just surprised you don't remember given your—how did you describe it—your razor-sharp mind?"

She could see his sudden faltering memory was just an act.

He obviously remembered and didn't want to talk about it.

"Like I said, I can tell you the tiniest details about the movies, but when it comes to real life, especially my life, I'm not so interested in remembering everything."

"I understand. It's just that I ran into Zelda Vickers at the Sonora Estates recently, and she could recall in exact detail the loan you and Dwight applied for with her husband Dudley at the bank in order to open a restaurant."

Albie twitched slightly. He knew there was no squirming out of this one with a sharp denial. Instead, he hemmed and hawed, pretending to comb the recesses of his mind, before awkwardly copping to it. "Yeah, I guess I do remember that. But we were just kids back then. Dudley was probably wise not to give us that loan. As I recall, Dwight left town shortly after that and so I guess our short-lived partnership was down the tubes at that point."

"Were you upset when Dwight left?"

"No, of course not. I can't say I wasn't disappointed. I was basically a kid. I looked up to Dwight and wanted to be involved in any venture he wanted to try, but the restaurant brainstorm wasn't meant to be. It was bad luck and bad timing. So Dwight set out in search of other opportunities in the world and I stayed behind in Bar Harbor to figure out what was next for me. I promise you, there was never any bad blood between us." He nervously scratched his head. "I don't mean to be rude, but the box office is going to open soon and I need to tack up the poster in the display case." He shuffled off inside the theater, leaving Hayley standing on the street next to the abandoned ladder.

Albie was adamant about not wanting Hayley to infer any bitterness between him and Dwight after the long-ago collapse of their business partnership.

Which, of course, just made her more suspicious.

It just did not add up that Albie Schooner, with his amazing steel-trap mind, was this vague and forgetful when it came to such a seminal painful moment from his past.

He was hiding something.

Chapter 38

Jordan's Restaurant, a local homestyle eatery, was started by the Paine family to feature wild blueberry products back in 1976. The Paines decided to retain the name of Jordan in honor of the original property's grocery store, owned and operated by Dwight's grandfather and Hayley's great-grandfather, Lowell Jordan and his dear, beloved wife Leona Paine, a descendant of the current owners. Jordan's had been a Bar Harbor staple since its doors first opened, boasting their signature blueberry pancakes.

Dwight had shown up at Hayley's door at six-thirty in the morning, ringing the doorbell and rousing Hayley and Bruce out of bed to treat them to breakfast at his family's namesake establishment. He also wanted to say hello to an old classmate, Dave Paine, who still worked as a fry cook even though he had left the day-to-day running of the restaurant to his son some years ago. When Bruce tried to put Dwight off, at least until a decent hour, Dwight firmly reminded him that the restaurant had already started serving customers at five AM, and it was now going on seven o'clock, and even during the winter months, there could be a long line waiting to be seated in one of their booths.

Hayley gently told Bruce there was no point in arguing with Dwight, especially since they were both now fully awake and in desperate need of some caffeine. Plus, now that the thought of those blueberry pancakes had been planted in her head, she could not stop thinking about them.

Although mercifully there was no line snaking outside in the freezing cold, the booths were filling up fast and the hostess led them to the last available booth in the back. She had filled their coffee cups before they were even seated and told them she would be back to take their order in a jiffy.

None of them even had to glance at the menu on the paper place mats, and when Hannah, a large, imposing woman in her fifties with a stained Grateful Dead T-shirt and a red apron tied around her faded jeans, returned with her notepad and a pen, they were ready to order. Both Hayley and Dwight opted for the blueberry pancakes, while Bruce asked for the lobster, cheese, and veggie omelet. Hannah nodded, gave them a quick smile, and departed to the next table.

As they sipped their coffee, Hayley finally brought up the subject of Dwight's partnership with Albie Schooner fifty years ago.

"How did you hear about that?" Dwight asked warily.

"Dudley Vickers's widow, Zelda, is still sharp as a tack and remembers everything. She was the one who told me, and then I went to speak with Albie and he made light of it, as if he could barely recall the two of you going into business together, let alone any hostility between the two of you."

Dwight chuckled. "Is that how he's playing it these days?"

Bruce tore open a package of sweetener and dumped it in his coffee. "Why? How do you remember things going down?"

"I'm not going to sugarcoat it. Albie wanted to kill me after our partnership soured."

Hayley arched an eyebrow. "How do you know?"

"Because he told me. Several times. I can't blame the guy. I kind of left him high and dry. After Vickers rejected our loan application, our new restaurant was pretty much toast. But then I found out Albie had an uncle who had recently died and left him twenty grand, which he was saving for a rainy day, and I convinced him we were in a downpour and needed that money pronto if we were going to remain partners. I promised him if he invested it in the property, once the restaurant was up and running, we could pay him back in a matter of a few months with interest. I was basically talking out of the side of my mouth. I had no clue how much it was going to cost to get started, and it turned out it took every last penny buying all the equipment and supplies and just getting the kitchen up to code. But we finally did it and then . . ." A wave of guilt washed over Dwight's face.

"You skipped town," Hayley sighed.

Dwight nodded. "I know, not my proudest moment.

It got to be too much, and as you know, I had a lot of personal stuff going on—"

"Yes, I'm painfully aware of all your family drama," Hayley snapped.

Dwight shrugged. "I guess the idea of staying in Bar Harbor scared the bejesus out of me. I was feeling overwhelmed, I was suffocating with all the responsibilities that were crashing down on me, so one morning I woke up and I just left."

"And you left Albie high and dry," Hayley whispered.

"I was the talent, the chef. Without me he had no business, so the poor schlep had to close down before he even opened."

"I would've threatened to kill you too," Bruce said, scowling.

"Over the years one of his letters would find me, and I won't repeat the things he said to me, but the gist of it was, as far as he was concerned, I had ruined his life and one day, when I was least expecting it, he'd get his revenge, and then he'd go into graphic detail about how he was going to do it: no shot between the eyes. He wanted to watch me die a slow, painful death."

Hannah returned with more coffee. "Your breakfast will be out in a minute." And then she was gone again.

"When was the last time you heard from him?" Bruce asked.

"I don't know, ten, maybe fifteen years ago. I knew when I came back to town, he was still here. I occasionally read the *Island Times* online and would see his classic movie night ads. And when I ran into him at the

Criterion, I braced myself for a violent tongue-lashing, but he was so nice and polite, I figured he just wasn't mad at me anymore, that he'd finally let go of his anger toward me."

Hayley shook her head, unconvinced. "I would have a hard time forgiving you for squandering my entire life savings despite how long ago it happened. So why would he pretend it was no big deal and all is forgiven?"

"It could be an act. Maybe he decided to lie in wait, hold out for the right opportunity to strike," Bruce suggested.

Dwight slurped his coffee. "So you think he's our number-one suspect?"

"The problem is Albie has airtight alibis for both the incident at Long Pond and on the day of the shooting in the park. He wasn't anywhere near either location. He couldn't have moved that thin ice sign or taken those potshots at you," Hayley said.

Hannah arrived with their food, balancing the three plates on her arm before setting them down on the table.

"So Albie Schooner's not our guy," Dwight said.

Hannah smirked. "He's somebody's guy, for sure."

They all exchanged puzzled looks.

"What do you mean, Hannah?" Hayley asked.

"Albie's finally got a new girlfriend. They were in here having breakfast just the other day in that corner booth in the back, where they wouldn't be seen by the other diners. I saw them holding hands and whispering to each other. It was very romantic. Who knew Albie still had it in him?"

Hayley stopped pouring maple syrup on her pancakes and suddenly sat up straight. "Does this new girlfriend happen to be Dolly Halperin?"

Hannah nodded and smiled. "I guess the word is finally out. I have to admit, they look adorable together."

"I was the one who introduced them to each other right before Christmas at his classic movie night," Hayley said.

Bruce snickered. "My wife, the matchmaker."

"It's such a small town I can't believe they had never really met before," Hayley said.

Hannah gave them a curious look. "Christmas, you say? Not possible. I saw them in here canoodling together long before that, probably around Thanksgiving, maybe even Halloween."

Alarm bells suddenly went off in Hayley's head. "Hannah, are you sure?"

"As sure as I know my husband Duke is home on the couch watching TV, instead of shoveling the snow off the sidewalk in front of our house like I told him to do before I came in to work today."

"That's a firm yes," Bruce noted.

As Hannah shuffled off, Hayley's mind was racing. "Why would they lie about not having met before?"

Chapter 39

"**H**ayley, what a nice surprise," Albie Schooner said with a tight smile as he opened the door to his small duplex on Myrtle Avenue. He had not been expecting any visitors.

"I was just driving by and I said to myself, 'Hayley, you forgot to invite Albie to your New Year's Eve party at the restaurant,' and I saw your car parked in the driveway, so I thought, Why not just swing in and deliver an in-person invitation."

"That's very kind of you. I would be happy to attend," Albie said, slightly flustered, as Hayley stood firmly planted on his doorstep, not anxious to leave. "Um, would you like to come in for some coffee or tea?"

"I would love to!" Hayley said, brushing past him through the front door before he could change his mind.

Albie's home was small but quaint, sparsely decorated. The living room had a love seat and a couple of armchairs and a beat-up coffee table made out of a beer barrel. There was a large fifty-five-inch TV attached to the wall and a bookshelf stacked with DVDs of Albie's film collection.

"You have a lovely home, Albie, very cozy," Hayley noted as her eyes scanned the room.

"Thank you. I have some Earl Grey in the kitchen. I just need to put the teakettle on the stove. I have traditional, plummy or extra-strong. Which would you like?"

Hayley wandered over to the bookshelf and began reading all the titles. "Extra-strong. It's been one of those days."

"I will be right back," Albie said, withdrawing from the living room to the kitchen.

Hayley perused the shelves of movies, organized by categories, such as comedy, drama, mystery thrillers, international, musicals. By far the largest category was mystery thrillers, which took up three and a half of the six shelves, including a near complete Alfred Hitchcock collection from the sound version of *Blackmail*, released in 1929, to his final film, *Family Plot* from 1976, four years before his death.

Hayley noticed an empty space between the DVD of *Stage Fright*, starring Jane Wyman from 1950, and the DVD of *I Confess*, starring Montgomery Clift from 1953. She glanced around the room and spotted a DVD on the coffee table. She walked over and picked it up. Of course. It was one of the master of suspense's most iconic films, *Strangers on a Train*, starring Farley

Granger and Robert Walker from 1951. She opened the DVD case. It was empty. She read the back cover as she called to Albie, who was still in the kitchen. "By the way, Albie, feel free to bring a date to my New Year's Eve party."

"Uh, okay, thanks!" Albie shouted as she heard cupboards slamming shut and teacups rattling.

"I heard through the grapevine that you and Dolly Halperin finally found the time to get together."

"Oh? Who told you that?"

"It's a very small town," Hayley said as the teakettle suddenly began whistling.

She was still reading about the film on the back of the DVD cover when Albie walked in carrying a silver tray with a matching teakettle, two cups with Earl Grey tea bags, and a plate of tea biscuits. He set the tray down on the coffee table, poured hot water into the cups, and then noticed Hayley holding the *Strangers on a Train* DVD.

"After *Shadow of a Doubt*, that's my favorite Hitchcock film. I just watched it again last night. I'm going to screen it at the Criterion sometime in the new year."

"I will make sure to be there," Hayley said.

"It's based on a Patricia Highsmith novel. She was a wonderful author who also wrote *The Talented Mr. Ripley*. Very underrated. Did you know that Hitchcock sent a middleman to buy the film rights from her to disguise the fact that a big-time Hollywood director wanted to make a film of her book? She sold the rights for a song and when she found out it was

Hitch who was going to direct, she was furious," he said, laughing. "She was bitter about it for the rest of her life, especially after the film became a huge hit!"

"I did not know that," Hayley said. "I remember seeing it when I was a kid, but I can't really remember what it was about."

Of course she knew.

She had seen the film many times.

But she wanted to hear Albie himself describe the plot, because she had a gnawing feeling in the pit of her stomach that it was somehow relevant to recent events in Bar Harbor.

"Two strangers meet on a train. Tennis star Guy Haines, played by Farley Granger and Bruno Antony, played by Robert Walker. The two men exchange life stories, commiserating over their personal troubles. Guy wants to divorce his promiscuous wife to marry his beautiful girlfriend, the daughter of a United States senator and Bruno wants to free himself of his cruel and controlling father. Bruno is a smooth-talking psychopath who suggests they help each other out by swapping murders. Bruno will kill Miriam, Guy's wife, and Guy will take care of Bruno's hateful father. Each of them will murder a stranger, with no apparent motive, so neither will ever be suspected. It's the perfect crime. Guy humors Bruno, never seriously intending to take him up on the offer, but then Bruno goes through with his end of the bargain and murders Miriam, and then insists that Guy must honor the deal. I won't give anything else away. You really need to see it again to appreciate its brilliance."

Albie's eyes danced as he relived the film in his mind.

Hayley could not stop staring at him.

A cold chill shot up her spine.

Her hands froze and she dropped the DVD case and it landed on the floor with a thud.

Albie bent down and picked it up, placing it gently back down on the beer barrel coffee table. He picked up on her sudden change of mood. "Is everything all right, Hayley?"

"Yes, yes, fine," Hayley said, suddenly filled with a deep desire to get out of this house.

As he bobbed the tea bag up and down in the cup before trying to hand it to Hayley, she took a step back, refusing to take it.

"I'm sorry, Albie, I just remembered: I'm supposed to pick Bruce up at work and I'm already late. Can I take a rain check on the tea?"

"Sure." He nodded, eyeing her suspiciously. "I hope you're both still planning to come to my screening of *Shadow of a Doubt* tonight! Presales have been through the roof, but we still have some tickets left."

"Of course! We wouldn't miss it," Hayley said, slowly backing out of the living room.

Albie gave her a crooked smile. "See you tonight, then."

"Yes, tonight."

He picked up a tea biscuit and took a bite. The rest of it crumbled in his hand.

Hayley dashed out the door.

She still could not quite put all the pieces together,

but Albie's rapturous description of the film's plot had struck a nerve, like she was hearing a full-throated murder confession in the courtroom. She still had so many questions, but she was starting to feel like she was onto something, that she was on the verge of cracking this whole case wide open.

Island Food & Spirits
By
Hayley Powell

I was driving home today from the Shop 'n Save after picking up the ingredients to make my brother Randy's favorite carrot ginger soup that I wanted to take over to him, since he was suffering from a winter cold and needed cheering up, when I drove past the Glen Mary wading pool, which is located right around the corner from my house. Seeing all of the excited kids skating across the frozen pool always brings me a wave of nostalgia.

The Glen Mary wading pool has been around ever since I can remember and even years before I was even born. It's a Bar Harbor institution in its own right.

Every summer, parents take their kids to the large, round man-made pond, probably no more than three feet deep, where kids can cool off, play on the swings, and enjoy a picnic lunch before heading back into the water to splash each other and lounge on their brightly colored floaties. Then, in the winter months, the town turns the pool into a small skating rink, where kids lace up their skates and glide around in circles for hours.

When my kids were younger, during the winter

we would walk from our house to Glen Mary with our skates in tow after dinner and go around in circles until after dark and we were chilled to the bone and couldn't feel our toes. That's when we knew it was time to head home and warm up with steaming mugs of hot chocolate piled high with whipped cream.

In our formative years, Liddy, Mona, and I couldn't even recall all the wonderful times we had swimming in the summer and skating in the winter. However, there was one particular Glen Mary memory I couldn't shake even if I wanted to, one that came flashing back into my mind as I slowly drove past the wading pool.

Freshman year at Mount Desert Island High School is a little scary. It's exciting to be leaving the small confines of the Bar Harbor middle school and junior high in Bar Harbor to the much larger high school that brings together students from all the island schools, including Northeast Harbor, Southwest Harbor, and Tremont. It's a bit of a culture shock. You stick with your old friends at first before you get comfortable in your new surroundings, and then you start venturing out to make new friends from the other schools.

However, for me, Liddy, and Mona, despite our initial apprehension, we realized high school offered an opportunity to meet new boys, and not just the same immature blockheads we were stuck with in the eighth grade, who thought it was funny to stick gum in the back of our hair or put a live frog from science class in our locker. Suddenly we had dozens of new choices at MDI! By Thanksgiving, all those new-school jitters had vanished, and it seemed like everyone was meeting new crushes and dating kids from the other side of the island.

I was ecstatic because I had just met an impossibly cute boy named Evan in my algebra class, who was from Southwest Harbor. When I helped him solve a difficult problem he was stuck on, and he winked at me with these stunning emerald-green eyes while saying thank you—well, suffice it to say, I was hooked! And then, Mona heard from a girl in her English class, who heard from her twin brother in Evan's social studies class, that the feeling was mutual. Evan had a crush on me too, and had every intention of asking me out!

Mona, Liddy, and I were in the lunchroom excitedly dissecting this new critical piece of information, when I suddenly I had a horrible thought. My mother had told me that under no circumstances was I to date until I was fifteen, and I knew in my heart that she would never change her mind. My mother is as stubborn as a mule, which is something my ex-husband Danny used to say about me, which is ridiculous. I do not, repeat, do not take after my mother! Now, where was I? Oh, right. It looked like I was going to have to turn down poor Evan when he asked me out.

I was sadly digesting this depressing thought, when suddenly Evan appeared at our table and smiled at me, and said he would like to ask me something, and then, after hemming and hawing for a few seconds, working up the courage, he proceeded to ask me to go ice-skating with him Saturday night at Glen Mary. I stared into those pretty green eyes, and before I could politely decline, I heard myself saying, "Yes, Evan, yes, I would love to go out with you!" Grinning from ear to ear, his voice cracking, he said, "Great! It's a date!" And then turned and scampered away.

What had I gotten myself into? I was going to be the laughingstock of the whole school when people found out I wasn't allowed to date, or even just go skating with a boy unless it was with a whole group until I was fifteen. No other kid in my freshman class had to live under this draconian rule. Liddy and Mona's parents had not laid down the law in such an authoritarian fashion. It seemed as if just my mother was Bar Harbor's very own Mussolini! To make matters worse, once I bowed out of the date with Evan, I couldn't even commiserate with my besties at a sleepover that night, because Liddy and Mona were going to Portland for the weekend, Christmas shopping with their mothers. What was I going to do?

After school, I was sitting in the living room, practicing out loud what I was going to say to Evan when I called him to break our date. "Evan, I've contracted a weird toe fungus and the doctor says I can't go skating until it's healed" Gross! No! What about, "I'm sorry, Evan, my dog Wrigley chewed up my skates and now I can't tie them properly and don't want to risk a nasty fall!" No! What a stupid excuse. Besides, he could suggest we do something else. I was panicked!

Unbeknownst to me, my little brother Randy had been listening to me coming up with my excuses. When I caught him eavesdropping around the corner, I chased him down and grabbed him by the collar and seethed, "One word to Mom about this and I will make it my mission to torture you for the rest of your life, which could be pretty short, if you mess with me!"

Randy was unmoved. "Ha! You don't scare me. If it's my word against yours, we both know who Mom will believe. But hey, maybe we can work together, help each other out, so we both get what we want."

When did my eleven-year-old brother start sounding like Al Pacino from The Godfather?

Left with no choice, I asked him to explain. He told me that he and his best friend Jerry Sanborn wanted to go to the Criterion to see the new Stephen King horror movie *Misery* because they had heard there was a gory scene involving a sledgehammer and somebody's foot. But because it was rated R, Mom and Jerry's mother, Liz, refused to let them go because they were too young. Liz had also called the theater and told the woman in the ticket booth not to under any circumstances sell those boys tickets! So Randy suggested to me like a Mob boss that if I was to go and buy them two tickets, then they could see the movie and I could go skating with Evan, and then he would meet me afterwards at Glen Mary, and we would walk home together, and no one would be the wiser.

This actually sounded like a workable idea, except for one problem. We couldn't fib to Mom about our whereabouts because that woman was like a walking human lie detector.

"That's the best part!" Randy exclaimed. "She told me this morning that she's meeting some work friends for dinner in Ellsworth on Saturday night and won't be home until ten o'clock, plenty of time for us to get home."

I was impressed.

The kid had it all worked out in his head.

It was a pretty perfect plan.

What could go wrong?

Then I had a thought. "Wait a minute. Why did Mom tell you about her plans and not me?"

Randy chuckled. "Are you kidding? She didn't tell you because she wanted to make sure you wouldn't try and make plans to do something you shouldn't be doing, like ice-skating at Glen Mary pond with a boy!"

I couldn't argue with the truth.

"But she trusts me. She knows I'd never sneak around behind her back, trying to get away with something," Randy proudly declared.

Which was exactly what he was doing now.

But I kept my mouth shut because his plan appeared to be foolproof.

Saturday finally came, and just as Randy said, my mother asked me to watch him that night because she was going out to dinner with some friends. Of course, I happily told her I would love to babysit, winking conspiratorially at Randy when she left the room. I was surprised my mother was not more suspicious about my agreeable behavior. Normally I would huff and moan and stamp my feet at the prospect of being stuck with my little brother on a Saturday night.

As soon as our mother left for Ellsworth, Randy and I headed straight to the ticket booth at the Criterion Theatre, where I purchased his tickets and left him to wait for his friend Jerry. Then I made a beeline to Glen Mary, where I had already dropped off a bag with my skates and extra socks and gloves for my date with Evan.

Everything was going according to plan. Evan was already at the gate waiting for me when I arrived, and we headed to a bench to put on our skates. The evening was more glorious than I ever could have imagined. We glided around and around the pond. Evan even took my hand and squeezed it just as we skated past my archnemesis Sabrina Merryweather, who scowled because I was on a date with a cute boy and she was there with her six-year-old cousin. I thought I had died and gone to heaven, when suddenly I heard the unmistakable voice of my mother loudly yelling, "Hayley Jordan! Come over here right now!"

My stomach dropped.

I tripped over my skates and did a pratfall, face-planting on the ice and dragging Evan down on top of me. I could hear Sabrina giggling.

As Evan climbed off and helped me to my feet, I squeezed my eyes shut, hoping I was just imagining my mother's stern voice. But no, when I slowly opened my eyes, there she was, standing with her hands on her hips, eyes blazing, and Randy in the back seat of her car, a fearful look on his face.

"Is everything okay?" Evan asked, concerned.

I nodded and whispered, "I'm sorry, Evan, thank you for a lovely time, but I have to go." And then I skated away, over to my mother, my heart sinking, knowing I would probably never see Evan again by the angry look on my mother's face.

You might be wondering just how my mother found out about our little deception. Well, unfortunately for us, just as she reached Hulls Cove, about a seven-minute drive from Bar Harbor on the road to Ellsworth, Mom got a flat. She didn't have a spare, so she called Chuckie the tow truck driver to take her and her car to the shop. As they drove down Cottage Street, passing the Criterion Theatre, Chuckie had said, "Look at all those little rascals trying to get into an R-rated horror movie!" Well, when Mom glanced over, who did she see first in line but Randy and Jerry! She told Chuckie to pull over, scooped both boys up, deposited Jerry with his very unhappy mother, and then after getting a new tire at the garage, interrogated Randy, who caved immediately, blubbering all about the secret plan that I had coerced him into undertaking! That's when they drove straight to Glen Mary to ruin my very first date!

Mom read us both the riot act when we got home and we were grounded for two weeks. But the real punishment—or karma, as my mother would say—came the following week, when Sabrina rushed up to my locker to spill the beans that after I left him all alone at Glen Mary, Evan had started a conversation with Judy Carr, a sophomore, and now word on the street was, the two were an item! I couldn't blame him for not waiting for me until I turned fifteen.

Not a great start to my freshman year, but things began looking up a few months later when I finally did turn fifteen, and Johnny Gray asked me out to the winter carnival on Long Pond, but that's a story for another time.

So now for Randy's favorite soup and a special cocktail to go along with it. I hope you will give this recipe a try and let me know how you like it. It will warm you up real good after a cold night of skating at Glen Mary, that's for sure.

GINGER SPICED HOT CHOCOLATE

INGREDIENTS:
3 teaspoons unsweetened cocoa powder
2 teaspoons powdered sugar
⅛ teaspoon ground ginger
1 cup milk—your choice

In a saucepan, add cocoa powder, powdered sugar, and ginger and whisk until combined.

Add milk and heat on medium-high heat until hot, whisking occasionally to keep from scorching.

When hot and steamy, pour into a mug and top with whipped cream if so desired.

CARROT GINGER SOUP

INGREDIENTS:
1 tablespoon olive oil
½ white onion, chopped
½ teaspoon kosher salt
3 cloves garlic, smashed
1 pound carrots, peeled and chopped
1 teaspoon freshly grated ginger
1 tablespoon apple cider vinegar
3 cups vegetable broth
ground black pepper to taste
coconut milk (optional)

Heat your oil in a large pot over medium heat. Add the onions, salt, and pepper and cook until onions are softened and fragrant, stirring occasionally.

Stir in your ginger, apple cider vinegar, and vegetable broth. Bring to a boil, reduce heat and simmer for 30 minutes.

Let the broth mixture cool slightly, then add to a blender and blend until smooth. If your soup is too thick, add a bit of water until you reach your desired consistency.

Drizzle with a little coconut milk if desired.

Chapter 40

Hayley could not stop thinking about Albie's detailed description of the plot to *Strangers on a Train* he had so eagerly shared with her earlier that day. The fact that he and Dolly had both blatantly lied about meeting before Hayley had tried fixing them up suggested they did not want anyone knowing they were already connected in some way. Much like Guy Haines and Bruno Antony in the film after their chance meeting on the train. She was slowly starting to put the pieces of the puzzle together as Bruce wandered into the kitchen and asked if she still wanted to go to Albie's movie night at the Criterion featuring *Shadow of a Doubt*. He had swung by the theater and bought two tickets on his lunch hour. Hayley had a sense of dread in the pit of her stomach. After her earlier encounter with him in his home, she had no intention of ending up alone in a room with Albie ever again, at least not until all the facts of Carroll Flood's poisoning, Dwight falling through the ice at Long Pond, and the shooter in the park came into the light.

But she did feel the need to keep an eye on Albie and with Bruce as her protection, she felt safe enough going to the Criterion and watching a movie in a crowded theater.

As it turned out, the seats were only half full despite Albie's boast of a near sellout screening. Bruce excitedly bought a large popcorn and soda so he could take advantage of the free refills. They marched down the aisle to the sixth row up from the screen and settled into two seats on the end.

Albie walked out on the stage in front of the grand burgundy curtain and gave a brief introduction of the film, rattling off the same facts he had presented to Hayley earlier, about this title being Hitchcock's personal favorite, quick rundowns of the main cast, a few trivia facts, and then, pointing up to the booth where the Criterion's longtime projectionist Boyd, a sweet, unassuming local movie buff, was manning the digital projector. Boyd's wife, Connie, was a huge fan of Hayley's food and cocktails column and was constantly emailing her after trying one of her recipes, sometimes even catching her mistakes in the list of ingredients; one time pointing out that Hayley had listed two tablespoons baking soda when she meant two tablespoons baking powder. A quick correction had to be made and Hayley was most appreciative of Connie's eagle-eyed observance.

The lights went down and the curtain rose and after a few previews of upcoming attractions, the black-and-white splendor of Hitchcock's 1943 classic burst onto the screen, with Joseph Cotten fleeing a murder scene, on the run from some dogged police detectives. Bruce reached out and held Hayley's hand while shoveling popcorn in his mouth from the bucket in his lap with the other. About an hour and twenty minutes into the movie, Hayley suddenly realized she had not been paying too much attention to the film. She was still consumed with Albie Schooner lying to her and how his plot description of *Strangers on a Train* had so disturbed her. Bruce gripped Hayley's hand tightly as Teresa Wright's character slowly began to suspect her favorite uncle might be the vicious killer on the run and the handsome detective she had befriended might be right about him after all.

Bruce scraped the bottom of his popcorn bucket, then turned it upside down and emptied the rest out into his hand. He gave Hayley a puppy dog look. She knew what he wanted. Bruce had never seen the film before, but Hayley had, so he was hoping she might dash out to the concession stand and get his free refill so he would not miss any of the movie. Hayley sighed, grabbing the bucket, and then hauled herself out of her seat and marched up the aisle and out the door. In the lobby, the pimply faced high school kid working behind the counter took the bucket and scooped up a freshly popped batch, still hot, and handed it back to her with a bored, half smile.

"Thank you," Hayley chirped, turning around and suddenly finding herself face-to-face with Albie, who had a strange, off-putting, forced grin.

"Hayley, I hate to bother you, I know you and Bruce are enjoying the movie, but would you do me a huge favor?"

"Um, sure, Albie, what is it?"

"Boyd saw you come in, and you know how his wife Connie reads your column religiously. Well, apparently there was a mistake in the recipe that was published in yesterday's paper."

"Another one?" Hayley groaned.

"Yes, kind of a big one, according to Boyd. Connie can't stop prattling on about it."

"The carrot ginger soup?"

"I'm not sure, but she really wants you to correct it for the online edition of the *Times* before too many people try making it at home."

"Of course. Tell him to meet me in the lobby after the film and I would be happy to discuss it."

Albie frowned. "Unfortunately, he's ducking out a little early, so if you could just pop up to the booth for a second I'm sure he would appreciate it. You know how Connie is when she's got a bee in her bonnet. There is no living with her."

No, she did not know that.

And she did not feel at all comfortable going anywhere with Albie Schooner right now, especially with the nagging suspicions about him practically consuming her.

"Is he in the booth now?"

"He's always in the booth. Even when he's not, I still smell his pungent aftershave," Albie joked.

She hesitated.

Albie grinned again, causing the hair on the back of

her neck to stand up. "Do you know where it is? I'd go with you, but I have to have a little talk with Kenny about eating too much of the inventory during his shift." He pointed to the kid behind the concession counter, who had just torn open a box of Junior Mints and was plucking them out one by one and hurling them into his mouth.

"Excuse me," Albie said, spinning around and walking away.

Okay, at least he was not going to tag along with her.

And with Boyd in the booth, she would not be alone.

Hayley headed up the stairs to the balcony and hurried down the narrow hall to the door to the projection booth. She knocked, but did not hear anyone say "come in" because the sound of the film was so loud. She knocked again and then tried the door handle. It was unlocked. She stepped inside and had a nice view of the movie screen. But Boyd was not in his usual chair next to the digital projector.

"Boyd?"

She looked around, still holding Bruce's full bucket of popcorn.

The booth was empty.

Without warning, someone shoved her inside by the shoulders, causing her to stumble, pieces of popcorn flying. The door to the booth slammed shut and she pivoted to see Albie blocking her escape.

"Where's Boyd?" Hayley demanded to know.

Albie shrugged. "He must have gone on his break."

"Albie, what is this?"

"Oh, come on, Hayley. I knew from the moment your eyes fell on that DVD that it was only a matter of time before you figured it all out. That's what you do. Everyone in town knows you're Bar Harbor's very own Miss Marple!"

"I have no idea what you're talking about," Hayley squeaked.

Albie roared with laughter. "Of course you do. I can see it in your eyes. Stop trying to humor me. I've seen too many movies not to know you're feigning ignorance, pretending to still be in the dark. It's demeaning to yourself, Hayley. You know exactly what's going on."

She made a move for the door.

He threw his back against it to prevent her from leaving.

He had her trapped.

There was no point in playing games anymore.

"Okay, fine. You're right, Albie. It took me a while, but when you so gleefully recounted the plot to *Strangers on a Train*, almost daring me to solve the case, it all slowly started to make sense. You and Dolly played out the plot of that movie to get what you both wanted. That's why it was so critical for you to hide the fact that you two already knew each other. You wanted me and the police to think you were meeting for the first time at one of your movie nights, like the two strangers on a train with no connection whatsoever, but it was a really dumb move discussing your plans in a corner booth at Jordan's."

"We hatched the plan over breakfast that morning. After that, we were careful not to be seen together. We honestly didn't think anyone would notice, let alone talk about us! Nobody in this godforsaken town has ever paid much attention to either one of us, so we weren't too worried. How would our names ever come up in anyone's conversation?"

"But they did. When Hannah the waitress overheard me mention playing matchmaker for the two of you. I thought you and Dolly didn't know each other and Hannah innocently corrected me."

Albie scowled. "I hate gossips!"

"Dolly abhorred her ex-husband Carroll Flood and you wanted to crush Dwight Jordan for frittering away your savings and livelihood all those years ago. So you swapped murders, just like in the movie. You were at the gingerbread house contest and injected Carroll's bag of gumdrops with the poison. Then during the commotion, you slipped the vial of poison in Dwight's coat pocket so he would be the number-one suspect. You had nothing against Carroll so you were safe to assume you would never fall under scrutiny. Then it was Dolly's turn. She was selling her crafts at the Christmas carnival on Long Pond and had ample opportunity to move the warning sign about the dangerously thin ice from view and then lure Dwight out there with the note written on the napkin. But you two didn't count on Bruce rescuing him in the nick of time."

"I was furious! Dolly got scared and wanted to wash her hands of the deal at that point, but that would not have been fair to me. It was up to her to hold up her end of the bargain!"

"So you pressured her to try again. Which she did in the park. Only she was more nervous the second time, more prone to mistakes, and after firing wildly, only landing one bullet in the shoulder, she took off and got stopped for speeding by a park ranger. That ticket placed her directly at the scene."

"She came to me in a panic. I assured her she had nothing to worry about because of our pact. If the cops questioned her, what would be her motive to kill Dwight? She had none! The cops were running in circles trying to come up with suspects. We were going to get away with it scot-free. Until you had to stick your nose into it!"

"I already told Sergio my theory of what happened. I'd be surprised if he wasn't already downstairs in the lobby waiting to arrest you," Hayley fibbed, putting on a brave face.

Albie sneered menacingly. "I think you're lying." He took a step toward her, unfurling his clenched fists. "You haven't told anybody yet. And you never will." He raised his hands and lunged at her, trying to get a stranglehold around her neck.

Hayley jumped back and hurled the bucket of popcorn at him. It didn't stop him, but the rain of popcorn momentarily blinded him, so she was able to push past him and race for the door. As she grabbed the knob and was about to open it, he was suddenly grabbing her from behind, encircling her neck with the crook of his arm, yanking her back. She clawed at his elbow with her nails, scratching and biting down on it. He howled in pain, tightening his grip, but then she headbutted him in the face, cracking his nose. He let go and she was out the door, screaming at the top of her lungs.

But the movie had reached its climactic scene, the

moment in the film where Teresa Wright now understands her Uncle Charlie is a cold-blooded killer and is trapped on a train with him, the chugging and whistling of the train drowning out her desperate cries for help, as well as Hayley's own desperate cries for help. Albie was out of the projection booth like a shot and chased Hayley down the steps of the balcony to the edge that hung over the orchestra section. He clutched a fistful of her sweater and violently shoved her against the brass railing that ran across the balcony, trying with all his might to lift her up and send her hurtling over to the oblivious crowd below.

Hayley fought like a wildcat, struggling and scratching and screaming, mirroring the image of Teresa Wright fighting her Uncle Charlie between train cars, his hand clamped over her mouth, her desperately trying to cling to the door as he tried shoving her out of the train to the tracks below and certain death. Hayley faced a similar dire situation as Albie managed to lift her up off her feet as she savagely fought to keep hold of the brass railing. On-screen, just as Teresa Wright wiggles from his grasp, spinning around, Joseph Cotten slips and falls, flying off the train into the direct path of an oncoming train hurtling down the next tracks. At the same moment, Albie pushed all his body weight against Hayley, who used her grip on the brass railing to pull herself down, slipping out of Albie's grasp and sending him careening over the railing. But unlike Cotten, Albie managed to grab ahold of the brass railing to prevent himself from falling into the crowd below, whose eyes were all still fixed on what was happening on the large screen, completely unaware of their host dangling perilously over the balcony, legs flailing above the heads of the audience.

As Albie, eyes wide with fear, begged Hayley to get help, she ran downstairs to find some strong men who could lift him up to safety, taking comfort in the fact that, unlike Joseph Cotten after his string of grotesque and heartless murders, Albie Schooner would actually live to pay for his crimes.

Chapter 41

"Do They Know It's Christmas?" was a charity song written in 1984 by Bob Geldof of the Boomtown Rats and Midge Ure to raise money for the devastating famine in Ethiopia. Such pop luminaries as Paul McCartney, Boy George of Culture Club, Phil Collins, David Bowie, George Michael (still of Wham!), Bananarama, among many others sang on the record, making it a worldwide hit. Millions of dollars poured in for the relief effort. Now, many years later, the Bar Harbor's Congregational church choir was rehearsing the song to perform at the following Sunday service, even though it was almost a week past Christmas. The choir was not ready to give up their holiday spirit and insisted on one last hurrah of Christmas carols before the new year rang in the dreary, cold, gray days of January.

Hayley sat in the back pew of the church as the choir belted out the number during their late afternoon rehearsal. Picking up Boy George's solo, Dolly Halperin gave it her all, singing, "*And in our world of plenty, we can spread a smile of joy, throw your arms around the world at Christmas time!*"

Flawless.

Pitch-perfect.

And she knew it, breaking out into a wide, self-satisfied smile, as two of her fellow male choir members continued the George Michael and Simon Le Bon (of Duran Duran) part, a duet.

When they finished, there were lots of backslapping congratulations from the exhilarated choir, with most of the accolades going to star soloist Dolly, who also nearly raised the roof of the church off with her rendition of "White Christmas" earlier in the hour. Dolly was on cloud nine as she gathered up her tote bag and wiggled into her winter coat, floating down the aisle of the church, catching sight of Hayley, who stepped out from the pew to greet her.

"Hayley, what are you doing here? Are you interested in joining the church choir? We need another soprano now that Joyce Higgins has strep throat and has to stay quiet, which is a first in that woman's life—but oh well, doctor's orders!"

"If I could carry a tune, I would actually consider it, Dolly," Hayley laughed. "No, I just popped by, hoping you might be here, and as luck would have it, I arrived just in time to witness your powerful performance. My goodness, Dolly, you certainly have a set of pipes on you! You steal the show!"

Dolly blushed, feigning modesty. "Hayley, you're too kind. But it's really a team effort. This choir is at the top of its game, never been better; their backup vocals really make my voice sound better."

"Well, I'm impressed. It makes me want to attend services this week if I can manage to drag Bruce to church on a Sunday."

"Maybe you can bribe him with the gingerbread cake Gladys Hopkins is planning to bring to the after-service social. It will be first come, first served."

"That just might do the trick," Hayley said with a wink.

"You said you wanted to see me?" Dolly asked, her face still flushed with euphoria from the ego-stroking reaction to her standout vocals.

Hayley nodded, solemnly. "Yes, I wanted to make sure you heard the news."

Dolly's smile froze. "News? What news?"

Hayley exhaled a deep breath. "Albie Schooner has been arrested for Carroll Flood's murder."

Dolly gasped, eyes widening. "What? Oh, Hayley, no! You can't be serious."

Wow.

Dolly was a better actor than Hayley could have imagined.

"Yes, I'm afraid so."

Dolly shook her head, playing dumb. "I'm so surprised! Albie would have been the last person I thought would—I mean, I got the impression they hardly knew each other."

"I just feel so awful setting you up on a date with a murderer. I mean, who knows, Dolly? You could have been his next victim!"

"Hayley, dear, you couldn't have known, and we just had the one date. I wasn't even sure I was going to commit to a second one. I mean, Albie was nice and all, but I just had this strange feeling, like something was a little off, and my heavens—now I know why! Always trust your instincts is the lesson, I guess!"

"Yes," Hayley said, her eyes fixed on Dolly, who suddenly seemed uncomfortable and anxious to leave.

"Well, I better run. I have a million errands to run. Nice seeing you, Hayley, and thanks for letting me know."

"I will walk you to your car," Hayley kindly offered.

"No need. You said yourself that the police have arrested Albie, so he's no longer a threat, right?"

She flew out the door with Hayley on her heels. Her car was parked at the curb directly in front of the church and not the side gravel lot next to the building where everyone else parked.

"I was running late for rehearsal and grabbed the first space I could find," she felt the need to explain. She fumbled in her tote bag for her car keys as Hayley stood patiently next to Dolly's blue Honda Civic. Once she retrieved her keys, she turned to see Hayley was still there. "Honestly, Hayley, don't feel bad. All is forgiven. It's not your fault about that Albie business. You were in the dark like the rest of us. Please don't beat yourself up. Now, if there is nothing else, I better go."

She pressed the fob with her finger and the car doors unlocked. She flung open the driver's-side door and was about to climb inside when suddenly a police squad car pulled into the empty space behind her and Chief Sergio got out.

"Good afternoon, Chief," Dolly squeaked uneasily, her mind racing to figure out exactly what was going on here.

"Afternoon, Dolly," Sergio said, a grim look on his face.

There was an awkward silence.

"Is there something I can help you with?" Dolly asked warily.

"As a matter of fact, there is," Sergio said. "Would you mind if I take a quick look in the trunk of your car?"

Dolly's eyes nervously darted back and forth between Sergio and Hayley. "I don't understand. Why?"

"You must be aware that someone tried to shoot Dwight Jordan in the park?"

"Yes, everyone in town knows, but what does that have to have to do with what's in my—?"

"On the same day you were pulled over by a park ranger for speeding."

"Chief, I do not like what you're implying. I had no ill will toward Dwight Jordan. I had absolutely no reason to harm him. I am completely innocent!" Dolly protested, too much.

"Then you shouldn't mind if I take a quick peek in your trunk . . . if you have nothing to hide."

Another uncomfortable pause.

Her face darkened. "Do you have a warrant?"

Sergio reached into the inside pocket of his navy-blue police jacket and produced a folded-up piece of paper. "As a matter of fact, I do."

Dolly's whole body seemed to go limp, as if she was about to faint. Hayley stood ready to catch her if she swooned and pitched forward.

"My officers already searched your house earlier this afternoon and didn't find anything, so I had a hunch that if you did take those potshots at Mr. Jordan, then you might still have the weapon stowed in your car."

"That's p-preposterous, how dare you!" Dolly sputtered, turning to Hayley for support, suddenly realizing she was in on the whole thing. "You didn't come here to tell me about Albie Schooner. You came here to delay me until Chief Sergio could get here."

"Guilty as charged," Hayley admitted.

"Hayley, would you do the honors?" Sergio asked.

Hayley leaned inside the Honda Civic and popped the trunk open. Sergio walked around to the back of the car, staring into the trunk.

Dolly started weeping, wiping her nose with the brown leather gloves she was wearing.

She knew it was over.

Sergio, also wearing gloves, carefully lifted a twelve-gauge shotgun out of the trunk, taking care not to compromise any fingerprints that might still be on it.

"Dolly, you're under arrest for attempted murder," Sergio said.

That's when Dolly Halperin's eyes went up into the back of her head and she pitched forward, as Hayley managed to catch her by her limp arms before her face hit the pavement.

Chapter 42

Try as he might, Dwight Jordan could not hold back the flood of tears that gushed down his cheeks as he sat at Hayley's dining room table, his eyes fixed on her laptop's screen during the Zoom call he was having with his grandchildren, Gemma and Dustin, their respective spouses, Conner and MacKenzie, and his great-grandson, the rambunctious, adorable Eli, Dustin's three-year-old son. Hayley stood off to the side, observing, with a warm smile. She had scheduled the call at Dwight's request. Sheila was understandably nervous that reconnecting with the grandkids was a risk, fearing they all might invest emotionally in this rather unreliable man who might take off again, but she made a point of not standing in the way, allowing this tentative meet and greet in order to keep the peace.

Dwight was nervous at first, responding to their questions with quick, one-word answers. But Hayley knew the innate charms of her two children, the vibrant, quick-witted Gemma and her more thoughtful, talented artist Dustin, would soon win him over. Within minutes, he was the one asking questions, sincerely fascinated with their lives and accomplishments, Gemma working as an executive at the Food Network in New York with dreams of one day hosting her own cooking show, and Dustin, an animator in Los Angeles, working for a start-up digital company on the cutting edge of computer animation.

Dwight was enjoying the virtual meeting immensely, and finally his emotions had gotten the best of him and the waterworks began. Hayley plucked a few tissues from a Kleenex box and handed them to him. He thanked her with a nod and then blew his nose, honking so hard Eli erupted into a fit of giggles.

"And what about you, Conner, what do you do for a living?" Dwight asked.

"I'm an actor," Conner answered proudly. "Mostly commercials and small guest spots on whatever *Law and Order* show is casting, but I get by."

"He's being modest. He's a very successful actor. He just finished a show in London and now he's rehearsing for a new Broadway play that opens in February," Gemma boasted.

"Off-Broadway!" Conner corrected her.

"That's pretty impressive," Dwight marveled. "I used to do a little acting back in the day. Nothing like you, just some community theater wherever I might be living at the time."

"He's being modest too. Your grandfather is always acting—every day of his life, it seems!" Sheila could not help but acidly interject as she wandered in from the living room.

Hayley shot her an admonishing look. "Mom!"

Carl, who was on the couch, scrolling through Instagram posts on his phone, glanced up with a weary look. "Sheila, come back in here and leave them alone."

Much to everyone's surprise, Sheila obeyed her boyfriend's command, but not before sticking her head in front of the laptop camera and waving at her grandchildren. "Bye, kids! Nana loves you all very much!"

They all happily waved back.

Sheila glared at Hayley. "I just came in to say good night."

Hayley nodded, knowing her mother could not resist one last jab at her ex-husband.

"Sheila!" Carl bellowed, eyes still glued to the phone.

"I'm coming, I'm coming!" Sheila huffed, marching back into the living room and plopping herself down on the couch next to Carl.

"I better get going. I need to go over my lines before rehearsal in the morning," Conner declared, standing up from the kitchen table in their small, but cozy New York apartment.

"We better go too," MacKenzie said. "We need to put Eli down for the night. It's way past his bedtime. Say bye-bye to Great-Grandpa!"

Eli waved his chubby little hand. "Bye!"

MacKenzie leaned down and whispered in his ear. "Can you blow him a kiss?"

Eli pursed his lips and blew as hard as he could.

It was more of a raspberry than a kiss, but it managed to do the trick.

Dwight choked up all over again.

"Goodbye, everyone. This call meant the world to me. Thank you for taking the time. I know how busy you all are!" Dwight said, sniffing.

"We'll do it again soon!" Dustin promised.

"Good night, Grandpa!" Gemma said, beaming.

And then her screen went dark.

MacKenzie had already led Eli away and Dustin tapped a key and then their screen went dark as well.

The Zoom call was over.

But Dwight continued staring at the computer screen, overcome with emotion. Finally, he whispered, barely loud enough for anyone to actually hear, "That was nice."

Hayley put a hand on his shoulder.

He looked up at her. "Thank you for making that happen."

"My pleasure. And it doesn't have to be a onetime thing. I will get you everyone's numbers so you can all keep in touch." Hayley casually glanced over in her mother's direction to gauge her reaction to this, but she did not seem to flinch.

On the outside, anyway.

"Can I get anyone coffee?" Hayley offered.

"No, I will be up all night," Dwight replied.

"How about a shot of whiskey?" Carl piped in.

"Carl! It's way too late to start drinking!" Sheila scolded.

"It's not even eight o'clock!" Carl whined.

Hayley shook her head, laughing. "How about I make gingerbread whiskey sours for everyone?"

"Sounds good to me!" Carl said, determined to have the last word, daring Sheila to say no again.

She wisely chose not to try and stop him.

"Good. I've got some tasty hors d'oeuvres I can pop into the oven too. We'll make it a little pre–New Year's Eve party right here at home," Hayley said. "Just let me go upstairs and get Bruce to come down and join us. He should be almost finished with his column by now."

Dwight reached out and touched her arm. "Hayley, I just want to thank you for making room in your life for me." He sniffed back more tears. "I know you didn't have to. I haven't exactly been Father of the Year."

She patted his hand. "I'm happy you're here."

She was about to pull away, but he maintained a gentle grip. "I've missed so much. So much . . ." His voice trailed off.

Both Sheila and Carl watched the scene with keen interest.

He managed to collect himself and continue. "But I promise to do better from here on in. And, if you don't mind, I may give Liddy a call tomorrow, see if she can find me a small, short-term rental, nothing fancy, so I can stick around town for a few months, maybe longer. I guess we'll see how it goes."

"I would like that very much, Dwight," Hayley said.

All eyes moved to Sheila, who sat stiffly on the couch next to Carl, stone-faced.

"I mean, if your mother doesn't mind," Dwight added.

There was a long pause.

"Why would I mind? Carl and I are going back to Florida in a few days. It's your life. You can do whatever you please. I'm not going to stop you."

There was a release of tension in the air.

"And you're welcome to come down to Florida and visit us anytime you'd like, Dwight!" Carl chirped.

Sheila elbowed him in the rib. "Don't push it, Carl."

She may have been open to Dwight staying in Bar Harbor, but she was still struggling with the notion of her ex-husband and current boyfriend becoming bosom buddies.

"There's one more thing, Sheila," Dwight muttered.

Everyone braced themselves.

"It's about Celeste . . ."

"One of the reasons you want to stay is because you want to build a relationship with one of my best friends and you want my blessing? Is that it?"

Dwight took a moment before nodding. "Yeah, I guess so."

"Celeste can be a handful. Snobbish, flighty, and maddeningly late all the time, but she's a lovely person with a heart of gold, and if you hurt her, I will hunt you down and make you wish you never came back to Maine, do you hear me?"

"In other words, you have her blessing, Dwight," Hayley said, chuckling. As she headed up the stairs to find her own husband, Hayley could hear Dwight say to Sheila and Carl, "It's good to be home."

Chapter 43

For the first time in her life, Hayley was grateful for her mother's obsessive-compulsive disorder, her overpowering need to keep her house spotless, not to mention any home where she might be staying, including Hayley's. Growing up as a messy teenager was a challenge. Her mother was constantly nagging her to clean her room, and even during the last two weeks her mother and Carl had been visiting, she felt guilty when a dirty dish was left in the sink or a stray coffee cup discarded in the living room. Sheila would zero in on the offending object like a laser beam and quickly scoop it up and load it in the dishwasher. But today, the day of her New Year's Eve party she was hosting at the restaurant, Hayley only felt relief watching Sheila sweeping the floors of Hayley's Kitchen, determined to round up every last dust ball and speck of dirt. Once she was finished with the dining room, she marched off to the kitchen to start scrubbing all the counters and large appliances. Carl was her first lieutenant for her

mission, following closely behind her with a bottle of
Windex and a rag, spraying and wiping all the glass
surfaces and windows he could find. Liddy showed up
with a trunk full of fresh flowers to place around the
dining room. Randy was in the kitchen, busy mixing
batches of his famous New Year's Eve champagne,
loaded with triple sec, blackberry brandy, Chambord,
pineapple juice, ginger ale, and of course, champagne.
Hayley remained chained to the restaurant's kitchen,
wiping the sweat from her brow with the back of her
arm, as she tirelessly prepared all the food for the
party, precooking some of her hors d'oeuvres and finger foods, while refrigerating some dishes that needed
to be baked closer to party time. By midmorning,
Elmer and Rocco arrived to help Carl move tables
from the middle of the dining room to the side to allow
guests plenty of room to mingle.

When Mona showed up at lunchtime with lobster
rolls for everyone, Hayley insisted they all take a break
and have lunch.

Elmer's husband, Rocco, excitedly pulled Hayley
aside. "I have a wild idea I want to run past you."

"Shoot," Hayley said, taking a healthy bite of her
lobster roll.

"See that large empty space over by the fireplace?"

Hayley nodded.

"It is just screaming for a baby grand piano!" Rocco
exclaimed.

Hayley raised an eyebrow. "A piano?"

"Think about it. Live music at Hayley's Kitchen on
the weekends. We could transform this place on
Fridays and Saturdays, maybe add some overhead pen-

dant lights that would cast a gentle radiance across the room, creating both an intimate and lively atmosphere! Picture it. The hum of conversations and the clinking of cutlery as people enjoy your amazing menu, creating a harmonious backdrop of what is about to unfold. Then, at seven-thirty sharp, the lights dim and a spotlight illuminates the piano by the fireplace. The pianist, in a classic black suit, poised on the cushioned bench, his fingers hovering over the ebony and ivory keys, make their first contact, producing a soft, enchanting prelude. As the music swells, every note seems to resonate with the heartbeat of the room, captivating diners mid-bite and drawing them into the pianist's spell. He transforms the dining experience into a sensory journey of your gastronomic delights and his soul-touching symphonies!"

Hayley stared at Rocco, slack-jawed. "Wow, that's, um, that sounds totally . . . fabulous, but there's just one problem. Where do I find this ivory-tickling maestro?"

"Me! I could fly up here from New York Thursday night, perform Friday and Saturday and fly home on Sunday. It's perfect! I've been looking for a fun side gig like this!"

Hayley had to admit Rocco was talented.

He had rocked Liddy's Christmas party with his piano prowess. He was a true talent. Perhaps this was not as crazy an idea as she first believed.

She opened her mouth to speak, but Rocco anticipated her question. "I saw an ad in the *Island Times*. A retired couple in Ellsworth are moving to Florida and have a baby grand for sale real cheap. Their son has a flatbed. Delivery is included. I know it's a lot to bring up, but they're leaving soon and—" Rocco stopped himself. Hayley could tell he felt he was pushing too hard. "Just give it some thought. No pressure. Elmer is always rolling his eyes over my harebrained schemes!"

Hayley considered his proposal and smiled. "Let's talk tomorrow after the party when I have more time to think."

Rocco hugged her. "Thank you, Hayley!"

She noticed Sergio, in his police uniform, had just arrived. He was hovering by the front door, a somber look on his face.

"Excuse me, Rocco, I'll be right back."

She walked over to Sergio. "You here to help get ready for the party?"

He shook his head. "No. I'm here on business."

A wave of apprehension swept through her. "What's wrong?"

Sergio bowed his head, not anxious to deliver the news. But then, he sighed and raised his eyes to meet hers. "I have two FBI agents sitting in my office at the police station."

Hayley gulped. "What do they want?"

"They're looking for Dwight. They want to talk to him about a scam he was involved with five years ago. They didn't go into detail, but it sounds serious, Hayley."

Her shoulders sank.

"Do you know where I can find him?"

"Try Jane and Bubba's house. That's where he's been staying. He promised to drop by later and help with the setup for the party."

"This can't wait. I'm going to head over there now."

Sergio turned on his heel and left the restaurant.

Liddy approached Hayley. "What was all that about?"

"He needs to talk to Dwight. I sent him to Bubba and Jane's place," Hayley answered, watching Sergio get into his squad car and drive away.

"Well, he's not there."

Hayley spun around to face Liddy. "How do you know?"

"Because he's at my mother's house having lunch with her. Those two lovebirds can't stay away from each other. It makes me sick. My own mother has a more active love life than I do!" Liddy huffed.

"I have some spinach goat cheese pinwheels in the oven! Do me a favor and don't let them burn!" Hayley cried as she rushed out of the restaurant.

Chapter 44

W hen Hayley arrived at Celeste's home and rang the bell, her stomach twisted in knots, Celeste, in a flattering green blouse and beige dress pants, opened the door and lit up with a bright smile. "Hayley! What a lovely surprise. Please, come in. We just finished lunch."

She led Hayley into the kitchen where Dwight, in a plaid work shirt and khaki pants, stood at the sink, drying dishes with a towel.

"I know, it's shocking, right? I didn't even have to ask Dwight to help me clean up. He volunteered himself," Celeste laughed.

"She might be the first woman to domesticate me," Dwight cracked with a wink.

Hayley could see they were having fun together, enjoying each other's company, maybe even daring to set their sights on a life together, and so she hated what she had to do. Her heart pounded like a drum.

"So as much as he tried to avoid the topic while we

were enjoying our clam chowder, your father finally worked up the nerve to ask me to be his date to your New Year's Eve party tonight. Of course, I had to sweeten him up first with my homemade bread pudding."

"You should have some, Hayley," Dwight insisted. "She makes it with chocolate chips and dried cherries and a bourbon whiskey sauce that will knock your socks off!"

"There is a small piece left I could heat up in the microwave if you'd like, Hayley," Celeste said.

"No, thank you, I really can't stay," Hayley said in a tight voice. "I just need to talk to Dwight, if you don't mind."

Celeste's eyes widened, disturbed by her tense tone. "Of course." She stood there, waiting, then realized. "Oh, you mean alone. Yes. I have some laundry I need to put in the dryer." She scuttled out of the room, leaving them.

Dwight picked up a plate off the rack and started drying it with the towel. "Hayley, you look so serious. What's the matter?"

She took a deep breath, mustering the courage to break the news, then exhaled and plowed ahead, her voice trembling as she spoke. "Sergio stopped by the restaurant while we were preparing for the party tonight and he said there are two FBI agents down at the police station who want to talk to you."

As the words left her lips, she saw her father flinch ever so slightly. His grip on the dish he was drying tightened, a brief flicker of concern passing across his face. Hayley could sense his unease, but she knew her father well enough now to know he would do whatever was necessary to alleviate her worry and brush it off, which is exactly what he did.

"I think I may know what this is all about and trust me, it's just a misunderstanding." He placed the plate in a cupboard and wiped his hands on the towel, eyeing Hayley, gauging the level of her distress. "Honestly, honey, I got mixed up with a couple of shady businessmen a while back, thinking they were on the up-and-up and they ended up bilking some money out of an unsuspecting widow and took off before I even realized what they were doing. Luckily, she was rich so she didn't even miss it. But of course, that doesn't excuse any of it. They were scam artists and they're probably still on the lam. I'm sure those FBI agents just want to talk to me to find out if I know of their current whereabouts, which I don't, by the way. Once I knew they were bad men, I steered clear of them."

He studied Hayley's face and could see there was skepticism written all over it.

"You don't believe me," he whispered, disappointed.

"Can you blame me, given your past history?" Hayley sighed.

Dwight nodded. "You're right. You have no reason to believe anything I say. But trust me. This time I'm telling you the truth. Listen, I'm going to drive over to the station and clear this whole mess up right now." He flung the towel down on the kitchen counter. "Tell Celeste I'll be back at six to pick her up for the party." He stepped forward to hug Hayley, hesitating a moment to see if she would accept it, but Hayley reached out first and they embraced. After a moment, Dwight took a step back and stared at Hayley with an adoring smile. "See you tonight?"

"Yes. Tonight." Hayley's voice cracked. She felt as if she was on the verge of crying because a small part of her believed that this would be the last time she would see her father for a long, long time.

She watched through the kitchen window as Dwight hopped in his car and peeled away.

Where he was actually going, she could not be sure.

Chapter 45

It was ten minutes to midnight at Hayley's New Year's Eve party, and despite the sobering realization that Dwight Jordan had once again fled town without saying goodbye, Hayley's guests did their best to keep the mood festive. Mostly that involved keeping a heartbroken Celeste's champagne glass full as she sulked in a corner while her daughter, Liddy, as well as her best friends, Sheila and Jane, surrounded her with words of encouragement and support.

"I should've listened to you, Sheila, I'm such a fool!" Celeste declared, wiping away a tear from her eye. "Dwight Jordan will never change!"

"Chin up, Celeste, you're not the first one to fall for Dwight's irresistible charms. I was the trailblazer way back in the day; I believed every lie he told me!" Sheila said, patting her on the back.

"But you were in high school. I'm an old—" She quickly corrected herself. "Mature woman. I should've known better." She turned to Liddy and stroked her cheek with her hand. "Poor Liddy. Now I know where you get your terrible taste in men from."

Liddy stiffened, removing her mother's hand from her face. "Let's not make this about me. Let's focus on you and how you're going to get over this. The best course of action now is for you to get right back up on the horse."

Celeste's mouth dropped open. "Are you serious? I am done with men. Full stop. They're all good-for-nothing louses! Every last one of them!"

"Carl's not so bad," Sheila pointed out.

"Carl is a lot more than that. He's a catch, Mother. You're lucky to have him. He worships the ground you walk on!" Hayley reminded her.

Celeste downed her champagne and held out her empty glass. Hayley quickly picked up on the cue and refilled it to the brim.

"I have some good news," Liddy chirped. "I just spoke to Dad and he and Rocco know a guy, very sweet, in his seventies, so an appropriate age range, jaw-droppingly handsome, wife died about six years ago, looking for love again, a regular Golden Bachelor!"

Celeste let out a heavy sigh and shook her head as she slammed down her champagne glass on the table. "No! Absolutely not! In what world would I ever allow my gay ex-husband to play matchmaker for me? That sounds like the pinnacle of humiliation! No! For-get it!"

Liddy was quickly on her phone and bringing up his Instagram page. "At least look at his picture!"

Celeste waved her off, but Sheila and Jane eagerly crowded around Liddy to get a good look. Hayley also peeked over their shoulders, curious. He was definitely tall, gray, and dreamy, wearing a polo shirt and standing in front of what she assumed was his personal yacht.

"Celeste, he's a silver fox!" Jane exclaimed.

"I don't care," Celeste sniffed, refusing to look.

"I think he might be the most handsome man I've ever laid eyes on," Sheila cried. "I mean, Carl's a seven, maybe eight, but this man is a ten!"

"Eleven!" Jane crowed.

They were slowly getting to Celeste. Finally, unable to resist a quick look, Celeste glanced at the phone Liddy held out toward her. She shrugged. "He's all right, I guess. What does he do?"

"Retired hedge fund manager," Liddy said.

Celeste pursed her lips, considering. "He'll probably turn out gay like Elmer."

"He was married to his wife for thirty-seven years before she sadly passed. He's only now ready to dip his toe in the dating pool again. Come on, Mother, you must be just a little bit intrigued."

Celeste folded her arms defiantly, but couldn't help ask, "Any children?"

"Two daughters. One grandchild. An adorable four-year-old boy. Dad already texted him about you and sent a picture and he's very interested in meeting you. Come on, Mother, how many opportunities are you going to have to meet a gorgeous rich man who actually has a heart?"

"If you think I'm going to drop everything for the first millionaire who comes calling—"

"Billionaire," Liddy said.

Celeste sat up in her chair. "I beg your pardon?"

"I said *billionaire*. With a B. If you do take some of your precious time to look at his Instagram page, make sure not to miss the stunning photos from his villa in Tuscany."

Celeste snatched the phone from Liddy's grasp and began furiously scrolling. "Fine, Liddy, if it will get you to stop harassing me, I will meet him for a drink the next time I'm in New York!"

As Celeste kept her eyes glued to Liddy's phone, Liddy glanced over at her father and Rocco, who were by the bar conversing with Carl, Bruce, and Bubba, and gave them a thumbs- up. They toasted her with their cocktails.

Hayley checked the time on her phone.

It was close to midnight.

She looked up and noticed Betsy Shaw hovering near the door, looking awkward and nervous.

Hayley rushed over to greet her. "Betsy, I'm so glad you made it. I was afraid you weren't going to come!"

"I made it just under the wire," Betsy said.

Hayley, still holding the bottle of champagne, grabbed a clean glass from the host station and poured some for Betsy.

"Thank you," Betsy said. "I wasn't sure I should come. I'm still processing everything, as I'm sure you are."

"Yes. Both Randy and I have promised to have a sit-down after the New Year and discuss the whole situation. But one thing we know for certain, Betsy, is that we both want to get to know you better. I understand that it's a lot to handle, saying hello to you at the

Shop 'n Save whenever we checked out with our groceries for all these years, and never having an inkling that we were related. But, Betsy, believe me when I tell you, we both see this as a good thing. We haven't lost anything. We've gained something wonderful. We found a sister."

The party guests at Hayley's Kitchen began the count down. "Ten . . . nine . . . eight . . ."

Betsy, trying to keep her emotions in check, smiled. "That means so much to me, because, as an only child, I always dreamed of having siblings but thought it could never happen, and you've been so nice and warm and welcoming, it's been a little overwhelming . . ."

"Seven . . . six . . . five . . ."

Hayley enveloped her in a hug. "Welcome to the family, Betsy!"

"Four . . . three . . . two . . . one . . . happy New Year!" The party revelers roared as they blew on kazoos and tossed confetti in the air and gulped down their champagne and kissed those nearest to them.

Hayley grabbed her own flute from the host station and clinked glasses with Betsy as she shouted above the cheers of the crowd, confetti raining down upon them. "Happy New Year, sis!" Then she turned to find her husband hustling up behind her in order to plant a big one on his wife's lips to ring in the new year, one she hoped might be slightly calmer and not usher in as many shocking and life-changing surprises.

Island Food & Spirits
By
Hayley Powell

This afternoon, as I gave my husband Bruce a quick goodbye kiss before he headed out the door to Ellsworth with his boss Sal to look at snow-mobiles, I had to chuckle because the two grown men were acting like a pair of excited teenage boys going to buy their first car. Even though I had been warning Bruce all morning that he was only allowed to window-shop and not come home with one, I had a sneaking suspicion he wasn't listening to one word that I was saying. But seeing him cheered up since losing his brand-new snowmobile through the ice in an unforeseeable accident was enough to warm my heart, just as long as he didn't go back on his promise of waiting until next year before making such a big purchase.

Once Bruce and Sal were well on their way, I started rummaging through the fridge and spotted some cranberry juice and a chunk of fresh ginger left over from the holidays, so I decided to mix myself a tasty cranberry ginger cocktail, even though I had promised myself when I woke up this morning to start my annual New Year's resolution of going on a diet, since I had indulged way too much during the holiday season. True to form, that particular resolution had lasted until January 2, when I had a hankering for some chocolate chip pancakes.

I sank down on a kitchen chair, set my drink on the table, and stared out the window, lost in thought. Hypnotized by the snowflakes silently floating down and dancing in the wind, I noticed how quiet the house was, and that's when I realized that this was the first time I had been alone here since before Christmas, and it was now already the middle of January. So much has happened in such a short time that I have hardly had time to process any of it.

First of all, as many of you know by now, thanks to our stable of town gossips, the sudden return of my father Dwight and all of the drama that ensued with his arrival, including someone hell-bent on murdering him, not to mention Carroll Flood's sudden death at the gingerbread house contest, was enough to dampen any Christmas cheer, but somehow we all persevered. Next there was Dwight using his charms like a superpower to win over Liddy's mom, Celeste, who has never been easily won over unless you have a lot of zeros ending in the amount of your bank account. I must admit, I didn't see that one coming. Neither did Liddy. Or anybody, for that matter. Of course, then poof, he was gone. Our magician father performed the same disappearing act that he had when Randy and I were kids. Except this time it didn't hurt as much, because my brother and I both realized that Dwight has been out of our lives for much longer than he was ever in them. And that's okay. Even though he was only here for a short time, it really felt as if we all finally connected again, something I never expected would ever happen, and yet it did. And that was one of the best, unexpected Christmas present I could receive.

But I can honestly say that I feel in my bones that we have not seen the last of Dwight Jordan, especially since he left Randy and me with an even better Christmas gift than seeing him after all these years. We got a new sister! Yes, the local gossips have been in overdrive spreading this latest piece of local news around town.

Randy and I were finally able to meet up with Betsy a week ago at my restaurant Hayley's Kitchen for dinner so we could start getting to know each other better, and it was surprising how much we all had in common as we shared our likes and dislikes. For example, both Betsy and Randy have an intense dislike for lobster, cross-country skiing, ice fishing, and kayaking, all things that the island is noted for. On the other hand, they both share a love of old TV shows, comic books, and meat loaf with mashed potatoes. I just sat there, shaking my head in disbelief at how much the two of them could have been twins.

As for me, Betsy and I both love cooking and

eating and could spend the entire day just talking about food! Something we undoubtedly get from our father.

The three of us siblings have already made plans to have a family dinner once a week during the winter months, before we all get busy when the tourist season rolls around in the late spring. It's going to give us plenty of time to explore this new relationship.

Lastly, our time with Dwight may have been short and filled with one too many unpleasant surprises, not to mention a plethora of I told you so's from our mother, but still, I honestly believe Dwight is going to keep in contact with us from afar after our time together, especially since I received an unsigned postcard in the mail yesterday from Minnesota with the scribbled words wish you were here, followed by a recipe for ginger chicken, which I would like to share with you.

But before I do, I also now need to go grab my coat and get outside quickly, because my husband just backed his truck into our driveway past the kitchen window and up to the garage, and I can plainly see a very large object covered in a tarp in the flatbed. And if it is what I think it is, someone is about to be in very big trouble. Men!

Happy New Year to you all!

Love, Hayley

CRANBERRY GINGER COCKTAIL

INGREDIENTS:
3 ounces gin
2 ounces real cranberry juice
1 ounce ginger simple syrup
1 ounce orange juice
2 ounces club soda
cranberries for garnish (optional)

In a cocktail shaker filled with ice, add all ingredients except club soda and cranberries, if using.

Shake until well blended and strain into a glass filled with ice. Add club soda and cranberries for garnish and enjoy!

GINGER CHICKEN

INGREDIENTS:
1 pound boneless skinless chicken breasts cut
   into one-inch pieces
2 tablespoons vegetable oil
2½ cups broccoli florets
1 tablespoon freshly minced ginger
¼ cup oyster sauce
¼ cup chicken broth (no broth, I use water)
1 teaspoon granulated sugar
2 teaspoons toasted sesame oil
1 tablespoon cornstarch
salt and pepper to taste

Heat 1 tablespoon of oil in large frying pan over medium heat. Add your broccoli and cook for about 5 minutes or until tender.

Add the ginger and garlic to the pan and cook for about 30 seconds.

Remove the broccoli mixture and place on a plate.

Wipe the pan clean with a paper towel and turn on medium-high heat. Add the remaining tablespoon of oil.

Season the chicken with salt and pepper and add to your pan and cook for 4 to 5 minutes until all sides of chicken are golden brown.

Add the broccoli mixture back to the pan with the chicken and heat until all warmed through.

In a bowl, whisk the oyster sauce, chicken broth (or water), sugar, sesame oil, soy sauce, and cornstarch.

Pour the sauce over your chicken and vegetables and bring to a boil, and cook until sauce starts to thicken.

Remove from heat and serve with your rice and enjoy!

Index of Recipes